The Naughty List

By Cassie Cole

Copyright © 2019 Juicy Gems Publishing

All rights reserved. No part of this publication may be reproduced, distributed, or transmitted in any form without prior consent of the author.

Edited by Robin Morris

Follow me on social media to stay up-to-date on new releases, announcements, and prize giveaways!

www.cassiecoleromance.com

Books by Cassie Cole

Broken In

Drilled

Five Alarm Christmas

All In

Triple Team

Shared by her Bodyguards

Saved by the SEALs

Forbidden Crush

The Proposition

Full Contact

Sealed With A Kiss

Smolder

The Naughty List

1

Leslie

In my five years working at Allegheny Supply, the office printer had always been my nemesis.

"Oh *come on*," I growled under my breath. "I sent the print job five minutes ago. Start, damnit!"

Unconvinced by my curses, the printer remained silent. It was one of those big multifunction printers that was three feet tall and occupied one entire corner of the Operations Department. I wanted to kick it, but it was heavy enough that I would probably break a toe.

I took a deep breath and pressed the yellow "REFRESH" button again.

I'd been overwhelmed at the office lately. I was essentially working two jobs at the same time: my current role as Operations Analyst, and training for the new job I had applied for. I hadn't officially gotten it yet, but I expected to, and I wanted to hit the ground running if and when I was notified. But it meant juggling twice the workload in the meantime. Something which was hard to do when printer-related complications kept adding delays in my workday.

The hourglass on the printer screen spun, then disappeared. Nothing happened.

"Son of a..." I gripped the printer with both hands like I was going to shake some sense into it.

"How about I hold it still while you beat it with a baseball bat?" suggested a voice behind me.

I turned and immediately smiled. "Liam?"

I hadn't seen Liam Harford since we worked in the sales pit together two years ago. He was tall and slender, with a crisp white dress shirt and an emerald tie that brought out the color in his eyes. His boyish good looks and his mop of shaggy brown hair always reminded me of Jim from *The Office*, but sexy instead of just cute.

He hugged me without hesitation. He was taller than me, so even standing on my tip-toes my cheek pressed into his chest. Seeing him instantly raised my spirits.

"Leslie! It's been too long." He gestured at the printer. "Still trying to fight the printers around here?"

I rolled my eyes. "It should be simple. Click *print* on your computer, and then paper comes out here. Why isn't it simple!"

He leaned in close and gave me a secret smile. "There's a giant conspiracy among the printers. They get together on Tuesdays and think of all the ways to frustrate Leslie Hill."

"I knew it!"

We laughed together, and for a few moments it was just like old times. Shooting the shit in the office, teasing one-another... *flirting* together. I'd forgotten how much I missed him.

And then Liam did the thing he always did after joking with me: he helped.

"Let's take a look at this bad boy..." He bent over to open one of the paper trays. His dress slacks fit tightly over his cute little butt, and then he crouched down and opened up a compartment on the side.

"I think the feeder mechanism has something jammed in it." He rolled up the sleeves of his shirt and stuck his hands inside the printer like a doctor delivering a C-section.

Not all guys knew how to look good while dressing up. Many of the men I worked with wore suits that were too baggy, either because they had never visited a tailor in their life or because they needed big clothes to cover up a gut. Not so with Liam. His shirt and pants fit well-enough that he could have been a model in a clothing catalog. He made it look natural.

It didn't hurt that he still looked lean with muscle underneath, too.

He yanked inside the printer, and removed a crumpled piece of paper covered with black ink. "Found the problem." He tossed it in the trash can and closed the printer up. "Try it now."

I hit the "REFRESH" button. This time, the printer immediately hummed to life and began spitting out pages of the training document that I had sent to it fifteen minutes ago.

I clapped my hands excitedly. "You're a miracle worker!"

Liam grinned and rolled his sleeves back down. "That's why they pay me the medium bucks."

I laughed again. Liam had that effect on me—and on *all* the girls in the office. Five minutes around him and all the stress from my busy morning had disappeared.

"What brings you to the Operations Department?" I asked while the pages printed.

Liam jerked his head. "Got a meeting with John."

I glanced across the room of cubicles toward my boss's office on the far wall. My heart leaped. Was Liam moving out of sales into our department? Getting to see him every day again, just like old times...

Before I could ask, Liam put his hand on my forearm. "Hey, do you want to grab lunch today? Like we used to?"

I winced. The stack of printed papers was already thirty sheets high and growing, and it was all training information I needed to review. I was behind on all of that work and needed to know it inside and out before a meeting in the morning.

I gave Liam an apologetic frown and said, "I brought my own lunch today. I was going to eat it at my desk and get a head start on what I have to do this afternoon..."

"Bring it to the cafeteria and eat with me," he said smoothly. "I'd love to spend some time catching up. It's been too long."

It *had* been too long. I didn't have a lot of workplace friendships in the Operations Department, and seeing Liam today reminded me that I missed it. And I was dying for an excuse to put-off reading these training documents.

"Just for half an hour," I said.

He smiled warmly. "Plenty of time to eat your spring salad."

I gave a start. "How did you know?"

"Same thing you used to eat every day in the sales pit." He began walking away, but pointed back at me. "I'll come grab you when I get out of my meeting with John."

More than one woman turned to watch Liam walk across the office. I smiled to myself while waiting for the rest of the pages to print.

2

Leslie

Liam's meeting with John lasted twenty minutes. Twenty *long* minutes while I mentally noted all the things we could talk about. When he finally emerged from the office and we walked to the cafeteria, I had an entire new outlook on my day.

Our company, Allegheny Supply, took up four floors in a building in downtown Pittsburgh, just across the river from the Pirates stadium. The company barely survived the 2009 recession, but had been booming since then. We had opened ten new branches across Pennsylvania and Ohio, and business was growing at a hectic pace.

The cafeteria boasted vending machines with typical snacks and even some pre-made sandwiches that were stocked daily. Liam bought a turkey sandwich from the latter and joined me at one of the tables in the corner by ourselves.

"So how's the sales pit?" I asked while opening my salad.

"Same as it always is," he said while biting into his sandwich. "A little less bright without you, of course."

I waved a hand at him. "Stop it. Commissions are still good?"

"Better than good. They're *fantastic*. I've been busting my butt all summer during the busy season. After the quarter we had, I can't wait to see what my paycheck looks like."

"Part of me misses those days," I said wistfully. "It was always so exciting chasing sales, and the immediate gratification that came from seeing the sales total increment every day. But I *don't* miss the stress. Especially hustling at the end of each quarter to hit our numbers."

"Yeah, there's still the stress," he replied. "But you look awfully stressed yourself right now."

"I *am* stressed," I admitted. "I'm sort of working two jobs at the same time right now."

Liam grinned his perfect smile. "You moonlighting at the strip club?"

I giggled. It was an old inside joke from years ago, when I'd had one too many drinks at the company Halloween party and had showed off my dancing skills in front of the whole department. Nothing raunchy or embarrassing, but enough that Liam had complimented-slash-teased me about it for years after.

"No stripping... yet," I said. "It's all inside the company."

"Oh?" he asked, inviting me to elaborate.

I started to answer, then stopped myself.

Allegheny Supply had been using old software to keep track of sales. That was fine when the company was small, but we had grown so fast so suddenly that now it was holding us back. A project was kicking-off to evaluate new software, choose the best one, and then migrate the entire company to it.

The project was called the STT: Systems Transition Team. As someone who had worked in sales for three years and operations for two, I had a well-rounded view of what software would be best. So I had applied for the management position to lead the entire STT.

I'd kept it close to my chest for so long that I was itching to tell someone about it. But I didn't want to jinx it before I got the job.

I can brag about it once it's all official, I thought.

"I'm working on two different projects simultaneously," I said vaguely. "Twice the fun for half the pay."

"Which projects?" he asked.

"Oh, boring stuff. Internal to the Operations Department." I shrugged it off. "How's Polly?"

"She's doing fine," Liam said. "Although we sort of broke up."

They broke up.

Liam and his girlfriend had broken up!

My heart raced. I'd had a workplace crush on Liam since starting here. Back in the sales pit days he joked that I was his "work wife," and I called him my "work husband." Plus a healthy amount of teasing and flirting about our sales numbers. But we were never single at the same time, so we never had a chance to go on a date.

Except he was single now.

"Oh, no," I said in what I hoped was a genuine-sounding voice. "I'm sorry, Liam. How'd she take it?"

"Well, she broke up with me. Said I was working too much." He shrugged it off. "It happened a few weeks ago. I'm over it. We weren't together *that* long."

I frowned. "Hadn't you guys dated for, like, two years?"

I was being coy. I knew *exactly* how long they had been dating: since the company Halloween party of 2017. I remembered because I had just broken up with my boyfriend, and it was a rare window of opportunity where both Liam and I were single. I had hit the punch hard that night in the hopes of flirting with Liam enough to make something happen. I wore a sexy cat costume to the party, something I normally would have deemed too risque for an office gathering. Liam was dressed as a pirate, the same costume he wore *every* year, because it gave him a chance to use his cheesy pirate accent. The stars aligned, and all I had to do was ask him to dance.

But *she* had gotten to him first. Polly Graham, an intern from Human Resources. She invited him to dance, and they never stopped, and my chance was lost.

"I guess it was two years ago," Liam said to himself. Then he leaned across the table toward me. "Between you and me? Polly and I have been running on fumes for the last six months. So it's almost a relief to be officially over."

"Well, I'm still sorry it didn't work out," I said diplomatically.

"What about you and your boyfriend?" Liam asked. "The physical trainer dude with the ocean name. Mediterranean?"

"Caspian," I laughed. "And we broke up three months ago."

He put down his sandwich. "Leslie, I'm really sorry to hear that. I know you two were serious."

I made a face. "Had you ever met him?"

"You brought him to the holiday party last year," Liam said. "And I heard you two were running a lot of races together. I know I was making fun of his name, but he seemed like a really cool guy."

Whereas I felt fake in my sympathy for Liam and Polly's dead relationship, Liam seemed genuinely sorry to hear about mine. It was touching, in a way.

"He was a cool guy," I agreed. "But we were at different stages in our lives. Caspian wanted to settle down, have a family, get serious..."

"And you didn't?"

"I don't know what I want." I picked at my salad, then looked up. "Does that make me weird?"

He shook his head. "Lots of people don't know what they want by the time they're twenty-six. I sure as hell don't."

"Except for making that sweet commission money."

"Of course. I'll always want that."

We shared a moment, grinning together in the cafeteria.

"So." Liam crossed one long leg over the other. "If you're not with Aegean..."

"Caspian!" I laughed.

"...does that mean you're not big into running anymore?"

I winced. "Funny story. I'm actually running a marathon in two months."

Liam coughed on his sandwich. "Seriously?"

"I was already halfway through training when Caspian and I broke up!" I argued. "I want to see it through to the end. And I kind of enjoy running now."

"Nobody likes running," Liam replied. "Except people who are otherwise totally boring. Which you are not."

I rolled my eyes at him. "It's a good way to relax after work."

"A better way is to have a few drinks at the bar." He pointed at me. "Which we should totally do sometime."

"We should."

I tried not to smile too hard. I could feel a spark between us, just like old times. Except now we were both finally single and could do something about it. Granted, I was insanely busy between work and marathon training. But I wasn't going to let that stop me. I couldn't let him get away this time.

And I could tell by the look in his eyes he was thinking the same thing.

"How did your meeting with John go?" I asked.

"It went great," he said excitedly. "They're looking for a sales expert to join that new Systems Transition Team. To help evaluate the new software from a sales perspective."

The STT.

The team I thought I would soon be managing.

He would be reporting directly to me. There would be a conflict of interest if we started to date.

My heart sank. "Oh really? The STT?"

His shaggy brown hair bounced as he nodded. "It means giving up next quarter's commissions, but it's the right career move. Put some balanced experience on my resume besides just sales."

"That's great," I said numbly. "The STT is going to catapult a lot of careers in the company."

"If it's a successful transition," he said skeptically. "Rumor has it the board is pushing for an aggressive timeline. They want us on a new software system before the end of the year. If the transition goes poorly, it could *tank* a lot of careers."

"Good point," I said. I knew the truth of that statement more than anyone. The stakes were high for everyone who moved into the STT project. "It seems like a lot of risk for you. Is it worth giving up your cushy sales job?"

"Nothing ventured, nothing gained," Liam said. "I've given it a lot of thought, and it's the right move for me. John said I have it in the bag. I just hope whoever gets the manager role knows what they're doing."

"I hope so too," I said with my best poker face.

He finished his sandwich and crumpled up the wrapper. His emerald gaze was intense as he leaned across the table toward me, giving me a whiff of his musky cologne.

"Listen. Leslie. It's been great talking to you. It reminds me of the good old days in the sales pit. Forget the drinks I mentioned earlier. Do you want to get dinner with me? Tonight, or this weekend, or whenever. It doesn't matter. Whatever works for you. I was thinking Lili's Bistro, downtown."

It was what I'd dreamed of Liam asking me since I started working at Allegheny Supply five years ago. No more teasing, and flirting and sharing smiles from across the office. He was asking me out on a date.

But I had to say no.

I was probably going to get the job as Manager of the Systems

Transition Team. It would hurt too much to go on a date, get the job, and then have to break things off with him. Or worse: it would force *him* to turn down a position in the team so that we could date without there being a conflict. Such a sacrifice wasn't a healthy way to start a relationship. It was the kind of thing that would breed resentment.

If only you weren't joining that group, I thought sadly.

I couldn't tell him the truth, not until it was official that I was getting the manager job.

I reached across the table and put my hand on his. "Liam."

A crack appeared in his charming smile. "Uh oh. This doesn't sound good."

"I can't," I said regretfully. "My life is too crazy right now. Between the two jobs I'm working here and the marathon I'm training for, I barely have time to eat and sleep. It wouldn't be fair to you."

Even as I forced myself to say the terrible words, I was hoping Liam would reject them. I wanted him to shake his head and pound the table and tell me that he wouldn't accept what I had said, that he was taking me out to dinner that weekend. I desperately wanted him to tear apart my excuses like they were pieces of paper jammed in a printer.

Liam smiled sadly. "I'm sorry to hear that. But I understand." He patted my hand. "Maybe when your schedule is a little less crazy? Next year, when the marathon is done and your work isn't killing you?"

"Yeah," I said. "Definitely."

I spent the rest of lunch smiling politely at the beautiful man across from me, and wishing things had turned out differently.

3

Liam

Since the moment I first met her in the office five years ago, I'd had a thing for Leslie.

I'd been with Allie then, my college sweetheart. By the time she and I broke up, Leslie was dating some guy from Accounting. Then when they were done, I was with a woman named Rose. We leapfrogged through our careers like that, never aligning the way we should have.

She was the one who got away.

Despite that, we always had a great working relationship in the sales pit. We teased each other and flirted. There was always a sexual chemistry between us that we could never act on. Even our co-workers commented on it.

I'd known for a while that she and Caspian had broken up. I remember wanting to fist-pump in the office when I overheard a friend of Leslie's talking about it. I wanted to sprint to her desk and ask her out that very moment. But I bided my time. Gave her a respectful three weeks. Twenty-one days was the number I decided on, and I counted them off my calendar every night before going to bed.

Twenty-one days, and not a day longer.

I had arranged our bump-in at the printer. The breakroom for her floor was right outside the Operations Department where I could watch her. I spent eight minutes pretending to make a cup of coffee before she got up to visit the printer. Only then did I make my entrance, so I could "accidentally" run into her.

She was as gorgeous as I remembered: a waterfall of auburn hair running past her shoulders, with cherry-red lips that always pursed like she was trying to hold back a smile. She was somewhere between curvy and skinny, with a voluptuous body that hadn't changed since the days in sales when I'd stolen glances of it whenever she wasn't looking. Back in those days the sales team dressed more casually, but now she was wearing a tight black dress that hugged her body in a way that made me want to throw her over my shoulder and carry her into a supply closet somewhere.

I was nervous to talk to her after so long. But then my awkwardness melted away, and as we chatted we fell into the same friendship groove as if we had never stopped working together.

...And then she rejected me.

I smiled and nodded along as we ate our lunch and talked about the company. Sales numbers and expansion projects. The weather for her marathon, and whether she would be running on snow-covered ground. But deep inside? I was crushed. Maybe I had imagined everything.

Maybe she never liked me after all.

"Twenty miles, wow," I said. "And you don't run more than that in training?"

"Nope, that's the longest training run. Then two weeks of tapering, then the marathon."

I flashed her my best smile as if nothing was wrong. "I'll have to come cheer you on. See it with my own eyes and bring you a cup of cocoa."

She smiled back at me. That same smile I fell in love with years ago, which only caused me agony now. "I'd like that."

The hole in my chest was spreading, twisting in on itself as I stared across the table at the woman I'd been pining over for the past twenty-one days. For the past five years. As nice as it was to see her again in a platonic way, I wanted nothing more than to go somewhere else and feel sorry for myself in peace.

The other employees in the cafeteria were getting up and leaving all at the same time. I glanced at the calendar on my phone. "Oh, the department meeting is about to start. I'd better grab a seat before they're all taken."

She cursed under her breath. "I forgot about the department meeting."

"Are you going?"

Leslie glanced at her cell phone and made a noncommittal noise. "I don't want to go. But I hate to skip."

I tossed my trash away and then turned to say goodbye. Leslie surprised me by giving me a hug. She clung tightly to me, allowing me to savor the feel of her body against mine. I wrapped my arms around her and hugged her back.

Not a normal hug. The kind between more-than-friends that lasted a little longer than other hugs. The kind of hug that makes you all tingly inside.

"I'm glad you pulled me away for lunch," she said. "It was great catching up with you, Liam."

"Yeah, you too, Leslie," I said as we parted ways.

I headed to the big conference room feeling confused and dejected.

4

Leslie

I hated department meetings.

We had them once a month. Twelve times a year. That was about eleven times too many. The managers of all the departments or individual projects got up and told everyone what they were working on and how things were going. On paper, this might seem like an opportunity for employees at our Pittsburgh HQ to get a holistic view of what everyone else was doing. In practice, it ended up being little more than an inter-departmental team meeting.

Three hours down the drain when I could have been doing something far more productive.

Especially after lunch, I thought. It was refreshing to catch up with Liam, but now I was *really* behind on my work for the meeting tomorrow. So I grabbed my laptop from my desk and brought it to the big conference room so I could try to get some work done discreetly.

The conference room was the largest we had on the floor, with a huge projector screen on one wall and enough room to fit a hundred employees in chairs and tables. The room was already three-quarters full, but I was able to find a seat in the corner where nobody would be looking over my shoulder as I did other work on my laptop.

I gazed around the room and found Liam. It wasn't hard since he was taller than most men. He sat on the far end closer to the projector screen, chatting with one of the other outside sales people. A young woman with blonde hair and annoyingly-large boobs. Liam was smiling, and laughing. Like he'd just told a joke. He brushed back his chestnut hair and I sighed to myself, alone in the corner.

I wished things didn't have to be this way. It felt so *good* to catch up with him at lunch! Slipping back into our old friendship from long ago. It made me fantasize about ignoring the fact that I might soon be his manager. Have some sort of relationship with him in secret, sneaking around like Romeo and Juliet under the cover of darkness.

Liam swiveled his head and caught my eye. He smiled, but then looked away.

He probably thinks I'm not interested. It ate me up inside to have to decline his date. And worse: to give him a mostly-false reason for declining.

John Fadringham, my boss and our department head, got up and smiled at the collective group. "Alright, let's get started. How's everyone doing today? I don't know if you all have seen the numbers, but we had a great quarter. First we'll go over the financials and then turn it over to the managers to give progress reports..."

On my laptop, I opened up the document I needed to study before tomorrow's meeting. But as Fadringham spoke about budgets and gross net profit, I found myself gazing at Liam across the room.

It stung that I had to make an excuse about being busy, but it was still mostly true. I was swamped right now! As an Operations Analyst, I had to review all of the sales reports for my region—which stretched from Kentucky all the way to Maine. Checking all the big reports for financial discrepancies and cleaning up any sales orders that included rebates or charge-backs. I was *very* good at my job, which meant I could clean them up in about eight hours... If I busted my ass all day without a break. So in the best of circumstances, that left me with only one hour a day to study the software manuals for the potential new software systems for the STT job.

I was overworked. I was burned out. The days bled together, and I found myself constantly in a state of catching-up. I'd been taking my laptop home on the weekends and doing ops reports while watching the Steelers on Sunday just to feel like I wasn't behind every Monday morning. The stress was getting to me. I couldn't wait to officially get the STT manager job so I could leave all my old responsibilities behind and focus all of my efforts there.

After Fadringham discussed the company's quarterly financials, two more managers spoke about their little departments. I reviewed a few pages of the training document on my laptop while pretending to pay attention to the managers speaking at the front of the room. Then the head of Human Resources, a portly woman with a round face and wide mouth, got up and turned her too-large smile at the group.

"It's that time of year again, everyone! The holiday party is just around the corner! Work hard, play hard, am I right?" She paused for cheers. When they didn't come, she went on. "Each year, HR relies on volunteers to help us plan and organize the holiday party. This year, I'd like to call out our volunteers to thank them for taking on the responsibility of making sure we all have a great holiday and new year!"

The slide on the projector changed.

I glanced at it, then back at my own laptop. Then I did a double-take.

PARTY PLANNING 2019 VOLUNTEERS
-Beth Carlson

-Arthur Durand

-Robbie Godwin

-Polly Graham

-Liam Harford

-Leslie Hill

-Charletta Reese

The party planning team! I had signed up for it after the holiday party last year, and totally forgot until now. There was a smattering of applause for the volunteers.

"I'm sending the seven of you a link to the shared drive with all the documents and information for the food, alcohol, and party equipment vendors," the HR woman continued. "If you have any questions I'll be happy to help! I know this year's party is going to be a doozy!"

A message popped up on my laptop in *Microsoft Teams*, our company chat client:

Harford, Liam: I thought you said you were too busy to take on anything else in your life? ;-)

I glanced across the room. He wasn't looking in my direction, but he was smiling down at his phone.

Hill, Leslie: I am too busy! I only signed up for this because I wanted some project management experience on my resume.

Harford, Liam: Sounds familiar: I only signed up for it because Polly made me. Things are going to be awkward now. Ugh.

Hill, Leslie: Oh damn, I didn't notice

she was on the list.

Harford, Liam: There's only one thing for us to do, Leslie

Hill, Leslie: What's that?

Harford, Liam: Suicide pact.

Hill, Leslie: LOL

Harford, Liam: I'll whip up some arsenic-laced punch and bring it by your desk later

Hill, Leslie: I know you're joking, but that sounds tempting right now

A new window popped up in *Microsoft Teams*. A group chat with everyone from the Party Planning Committee.

Reese, Charletta: Hey everyone! It's probably a good idea to get a group chat going to discuss the party planning :-)

Carlson, Beth: Good idea, Charletta!

Carlson, Beth: I'm excited to work with everyone this year. We're going to have the best party ever!!!

Way too many exclamation points, Beth, I thought to myself while gazing around the room. I knew everyone here by name, but didn't recognize most of them.

Godwin, Robbie: Well, who's going to be in charge?

Reese, Charletta: Not me—I'm a great second-in-command but I'm a terrible leader!

Carlson, Beth: What about Polly, since she works in HR?

Graham, Polly: Hey everyone. I was mistakenly added to this group. I am sorry, but I will have to bow out of the party planning committee. Have fun without me!

[Polly Graham has left the chat]

The private chat with Liam flashed.

Harford, Liam: Damnit. There goes my excuse for quitting the group.

Hill, Leslie: Nice try. Although I'm *definitely* going to need to drop out of the group too.

Harford, Liam: No! Don't leave me!

Hill, Leslie: Sorry. You're on your own with Beth!!! and Charletta

Back in the group chat:

Durand, Arthur: Should we meet after this department meeting to discuss everything?

I groaned. The thought of wasting any more of my day after this department meeting made me want to hurl my laptop across the room. Several other people were typing in the group chat, but my fingers flew over my keyboard to send a message before that:

Hill, Leslie: Hey everyone, my schedule is totally booked today. And I'm sorry, but I am probably going to need to back out of the party planning committee due to other obligations.

Reese, Charletta: I'm reviewing the HR documents and it looks like we need to get started ASAP. Vendors usually have to be booked two months in advance. We have to get moving on this.

Carlson, Beth: I agree—let's get the ball rolling!!!

I minimized the window because I didn't have the mental or emotional bandwidth to think about it right now. I pulled up my training document and tried to read for a few minutes, but the constant blinking of *Microsoft Teams* in my system tray was too annoying to ignore.

I opened it and saw that I had missed at least thirty messages. I skimmed the most recent page of messages:

Carlson, Beth: What about meeting after work? That way it doesn't interfere with anyone's schedule

Godwin, Robbie: I don't know if I can make that work

Carlson, Beth: Sure you can!!!

Reese, Charletta: Where should we meet? A restaurant?

Carlson, Beth: Someone's house would be better, so it's not loud and distracting

Durand, Arthur: I would host but my

apartment is very small. But wherever we go, I can bring wine!

Carlson, Beth: That's what I'm talking about!

Reese, Charletta: Leslie, what about your house? It kind of sucks that you're backing out of your obligation, but if you hosted the meeting tonight it would help. Especially since you live closest to the office.

I gritted my teeth. What kind of person just invited themselves over like that? But I didn't want to have this argument anymore, and if hosting the meeting meant I could drop out of it, then I would happily make that trade.

Hill, Leslie: Yeah, sure, my house works fine. 1181 Maple Street.

Carlson, Beth: Woohoo!

Durand, Arthur: I will bring the wine!

I turned my attention back to the room and saw Liam looking over at me. He gave me a *sucks you got roped into hosting* smirk.

The Chief Operating Officer of the company went up to the front of the room to speak next. She was a harsh-looking woman whose smile never touched her eyes.

"As you all know, our company is preparing to undergo a transition from our legacy sales software to a new system."

I perked up in my seat. Were they announcing the manager selection right now? It wasn't supposed to be made public until the end of the week.

"I don't need to explain the importance of this project," the COO went on. "Our old system was fine when we were a small company, but it's too slow and outdated now. Not only do we need to select a replacement as soon as possible, but we need to migrate to the new system quickly as well. Every day we're on the old system, we lose money. I speak for the entire board of directors when I say they want to start the new year fresh!"

They're announcing it. It was happening right now. If I had been turned down for the position, I would have been notified already. That meant the job was mine. Granted, I hadn't signed any of the paperwork or negotiated my salary, but that could always come later.

I tapped my foot and began practicing what my facial expression would be. Happy and determined.

The COO smiled and gestured toward me. "We are thrilled to announce that Oliver Edwards has accepted the role of Manager for the Systems Transition Team."

5

Leslie

Oliver Edwards.

I jerked as if I had been shot.

One row in front of me, Oliver stood up and waved. There was a smattering of polite applause for him, and then he sat back down.

"Now," the COO went on, "I'd like to discuss some new plugins to our Microsoft Office suite we will be rolling out this month. The first one is a data analytics tool..."

No point in studying the new system documentation now. I closed my laptop and stared at the back of Oliver's head as the COO's words washed over me. The rest of the department meeting passed by in a blur, and then we were being dismissed from the room.

Liam was moving toward me as we shuffled toward the door. He fell in beside me and whispered, "I still think suicide pact is our best bet."

"Heh," I grunted.

"What do you think of Oliver?" he asked. "I don't know much about the guy, but he seems nice enough. A good fit for the STT."

"I don't care about Oliver or the STT," I said more harshly than I intended. "I need to get some work done."

"Yeah, alright," Liam said as I pushed through the crowd.

I made a bee-line across the building to my department, but I didn't stop at my desk. I kept walking until I reached my boss's office. I closed the door and rounded on him. I'd worked for him for two years. He was the kind of boss who always had my back, and was genuinely interested in my career path in the company. I liked him.

Except for right now.

"Leslie..." he began.

"What was that?" I demanded. "I asked you for an update on the job *yesterday*. You said I was the leading candidate, and that I'd know by the end of the week."

John crossed his fingers on the desk and nodded at the seat across from him. He waited for me to sit down before answering.

"What I told you yesterday morning was true," he said calmly. "You *were* the leading candidate, and it was supposed to be announced by the end of the week." He sighed. "Then I heard they made the decision yesterday afternoon. I'm sorry, Leslie."

"So you knew I wasn't getting the job."

"HR was supposed to formally notify you. I couldn't tell you before then—there's a process for this sort of thing. If Oliver had turned down the job, you would have been chosen. I had to let HR do its thing."

I gritted my teeth and changed directions. "*Why* wasn't I selected? I thought I had it in the bag! Everything I've been working on in this department has been tangentially related to a system transition."

John shook his head ruefully. "I had a voice in the decision, but it was larger than just me. The entire company board was involved in hand-picking Oliver. This project is sensitive and will have a lot of visibility. They wanted to make sure it is done right."

I couldn't hide the pain from my voice. "They don't think I would do it right?"

"They think Oliver will do it better," John explained. "Leslie.

You would have been amazing at this job. That's why I convinced you to apply for it. It sucks that you were passed up, but it's not the end of the world. I'll make sure the next time an opportunity comes along, your name goes to the top of the list."

"I understand," I said, though I still didn't.

"At least you have the holiday party to plan," he said with a weak smile.

"I forgot I signed up for it," I replied. "Honestly, I'm probably going to ditch it so I can focus on my work..."

John winced. "I'm not sure that's a good idea. That committee would be a good feather in your cap when it comes time to shoot for another management position."

"I'll think about it," I said as I left his office.

I slumped into my chair back at my desk. I had thirty internet tabs open. One-by-one I closed the twenty that were related to new systems for the STT job. None of that mattered anymore.

At least I can focus on my normal job now.

Yet as I got back to my regular work, I couldn't get into a groove. I usually stayed in the office past five o'clock, but today I left at a quarter-till. I took the stairs down to the gym on the first floor, changed clothes in the locker room, and then carried my gym bag of clothes out to my car.

Our office building was nestled in the strip of downtown Pittsburgh where the Ohio River split off into the Allegheny and Monongahela Rivers. The running trails that bordered the rivers were my favorite in the city, so I left my car at the office and jogged to the trail and started running.

I loved Pittsburgh this time of year. The air was crisp and hinted that winter was just around the corner, but it hadn't begun snowing yet. Perfect running weather. I ran west until the trail curved back north and then east around Fort Duquesne, bringing Heinz Field and PNC Park into view across the river. Pittsburgh was known as the

City of Bridges—there were over 400 bridges in the greater Pittsburgh area. Crossing the river ahead of me was the Fort Duquesne Bridge, and then beyond that the Roberto Clemente, Andy Warhol, and Rachel Carson Bridges, all picturesque in their yellow painted steel.

Even though I had signed up for the Pittsburgh Marathon at my ex-boyfriend's insistence, I was glad that I had something to train for. It was a great way to unwind after the stresses of work, while simultaneously staying fit. Not to mention it had a meditative, calming effect after the events of today. As I ran north-east along the Allegheny River, all that mattered was the strip of pavement in front of me. One foot in front of the other, focusing on my breathing.

I ran in that direction for half an hour, then turned around and came back. Just eight miles tonight. I retrieved my car from the office, then drove the short distance home. I lived in Duquesne Heights, on the south side of the rivers. A small neighborhood with brick-paved streets and tall Cape Cod homes over a century old. My house was close enough that I sometimes walked to the office when the weather was especially nice, but today was a little too chilly for that.

I walked through the door and sighed. "After a crappy day, there's no place like home," I said out loud. I tossed my gym bag on the couch and opened the fridge. I reached for a Gatorade... then pulled out a bottle of Chardonnay instead.

"I definitely deserve this," I said while pouring myself a glass.

The last month had burned me out. Working my normal job, training for the marathon, and then spending every other minute of my day doing research for the STT job I expected to get. That position would have been *huge* for my career. It had been easy to work myself to the bone because I saw it as investing in my own future.

Now I just saw it as a waste of time.

It was a weight off my shoulders, to some degree. Now it was time to take care of myself again.

I carried my glass of wine upstairs and drew a bath in my clawfooted tub. I tossed in a lemon-spring bath bomb my mother had given me for my birthday that I had never used, and it filled the room with a strong citrus scent. I pulled up some peaceful music on my phone to set the mood, stripped out of my running clothes, and then submerged myself in the almost-too-hot water of the tub.

I sighed as every muscle in my body relaxed.

Thinking back on what my boss John had said, I knew he was right. There would be other jobs. There always were. But missing out on the STT manager position felt like a massive missed opportunity. Getting into that position and delivering a new software system would have catapulted my career forward.

It was like I'd found a Fast Pass ticket on the ground at Disney World, but then someone else cut in line at Space Mountain before I could use it.

I guess I'll just have to wait in line like everyone else.

I was still young. If I was being totally honest with myself, that's probably why Oliver got the job over me. He had less experience at Allegheny Supply, but more experience in the industry in general. Everyone liked him. Plus, he was fifteen years my senior. Meanwhile, I was still just twenty-six years old. The old men on the board of directors probably saw me as a kid.

If I was in their position, would I hire a twenty-six year old to manage the most important project in the company's history?

I sipped my glass of wine and decided that I didn't want to think about the answer just yet.

Downstairs, my doorbell rang.

FedEx usually made their deliveries around this time. I couldn't remember what package I was expecting. The box of monthly makeup samples? Trying out those might take my mind off things tonight. I'd been wanting to test out some new mascara.

The doorbell rang a second time.

I frowned and sat up in the tub to look out the window. It faced the street in front of my house, but there wasn't a delivery truck outside. I couldn't see my front porch from here.

The doorbell rang two more times in quick succession, and then there was a knock too.

"I just want to enjoy my damn bath," I grumbled while grabbing a towel and wrapping it around myself. I stomped downstairs and marched right up to the front door. Normally I would have checked out the living room window to see who it was, but I was too annoyed to take such precautions. I intended to give whoever it was—salesman, Jehovah's Witness, or Girl Scout—a piece of my mind.

I threw open the door.

And then I died of embarrassment.

6

Robbie

I wasn't good with social situations. Then again, what IT geeks were?

I'd been working with computers since I was a little kid and my dad brought home our first Hewlett Packard desktop. I was hooked the moment he showed me how to use the mouse and keyboard. Fast forward fifteen years, and I was still more comfortable in a dark room staring at a glowing screen than I was facing actual humans. In fact, my ideal day involved never having to interact with anyone in person at all.

But my boss had been insisting I branch out. Expand my boundaries and try something outside my comfort zone. It was healthy, he said. The only way to grow from a fresh-out-of-college geek and into an adult IT Analyst with a career.

Volunteering for the party planning committee was the last thing I wanted. The only thing worse than taking part in social gatherings was *organizing* social gatherings. But my boss insisted, so I had signed up.

And now we were banging on some stranger's door without an answer.

I cleared my throat and looked up at the house. "Are you sure this is the right place?"

Liam Harford, one of the guys from the sales department, rang the doorbell again. "I'm positive this is Leslie's house. And that's her car in the driveway."

This was my nightmare. I hated confrontation. Ringing someone's doorbell and awkwardly standing around? All I wanted to do was jog back down the steps, get in my car, and drive home.

And then the last thing I expected happened.

The door flew open, and a beautiful, semi-naked woman greeted us.

Leslie Hill was wearing only a towel, and her auburn hair hung wetly down her back. Her long eyelashes framed eyes that were round, surprised sapphires. The towel hugged her curves like a tight cocktail dress. A full chest and hips that were so shapely I immediately began thinking about running my hands along them, feeling where they went.

She was sexy as hell, in a way that knocked the wind out of my chest.

Oh, wow, I thought when I saw her.

Leslie blinked as if we were the last people she expected to see.

"Hey, Leslie," Liam said. "You, uh, did say we were meeting tonight. Right?"

The fair skin of her cheeks turned three different shades of red. "Oh my God. I forgot!"

Liam grinned. "I can see that."

I cleared my throat. "We can, um, come back another time. If you want."

Leslie sighed and stepped out of the way. "No, let's get this over with. The last thing I want is Charletta on my butt about canceling. Don't tell her I said that."

The house opened directly into the living room and kitchen area. A bottle of white wine was open on the kitchen island, and an attractive lemony smell filled the air.

"I'll be right back," Leslie said before hastily going back upstairs.

Liam glanced at me. "Well *that's* embarrassing."

"Yeah, heh," I said. "I would lock myself in my room and never come out."

He shrugged. "Leslie's a tough cookie. She'll get over it quickly."

"You two know each other already?"

"Worked together in sales," Liam confirmed. "We go way back."

Great. Now I felt like a third wheel. It was hard enough for me to make friends since I was so shy, but if people here already knew each other then I would be the odd man out.

"Hey, is she a runner?" I asked when I realized where she looked familiar from.

"Actually, yeah," Liam said. "Why?"

"I think we're in the same Saturday running group…"

A knock came at the door. Liam opened it to reveal Arthur, one of the financial analysts in the company. "Hello! I am here to plan the party!" he said in his subtle French accent.

Beth and Charletta, the other two women on the planning committee, came up the steps a few minutes after him. I'd never met either of them, and shook their hands and tried to introduce myself without mumbling or feeling awkward.

I winced afterwards. I had no reason to feel self-conscious. I knew I wasn't ugly, and I spent a lot of time in the gym to build some muscle and buck the trend of the scrawny IT geek. But I still felt so uncomfortable talking to strangers, especially women. Everything that came out of my mouth felt awkward and out of place.

This is good for me, I told myself as we lingered in the living room. *Branching out and pushing my comfort zone, like my boss said.*

Leslie came back downstairs soon after. She was dressed in jeans and a T-shirt, and smiled warmly at me. "Sorry about earlier. I didn't mean to answer the door in just my towel."

"It's, uh, totally fine," I said while shaking her hand. Her skin was soft and warm. "I didn't even notice you were wearing a towel."

"Ha ha, very funny," she said as she said hello to everyone else. I was glad that her attention was elsewhere, because I couldn't take my eyes off her. She was cute, and charming, and sexy as hell—all at the same time.

Maybe tonight will be alright after all, I thought.

7

Leslie

Somehow, I didn't die of embarrassment. I ran back upstairs and dried my hair, then put on some clothes. Even then, I didn't want to leave the confines of my bedroom. *Maybe if I stay in here for the rest of the night, everyone will leave.*

I made myself go back downstairs. Everyone else had arrived and were mingling in the area between my living room and kitchen. Liam glanced at me and gave me a look: *Nice of you to put some clothes on.*

Shut up, I sent back at him with a look. Then I went up to the one person I didn't know and shook his hand. He introduced himself as Robbie, and made a joke about how he hadn't even noticed the towel.

I groaned internally. It was bad enough that Liam saw me almost-nude, considering all the baggage the two of us had. But Robbie? Behind his thick glasses was a strong nose and a chiseled face. Unlike Liam, who had changed into jeans and a shirt, Robbie still wore a blue button-down tucked into tight slacks, both of which showed off the muscular build underneath. Aside from the glasses, he looked like he belonged in front of a barbell rather than a computer screen.

And now he was acting awkward around me. Because I'd

opened the door in a towel. Great.

"Leslie!" came a familiar French accent. "I see that you have already opened the wine without us!"

I grinned at Arthur. "Had to let the tannins breathe."

I'd worked with Arthur on one or two projects at Allegheny Supply, whenever a financial export was required. He was always a joy to be around, full of positive energy, big smiles, and exaggerated compliments. He was beautiful rather than handsome, like a cologne model in a magazine with a prominent hooked nose.

"Fear not!" Arthur declared, opening his bag. "I have brought two more bottles for us to share."

"I'll probably pass on the wine," Robbie said.

Arthur scoffed. "Nonsense, Robert! How can we plan a party if we are not in the proper mood? Come, Leslie, and show me where you have hidden your wine glasses!"

I couldn't help but smile as I showed him where they were. At least *he* hadn't seen me in a towel tonight.

"How about we order some pizza?" Charletta suggested.

While Arthur poured everyone wine, I hastily tidied up. My house was fairly clean, but it still wasn't "have company over" clean. I put away the gym bag I'd tossed on the couch, cleaned up a glass I had left in the living room the night before, and then moved the dishes in the sink to the dishwasher and wiped down the counter.

"Come have some wine with us," Liam told me. "We're all getting settled into the living room."

"As soon as I finish wiping this down," I said.

He snatched the cloth out of my hand. "If you don't think this is clean enough, you should see my place."

I tried to take the cloth away from him, but he hid it behind his back. I glared at him and said, "Your place is dirty? I would have taken you for a neat freak."

"I hide my true nature well. Come on."

He handed me a glass of wine and led me into the living room. Everyone was gathered around on the couch, the loveseat, and in chairs.

"Thank you *so much* for offering to host," Charletta told me. She was a little older than me, maybe around thirty, and looked like she was born to organize and plan events. "It's really unfortunate that we lost Polly from HR."

"Sorry about that," Liam said, raising his hand. "Our breakup is probably the reason she bailed."

I took a seat on the couch next to Beth. The petite blonde woman smiled at me and said, "Are you sure you have to quit the committee too? We could really use your help. Six is better than five."

I remembered what my boss had said about this being good experience if I ever applied for another management position. Maybe if I had been on the party planning committee last year, I would have gotten the STT manager job.

"Actually, I think I'll stay," I told her. "I didn't think I had the time in my schedule, but it appears that has changed."

Liam raised an eyebrow at that, but didn't ask.

"Yay!" Beth said happily.

"Excellent!" Charletta opened a binder. "I took the liberty of printing out all the documents and organizing them together, color-coordinated based on type of planning activity. We should get started by looking at last year's party..."

We listened to Charletta explain all the details of last year's party. That took twenty minutes by itself—there was a lot involved with planning a party for five hundred people. We made the decision to keep things simple tonight, and focus on broad decision-making. The smaller details and specifics could come later.

The venue for the holiday party was the easiest thing. It was always hosted on the fourth floor of the Allegheny Supply headquarters building, which had an open layout and housed the C-suite offices. We discussed food vendor options next, then alcohol. Should we serve only beer and wine, or have a full bar? What about beer, wine, and specialty mixed drinks like margaritas?

It helped that the office Halloween party was coming up in two weeks. That was already planned and scheduled, and gave us another idea of what we needed to plan for, and the scale compared to the holiday party.

As we discussed things, I began to loosen up. The wine helped. Even though I had started out the night wanting to wallow alone in my sorrows, it was nice to share some drinks with my colleagues. Beth was less annoying in person than she was in a chat room, since she couldn't attach five exclamation points to the end of every spoken sentence. Charletta was kind of anal, but she had taken charge of the entire planning committee and seemed to have a good handle on everything that needed to get done.

And the guys...

Robbie sipped his wine slowly and kept sending glances my way. He had this sexy nerd thing going on—shy and adorable.

Arthur was seated on the loveseat to my left, smiling and laughing and making jokes about the entire process. He spoke flawless English, but had just enough of a French accent to be sexy rather than distracting. From the few projects we'd worked on together, I'd learned that he had a reputation for being a ladies man. That didn't surprise me one bit. He was a notorious flirt, and was easily the sharpest dresser in the office. Arthur always wore a three-piece suit to work, and like Robbie he hadn't changed before coming here. Arthur had draped the suit jacket over the back of the loveseat, showing off the charcoal-colored vest underneath.

All the women in the office loved him. I thought he was sexy as hell too, though he had never made a move on me besides some harmless flirting. Having him sitting in my living room, drinking wine and smiling at me? It was like I'd brought home the most exotic animal from the zoo.

Then there was Liam sitting on the chair across from me. He made planning suggestions here and there while sending smiles in my direction whenever Charletta said something silly. It reminded me of the days working together in the sales pit, when we would share glances during our weekly status meeting in the conference room. Having our own private discussion together using only our eyes.

Like when Charletta suggested having a margarita machine instead of a full bar.

Margaritas? In December? Liam's eyes told me.

I know, right? I sent back.

Being around him reminded me of something else: my reason for not going out to dinner with him was no longer valid. Since I had been turned down for the STT manager position, there was nothing stopping us from dating. I needed to find time to tell him that I had changed my mind, that we should go out this weekend.

At the end of the night, I thought. *I'll tell him then.*

"We do need other activities at the party," Charletta was saying. "The party should not just be drinking and dancing."

"What about a raffle?" Arthur suggested. "Or a charity auction?"

"Oh, yeah!" Beth said. "There was a charity auction last year!"

Charletta flipped a page in her binder. "Oh, wow. It raised over twenty thousand dollars last year. We should definitely start reaching out to local businesses to donate items for the auction…"

"No, no, no," Arthur said unhappily. "I was referring to a human auction."

"I think we stopped doing that a century or two ago," Liam pointed out while glancing at me.

"It is a different auction." Arthur gestured, searching for the word. "Not for sale, for, um, lease? Single men and women only. People bid for a date with them… Yes?"

I took another sip of wine to cover my smile. Arthur's accent was becoming more pronounced the more he drank, and it was as smooth and sweet as French cream.

"Oh," Beth said. "A bachelor auction!"

"Yes!" Arthur snapped his fingers. "This is what I mean. An auction for bachelors."

"We could call it *the naughty list*!" Beth said excitedly.

"Oh, I love that!" I said.

"That's kind of risque." Charletta pursed her lips. "I'm not sure HR would allow that kind of thing in a corporate environment."

"It doesn't have to be risque," Liam suggested. "Instead of bidding for a date, it could be for a single dance at the party."

"We did one back in high school that was the same way: the winner won a dance," I added. "It was totally innocent, and a smash hit."

"Back in high school we also threw toilet paper at people's houses, and played *seven minutes in heaven*," Charletta argued. "That doesn't mean it's a good idea for the company holiday party."

Arthur frowned. "Seven minutes in heaven?"

"Have you ever played spin the bottle?" Liam asked.

Arthur nodded. "I have spun many bottles at university, yes."

"It's like that, but instead of kissing... You go into a dark closet together for seven minutes," I explained.

Arthur's hazel eyes widened. "And what occurs in this closet?"

I sipped my wine and smiled. "Whatever the two participants want to happen."

Arthur twisted his face in thought, then nodded once. "Very well. I would very much like to play this game."

Charletta laughed as if it was a joke. "We're *definitely* not doing this at the holiday party."

"No, no, no. I mean we must play it right now," Arthur clarified.

I thought about going into the closet with Arthur. Feeling those insanely kissable lips against mine. Wrapping my arms around him and pressing my body against his...

"Maybe some other time," Charletta said with another nervous laugh.

"Why not now?" Liam asked.

We all swung our gazes at him.

"Arthur and I are single," Liam gestured with his wine glass. "So is Leslie. And didn't you and Jesse break up last month, Charletta?"

"We did."

"I'm single too!" Beth chimed in.

Liam glanced at Robbie, who looked like he wanted to melt into his chair. "I'm not currently dating anyone, but I don't know if this is a good idea..."

"You do not have to play," Arthur said, sending a smile in my direction. "More fun for me."

I found myself smiling back at him.

I could see everyone thinking about it. Considering it. We were all in our twenties or early thirties, and none of us were dating someone. How often did an opportunity like this arise in adulthood?

The only negative I could see was the obvious one: we were all coworkers. Seven awkward minutes in a closet could lead to an entire *career* of awkwardness with another person. But to my surprise, I found the thought of fooling around with my coworkers thrilling. Tantalizing in a way that made my spine tingle.

They're all thinking the same thing, I realized as I looked around the circle. Everyone wanted to say yes... They just didn't want to be the first one.

Before anyone could answer, the doorbell rang.

"Pizza's here," I said, jumping up to answer the door.

8

Leslie

The topic was dropped as we ate pizza and resumed discussing the holiday planning. But I couldn't stop thinking about taking one of the guys into the closet and spending seven thrilling minutes with them.

Based on the faraway look on Liam's face, he was thinking about it too.

For the next half hour we discussed last year's party: what we liked and disliked, things that needed to be changed. We finished Arthur's two bottles of wine, so I opened up one of my own for us all to share. Slowly, the alcohol loosened us back up to the point that we were laughing and joking like before.

"A vodka fountain is *definitely* off the list," Beth said. "Remember Mr. Sinekund last year?"

I groaned. "The shirt thing?"

"Yes!" Beth laughed. "On his third or fourth visit to the vodka fountain, he spilled some on his shirt. So he ripped off his shirt right there and waved it around his head like a stripper!"

"Oh my gosh, I had forgotten about that," Charletta said. "That was the craziest thing I've ever seen since I started working here."

"How long have you been here?" Robbie suddenly asked. "Um, working at Allegheny Supply, I mean."

"Four years this November. You?"

Robbie rolled up his sleeves, revealing dark tattoos on his skin underneath. I found tattoos irresistible on a man, and it was so unexpected from someone like Robbie, that I couldn't stop staring.

"I just started here in the spring," Robbie said. "Not even a year."

"Arthur?" Charletta asked.

He sighed happily. "It has been three years since I arrived in your wonderful country."

"What about you?" Beth asked Liam.

Liam nodded at me. "Leslie and I both started in sales at the same time, five years ago."

"Five years," I said. "We were such *babies* back then. I don't know how we got any work done."

"You're still in sales, right?" Beth asked him.

"He never learned how to do anything else," I teased.

Liam glared back at me. "If you're good at what you do, why change?" He shook it off. "But I'm actually looking to branch out. I was just selected for the Systems Transition Team."

"The STT!" Beth exclaimed. "What role?"

"Sales liaison. I'll be helping choose the new software system."

"That's awesome!"

"Congrats," Charletta said. "I know a lot of people were vying for that role."

"Not just that role, but every part of the team," Robbie added. "I interviewed for the tech role, but didn't get it."

"When do you start?" Charletta asked. "Can you give us the inside scoop on what the new system will be like?"

"I would never jeopardize the integrity of the STT by divulging sensitive information." Liam scowled for a moment, then held out his palm. "For free. If you want to bribe me for the information, however..."

They all laughed and joked about the STT, but I felt my mood souring. I'd done a good job of not thinking about it all night, and now it was all any of them wanted to talk about.

I drank the rest of my wine and decided it was time to bring up another topic.

I went to the kitchen, refilled my glass, and then washed the bottle out in the sink. Then I grabbed my kitchen timer out of a drawer. When I returned to the living room, Arthur was giving me a knowing smile.

"So," I announced while hefting the empty bottle of Chardonnay and the timer. "Who wants to spin first?"

Everyone grew quiet. Arthur's smile deepened, and Liam cocked his head at me curiously. Robbie looked nervous, while Beth bit her lip and looked around to see what everyone else thought.

Charletta chuckled. Her cheeks were flush, and she was a lot looser than she had been earlier. "Are you serious?"

"We're all adults," I said. "And none of us work in the same department, so there's no conflict of interest..."

"You do not have to play if you do not wish," Arthur said. "You and Robbie may sit out..."

"I'll play," Robbie suddenly said excitedly. Then he seemed to realize he was excited, and blushed again.

He's so cute and shy, I thought.

Charletta made a show of thinking about it, then giggled. "Okay, I'm in!"

We moved aside the coffee table of pizza and sat in a circle on the floor.

"Wait!" Arthur said. "Pizza is good. Kisses are good. But pizza-kisses are not good." He passed around a pack of breath mints.

I popped one into my mouth and shared a look with Liam. *Is this really happening?* his expression asked.

I think so, I sent back. A tingle of excitement ran up my spine.

"Where are we going to... you know," Beth said with a nervous giggle.

"There's a coat closet behind the kitchen, around the corner," I said. "It's close... but not *too* close."

"The two people only have to do what they're comfortable with," Charletta said.

"Whatever that may be." Arthur winked at me.

I blushed and placed the bottle on the floor between all of us. "You go first," I told Liam.

"Why me!"

"My house, my rules," I said. "The most-senior person at the company goes first, which is you, since you started in sales two days before me. Then we'll go clockwise from you."

That meant the spin order would be Liam, Robbie, Arthur, me, Beth, and Charletta. Everyone gazed around the circle and nodded.

Liam leaned forward to grip the bottle in his hand. "No point in waiting."

With a flick of his wrist, he sent the bottle spinning.

Everyone was silent as the bottle spun rapidly on the rug. I glanced up at Liam and found that he was looking at me curiously. I smiled back and sipped my wine. *We both want this to happen.* I could read it in his expression as easily as if it was a text message.

Around and around the bottle went in a blur, then began slowing down. I watched with anxious eyes as it was nearly done. The end of the bottle passed me, then Beth, then Charletta, and was slowing to a stop as it came back around...

Land on me, I silently thought. *It's going to land on me!*

The bottle slowed to a stop just past me, halfway between me and Beth.

But *slightly* closer to her.

"Beth and Liam!" Arthur said in a slurring French accent. "You are the first two lovebirds chosen by the mysterious bottle!"

Beth giggled and stood up. "So... Are we doing this?"

Liam glanced at me, then quickly looked away. "I think so." He took her hand and led her down the hall.

I stared after them and tried to keep my disappointment from showing on my face. *Liam doesn't like ditsy blondes. They probably won't do anything.*

"So?" Arthur said, patting me on the leg. "What now?"

I shook off my rising jealousy and twisted the dial on the kitchen timer. "I set the timer for seven minutes. When it goes off, we tell them to come back out."

The timer began ticking down.

"So, it sucks what happened to Notre Dame, huh?" I said to take my mind off of what may or may not be happening in my coat closet.

Arthur clutched his vest like he had been stabbed in the heart. "Mon amour! I wept enormous tears of sadness when I saw the news!"

"I heard they saved all of the artwork inside," Robbie chimed in. "So that's, um, good. Right?"

We made quiet, awkward conversation while the timer ticked down. It was the longest seven minutes of my life. I convinced myself that Liam and Beth weren't doing anything inside. Maybe they shared a kiss, but nothing else. Liam wouldn't do that.

Except you just turned him down today, whispered the devil in my head. *He has no idea how you really feel about him.*

I tapped my foot and picked at my fingernail until the timer eventually went off.

"The time is up!" Arthur yelled excitedly. "Come out and show yourselves!"

I heard the door to the closet immediately open, and then the two of them came walking around the corner. They were still holding hands, and Beth was all smiles. Liam glanced at me, then quickly looked away as they took their seats in the circle.

"Well?" Arthur demanded. "Was it truly seven minutes in *heaven?*"

Liam shrugged coyly. Beth giggled and said, "It was very good."

Something definitely happened. It wasn't just a boring seven minutes with one quick peck on the cheek.

I put on a plastic smile. "Alright, you're next Robbie."

"Oh. Um. Okay." Robbie reached a tattooed arm forward to pick up the bottle. He tested its weight in his hand, placed it back down, and then gave it a spin.

Liam gave me a small smile. Almost apologetic. I glanced at Beth, who was still grinning like an idiot, then back at Liam. *Maybe they kissed a little bit. Or even made out.* Beth wasn't ugly. She was petite but had a round, innocent face. Guys would kill for seven minutes in a closet with her.

I was thinking of all the ways I disliked Beth when the bottle stopped on me.

"Oh," Robbie said.

Arthur clapped his hands. "The all-knowing bottle has chosen Leslie!"

I felt my cheeks redden with the excitement of being selected. Robbie smiled nervously at me. "If you don't want to..."

I got to my feet and took his hand. "We can't say no to the bottle. Come on."

His hand was big enough to completely envelope mine as I led him down the hall and around the corner to the waiting closet. He held the door for me like a perfect gentleman. The closet contained six of my coats, which I had to push aside to stand comfortably in. As Robbie joined me and closed the door, the closet was downright cramped.

Complete darkness filled the room. There wasn't even a sliver of light underneath the door. Just the two of us sharing the dark space, breathing quietly.

A light flashed on from Robbie's cell phone. He held it in his palm, face-up, so that it illuminated our two faces. "That's a little better," he said.

"That's sort of cheating," I pointed out.

He smiled. "I won't tell if you won't."

The harsh light from the phone accentuated the hard lines of Robbie's face, making him seem even sexier than before. I could barely see the ink from his tattoos on the hand holding the phone.

As we stood close together, I couldn't ignore just how gorgeous he was. And after the three or four glasses of wine I'd had, I was drawn to him. But still, I hesitated. Making the first move with someone was difficult, especially someone I had just met.

"I didn't expect someone like you to have tattoos," I said.

Robbie frowned behind his glasses. "Why not?"

"IT guys are always kind of quiet."

"I *am* quiet."

I chuckled and said, "Yeah, but getting a tattoo is kind of a *loud* thing, you know?"

He shrugged in the darkness. This close, I could hear his breathing and feel it softly on my skin. "I don't know. It's kind of a way for me to be more extrovert, but without saying anything. A silent form of personal expression."

"What are you trying to express?" I asked.

He moved the cell phone light and shone it on his arm. There was a tattoo of a maze, but the maze broke apart into digital ones and zeroes.

"I liked mazes as a kid," he explained. "If I had a piece of paper and a pencil, I'd sit quietly and draw mazes all day. And the ones and zeroes are because I'm a computer programmer. Everything is binary, at its core. Ones and zeroes. On or off. Give me enough memory space and nothing but ones and zeroes and I could write the constitution. Or Hamlet."

Robbie was suddenly so enthusiastic about himself that he seemed like a different person. Or rather, this was who he *really* was, and the quiet man behind a computer screen was someone else.

His enthusiasm was so infectious, so attractive, that I kissed him.

He was surprised, at first. He recoiled a bit, and dropped his phone on the ground. I almost stopped then and there. But then he began kissing me back.

And he was a *very* good kisser.

I melted into him as his arms wrapped around me in the darkness, lips moving gently against each other carefully. Thoughtfully. Deliberately.

When Robbie kissed someone, he didn't just go through the motions. He gave them all of himself.

Somewhere distant, a timer dinged. "C'est la fin!" Arthur called happily, voice muffled due to the door and distance. "Come on out!"

We both panted in the darkness, still holding each other in our arms. "You're a good kisser," I said just to say something.

His smile, illuminated by the phone light shining up from the ground, made my heart twist wonderfully. "I have a good partner."

Robbie retrieved the phone from the ground and we opened the door to return to the group.

Who would have thought the shy geek was the best kisser?

"There they are!" Arthur announced when we came around the corner. "I thought I would have to dive in to save you two, like the pool lifeguard! I can tell you had a wonderful time, Robbie, for you cannot stop smiling."

Robbie was indeed grinning, and being called out on it turned his cheeks crimson. Seeing him blush only made him *more* adorable.

Liam was watching me carefully. I smiled weakly and sat down, suddenly feeling guilty. *All we did was kiss*, I thought as I retrieved my glass of wine and took a sip. *Liam probably did the same with Beth, or worse.*

"At last, the time has come for me to spin the wine," Arthur said sagely. "I must warn you three charming ladies that I am a devilishly good kisser."

"Lot of talk before the action," Charletta said, biting her lip. "Hurry up so we can see what you've got."

"What I have *got* shall be seen soon enough!" Arthur picked up the bottle, spun it flourishingly in the air, then tossed it to the ground with an extravagant spin. It bounced once, but continued spinning rapidly on the rug.

I kept sharing glances with Robbie while we waited for the bottle to stop. I saw him in a totally different light now. Before, he had been cute in a nerdy sort of way, with some muscle to boot. But now? Everything had been dialed up to eleven. I wanted to kiss the tattoos on his arms and feel the biceps that bulged underneath his rolled-up dress shirt. I wanted to grab a handful of his hair and pull his lips to mine and kiss him so hard I drew blood.

The bottle slowed to a stop facing me.

"Ohh, two in a row!" Beth declared. "Lucky!"

Arthur bent down to extend his hand. "It is I who am the lucky one, to draw our beautiful host."

Arthur was beautiful and the line was cheesy, but when you were that hot, it *worked*. I bit my lip and took his hand, and he pulled me to my feet and led me to the closet. This time I didn't look back over my shoulder, because I knew there would be *two* men watching me go.

The door closed. Arthur's aftershave smelled strong and slightly sweet, and his fingertips ran up both of my arms.

I was so hot and bothered after my seven minutes with Robbie that I practically threw myself at Arthur, searching for his lips in the darkness. But he gripped my arms tightly and held me back when my lips were just an inch from his. So close that I could *feel* his smile in the darkness.

"No no no," he cooed softly. "This is not how it is done. I must taste you first." He pulled my hand to his lips and kissed my palm softly. The perfect amount of five-o'clock shadow on his cheeks brushed against my skin as he kissed my wrist next, then my forearm. "A woman like you deserves to be kissed not once, but many times."

His voice was a deep rumble in the darkness. "I bet that line has worked on a lot of girls over the years," I said, because it was *definitely* working on me just then as his lips kissed along my elbow.

"It is not a line. It is the truth. *Vous êtes belle*, Leslie. You are beautiful. Beautiful women deserve to be made love to, slowly and passionately."

I sighed deeply. "Is that what we're going to do in here? Make love?"

He put his face close to mine so that I could feel his breath on my lips. "We will see how far we get in seven minutes, *mon fleur.*"

His lips brushed against mine softly, and his tongue flicked out against my mouth. I parted my lips for him and gave him my tongue, not in a deep, passionate way, but in a soft, almost caressing manner. *Of course the Frenchman wants to French kiss*, I thought as I surrendered to the feeling of his tongue against my tongue and his lips against my lips.

Arthur's hands ran up and down my back, slowly pulling me against his body with increasing force. I was so hot and bothered from my seven minutes with Robbie that Arthur was exactly what I wanted, and then some. Soon I was kissing him harder, and moaning into his mouth.

Arthur's hand slid down to my hip, feeling the curve of my jeans. It lingered there, and I desperately wanted him to touch me, to escalate what we were doing to the next erotic step, so I reached down and felt the front of his slacks. I felt his hard cock immediately. The fabric of his pants was thin enough that I could feel every line and contour of his dick with ease. He wasn't wearing underwear.

As if by command, his hand moved from my hip to between my legs. He rubbed my pussy through my jeans and I moaned deeper into his mouth.

"*Mon Dieu*," he whispered. "*Te sens incroyable.* You feel incredible..."

"So do you," I breathed back.

It was clear Arthur was an expert at pleasing women. Even through the fabric of my jeans, he managed to find my clit with his fingers, rubbing with just the right amount of force. All the while his tongue swirled deeper in my mouth, French kissing me like there was no tomorrow.

I sighed as he cupped one of my breasts through my shirt, sending shivers of pleasure through my body. His other hand deftly unbuttoned my jeans, unzipped the zipper, and reached down into my panties to rub my wet slit. I began to reach for his zipper so I could take out his cock, to stroke him off properly and make him rumble with pleasure...

"Time's up!" Beth called from the other room.

"No," I whispered. "I don't want to stop..."

Arthur sighed unhappily. His hand stopped moving in my pants, but he kept it firmly on my pussy. Like it was happy there.

"We must stop," he said sadly. "Those are the rules, yes?"

"Rules are meant to be broken."

He made a clicking noise with his tongue. "Until next time, *mon fleur.*" He kissed me on the lips, then on the cheek, and finally removed his hand from my pants.

"Who says there will be a next time?"

He opened the door a crack, which made a sliver of light fall across his handsome French face. "I do. I say this."

He left the closet and rounded the corner. I followed close behind.

"Lovely people of the party planning committee," Arthur said in the living room. "I have an announcement to make. Leslie and I are now in love. We are unable to fulfill our obligations on this committee because we will be running off to elope together at once."

"Dang, Leslie," Charletta said, slurring her words. "Save some for the rest of us!"

Arthur took my hand and kissed it gently. I smiled back at him, aware that both Robbie and Liam were watching me closely now.

"Who wants more wine?" I asked, retreating to the kitchen area to get a hold of myself.

Beth joined me as I was opening another bottle. "You look like you two had a great time!"

I giggled in spite of myself. "Maybe."

"Come on," she whispered. "Give me some details! What did Arthur do?"

I looked sideways at her. "What did you and Liam do?"

Her smile disappeared. "Huh?"

"You and Liam went first." The words spilled out of me, driven purely by curiosity. "Did you two kiss? Make out? More than that?"

Beth glanced back at the living room. "I don't think I should say."

A dagger of jealousy stabbed me in the chest. She and Liam must have done more than just kiss for her to act this way.

I carried my fresh wine glass back to the living room. "Who's turn is it now?"

"It's your turn," Charletta said. The normally-organized woman was definitely beyond tipsy. "But the last two spins landed on you, so if you want to skip your turn and let someone else have a go..." She punctuated it with a wink at Arthur.

"I definitely don't want to skip my turn," I said, grabbing the bottle and giving it a spin. I glanced up at Arthur and said, "We can't break the rules."

He grinned back wolfishly.

As the bottle spun, I wondered who I wanted it to land on more. Arthur and I could finish what we started—the way his fingers were moving before, I was almost certain seven minutes would be enough. Or if it landed on Robbie, he and I could take things further than before. I'd love to see what he had going on underneath those pants.

But the bottle didn't stop on either of them.

It landed on Liam.

9

Leslie

The bottle didn't just stop in Liam's general direction. It ended facing directly on him, like a compass being drawn to a magnet. He blinked and looked as surprised as I was.

"Hat trick!" Beth said excitedly. "Finishing out the trio, huh Leslie?"

"Looks like it." I jumped up, grabbed Liam's hand, and pulled him toward the closet. Neither of us said anything as we opened the door, went inside, and closed it.

Everything was silent. I couldn't even hear him breathing. The moment dragged on and on. I didn't know what he was waiting for. Then again, what was *I* waiting for?

Five years worth of smiling, teasing, and office flirting passed in that single moment together in the dark closet.

"Well?" he finally asked. "What's going on, Leslie?"

"What do you mean?"

He sighed. "Today, after five years, I finally asked you out. And you told me you were too busy to date right now. It wasn't what I wanted to hear, but I respected that, because I know you're focused on your career and life is crazy right now.

"But then," he added in a different tone, "it turns out you're working on the holiday party committee. Which you said you were backing out of, then changed your mind about. So apparently you're *not* too busy. I spent the rest of the afternoon feeling sorry for myself and wondering if you ever had feelings for me at all, or if it was all just a game."

"Liam..."

He went on as if I hadn't spoken. "Then, out of the blue after a few glasses of wine, you suggested we spin the bottle and play seven minutes in heaven. All the while giving me bedroom eyes and confusing the hell out of me. Then going into the closet with Robbie and Arthur and grinning like a schoolgirl when you came out..."

"Hey, those are the rules," I protested. "I can't choose how the bottle spins."

"I'm not jealous," he clarified. "I don't care if you make out with either of them. That has nothing to do with my *feelings* for you. What I care about is that I feel like you're not being honest with me. What's going on with *us,* Leslie? Or is there even an us at all? If you don't want to be with me, just say it. I can handle rejection, Leslie. But I can't handle dishonesty."

His frustration, his passion, was like a physical presence in the closet with us. I felt simultaneously guilty and attracted to him for it. That he cared this much...

"I did lie to you," I admitted. "What I told you at lunch about being busy? It was partly true, but partly an excuse. The truth is that I turned down your date because..."

"What?" he asked softly. "You can tell me."

"I applied for the Systems Transition Team manager position."

I heard him gasp. "You would have been my boss."

"I didn't want to tell anyone before it was official. And I didn't want to go on a date with you, hit it off, and then be put in an uncomfortable position on the STT team."

His laugh was low and bitter. "If I had known, I would have quit the STT."

"Exactly the reason I couldn't tell you!" I insisted. "I didn't want you to have to make that decision. I didn't want to have to make it either." I sighed. "But they gave the position to Oliver."

"Which means..."

Liam took my hands in his. I wished it wasn't dark because I wanted to see the look in his eyes. And I wanted him to see the look in mine.

But the darkness reminded me of something else.

"Did you have fun with Beth?" I asked.

I sensed his body tense. "It was fine."

"Just fine? She seemed to enjoy it."

"I'm sure she did," he said carefully. "Leslie, why..."

"I asked her about it in the kitchen and she wouldn't tell me what happened. You must have really pleased her."

"Leslie, are *you* jealous?"

It was stupid. I had just been making out with Arthur, and Robbie before that, and here I was being jealous about Liam and Beth? Over a game that I had suggested?

But I couldn't stop myself. Today had been a shitshow from start to finish, and all I could think about was the way Beth had blushed when I asked her what they had done in the closet.

"I'm curious, is all," I said.

Liam sighed. "I can't believe you. I poured my heart out today at lunch, and again here in the closet, and you're asking about this..."

"Why are you avoiding the question?" I asked.

Before he could answer, the timer dinged in the other room. "Leslie! Liam! Your time in heaven has concluded!" Arthur shouted.

"Forget it," Liam said, opening the closet and marching out.

"Wait!" I whispered, but he was already around the corner.

I walked back into the room and wondered how I was going to pretend like everything was okay. Fortunately, I didn't have to. Charletta was standing and gesturing, and Beth was holding her arm and arguing with her.

"I think we need to get you home," Beth was saying to her. "You can barely stand."

"It's not my turn yet!" Charletta protested. "I want to spin the bottle!"

Arthur wrapped an arm around her shoulder. "Come, Charletta. Allow me to escort you to Beth's car."

"I don't want a car. I want a *kiss*."

Arthur gave her a lip-smacking kiss on her cheek. "*Voilà*! One kiss for Charletta. Is that better now?"

"A little bit..."

Arthur looked over his shoulder and gave me a wink. I waved goodbye as he and Charletta disappeared.

"I had, um, a really good time," Robbie said to me, as bashful as could be. "Thank you for having me over. Having *us* over, I mean. The whole group. Not just me."

I smiled at his cute awkwardness. "Happy to have you."

He grinned, then left. Liam was still in the living room gathering his coat and shoes, but Beth was standing next to me with a concerned look on her face.

"Leslie?" she whispered. "I want to tell you something. About what happened in the closet."

"It doesn't matter," I said. "It was just a game."

"That's the thing," she replied, glancing at Liam to make sure he wasn't within earshot. "*Nothing* happened. We didn't even kiss. I was all excited to make out with him, but he told me he couldn't do it. Because of *you*."

I gave a start. "What?"

"All he would talk about was you, Leslie! For seven minutes he told me everything about you..." She glanced over and quickly changed her tone. "So, yeah! Thanks for having us over! Can't wait to do it again sometime."

I frowned with confusion as she quickly left.

"Leslie."

Liam approached me while shouldering into his coat. With his mess of brown hair and boyish good looks, he was as handsome as the day I'd met him five years ago.

"It was good to see you," he said, moving to leave.

I quickly closed the door in his face. He frowned.

"You didn't do *anything* with Beth?"

"She's not my type. You should know that."

I trembled as I leaned against the door, blocking his path. "Do you really have feelings for me, Liam?"

His eyes widened. "I do."

I went to the living room and twisted the dial on the kitchen timer to seven minutes. It began ticking down.

"Prove it," I said.

With one shared look, we both knew what we wanted.

In four quick steps he descended on me hungrily, taking my face in his hands and kissing me like I'd always dreamed he would. I poured all of my love and affection into his lips, all of my frustrations of the day and of five years of always missing out on being with him, and based on the way he clutched my jaw and kissed me back he was doing the same thing.

We fell to the floor in a tangle, half on the rug in the living room and half on the tile of the kitchen, cool against my shoulder blades as he pressed his weight on me. He was wearing far too many clothes so I ripped off his jacket, then tugged at his oppressive shirt until he sat back and pulled it over his head. Despite looking tall and lanky, shirtless Liam was absolutely shredded with lean muscle. There wasn't an ounce of fat on his body that I could see; his abdominals and the muscles along his side rippled as he lowered himself on top of me again.

"Oh, Liam..." I moaned as he kissed my neck.

"I've been thinking about you all night." He kissed lower, pulling my shirt aside to nuzzle against my collarbone. "All day. Hell, I've thought of nothing but you since I became single."

"Yes," I whispered as he pulled my shirt over my head, revealing my bra and breasts. "Yes, Liam, touch me, kiss me..."

Guilt slammed into me like a door closing on my face. *He thought only of me, and yet when I was in the closet with Arthur and Robbie...*

"Liam." I pushed him back and sat up.

His face was flush with excitement. "What is it?"

"I have to tell you something. When I was in the closet with the others..."

"Leslie, I don't care."

"I made out with Robbie," I said in a rush. "Arthur and I went a little further, touching each other..."

I steeled myself for Liam's reaction, because I was certain he would look at me like he had been betrayed. Instead, he gave me that perfect lopsided grin he'd been giving me for five years."

"Leslie, I don't care." He cupped my jaw with one big hand. "I'm not the jealous type. It was only a game."

"Are you sure?" I asked in a weak voice.

His grin deepened. "I'm sure that our timer is ticking down. And I don't want to be interrupted this time."

He fell upon me again, kissing my neck and shoulder. I sighed with pleasure and excitement and relief, relief most of all. He unclasped my bra and then took my nipple in his mouth, circling it gently with his tongue while gently squeezing my other breast with his hand. I reached between us and grabbed his crotch, clutching it through his jeans, but that simply would not do so I unzipped his jeans and reached inside until I found his smooth, hot skin. He sighed around my nipple as I pulled his cock out and began stroking it.

Liam slid up and kissed me on the lips again, this time with tongue the way Arthur had. I scrambled out of my jeans and he did the same, until we were two naked coworkers on the floor of my living room, half on the rug and half on the tile.

His lips never left mine as he guided his cock into my pussy. I relaxed as his head entered me, then his long shaft, accepting inch after inch as he drove his hips into me. Then we were moaning together, sharing the ecstasy of our joined bodies after five years of foreplay.

I wrapped my arms around him and kissed him deeply as he fucked me. Long, slow strokes at first, but my body burned for his so I moved my hips faster, and he responded to the cues by fucking me faster and harder until every stroke was a sledgehammer of pleasure rocking my entire body while his tongue pressed wetly against mine. When I didn't think it could get any more intense, he reached between us and rubbed my clit with his thumb, a hard circle that flipped every remaining switch in my body to the "on" position and sent me screaming with ecstasy in my living room, and before long his own ragged voice joined mine, and I broke off our kiss so I could stare into his eyes as we came together again, and again, and again.

10

Leslie

"Alright, I can't take it anymore," I said.

"What's that?" Liam whispered.

"My ass is on the rug, but my shoulders are on the kitchen tile. And it's *cold*."

Liam rumbled with laughter. "Let's fix that." He rose off my body where he had been laying, and lifted me off the ground with him. He kept leaning backwards until his back was on the rug, and he pulled me with him until I was resting on his wide, warm chest.

"Much better," I murmured.

"All of this is much better," he agreed. "Specifically the part where we had sex."

I sighed happily. "Was it worth the wait after five years?"

"Eh," he said.

I sat up and punched him playfully in the arm. He gave me that lopsided grin of his and pulled me back to his chest.

"It was everything I could have imagined, and then some," he said.

I kissed his chest softly. "That's more like it."

He was right: it was everything I could have imagined, too. Sometimes a person built an idea up in their head for so long that it couldn't possibly hold up to their expectations. This wasn't like that at all.

If anything, the real thing was better than my imagination.

I looked over my shoulder at the kitchen timer on the coffee table. "Did we really do all of that in less than seven minutes?"

Liam shook his head, which shook me on top of him. "It went off while we were in the middle of everything."

"I didn't even notice."

"I must have done a good job."

I scrunched up my face. "Ehh."

He glared at me, then said, "So, about that date this weekend..."

"Now that I'm not going to be your manager? Count me in."

"Any preference?"

"Hmm." I traced lines on Liam's bare chest with my fingernail. "I have a long training run that morning, so I'm going to be hungry that night. Somewhere with lots of carbs."

"Pasta sounds great," Liam said. "I know of just the place."

"It had better be good. You're going to have to impress me for our first date."

He tilted his head up to look at me. "You're not impressed?"

I shifted my leg so that my knee rubbed against his soft dick. "I'm impressed with *this*. Now you have to impress me with the rest of the package."

"I'll see what I can do."

I crossed my arms underneath my chin and stared down at him. "Why did we wait five years to do this?"

"I know, right?"

I squinted at him suspiciously. "So let me get one thing

straight. You and Beth got paired up for seven minutes in heaven. And you spent the entire time talking about *me*?"

Liam shrugged. "What else would we have done with the time?"

"Oh, I don't know. Beth is a blonde bimbo with disproportionately-large tits for someone as small as she. I'm sure you could use your imagination."

He bobbed his head pensively. "Not gonna lie. I thought about it."

"But talking about me was sexier?"

"Way sexier." He pursed his lips. "I mean, if you're secretly crushing on someone for five years and finally get a chance to fool around with them, why make out with someone else?"

Liam gave me an extra long stare.

"That's a dig at me!" I said, shocked. "You're making fun of me!"

"A little bit."

"I only made out with Arthur and Robbie because I thought *you* did that with Beth!"

He ran his hand through my hair and smiled. "I'm just teasing you a little bit. It honestly doesn't bother me. It was just a silly game."

"Speaking of silly games." I moved my knee back and forth. "Want to fool around again? In the bed this time?"

Liam grinned up at me. "I really, really want to. But I have to be up super early tomorrow. I have to fill out paperwork with HR before starting my job with the STT."

I groaned and rolled off of him. "Rub it in, why don't you?"

He rolled over, smothering my nude body with his. "I've done plenty of rubbing tonight." He kissed me gently on the lips. "I'm sorry you didn't get the position. But I have to admit I'm selfishly happy it led to this."

"Trading one *position* for another," I teased. "I'm happy this happened too."

"I'm even happier it happened out here, when we were by ourselves. Not that I totally wouldn't go to town on you in a closet while our coworkers waited out in the living room..."

"A little privacy is always good," I agreed.

He kissed me again, this time longer and more passionately. "I'm sorry I have to leave. I'll stay longer after our date this weekend."

I raised an eyebrow. "Are you implying I'm the kind of girl who puts out on the first date?"

Liam frowned, and swept his hand across my nude body. "Yeah, you think?"

I was sad to see him get dressed and leave, but I got over it quickly. It had finally happened, after so many years of flirting and teasing. Liam and I had slept together!

And we had a date this weekend!

I went to bed as excited as a girl on Christmas Eve who had gotten to open one of her presents early.

*

It was a beautiful day the next morning, and sunny, so I decided to walk to work rather than drive. It gave me time to think about what had happened, replaying everything in my head. Not just with Liam, but the actual party planning too. Even though I hadn't wanted to be part of the committee, it wasn't so bad once we actually sat down and started planning. Making decisions about the food, drinks, and activities. Next we would start calling vendors, comparing prices, and booking them. As far as projects went, there wasn't much to a single holiday party.

The hardest thing would be settling back into my normal job as an operations analyst. As much as I didn't want to admit it, I had been slacking on my normal duties while expecting to get the STT manager position. Now that I was out of the running, I needed to play catch-up.

But it was tough to feel bad about that as I walked across the Three Rivers Bridge, savoring the early morning sunlight on my cheeks and thinking about Liam. There was nothing as perfect as a brand new relationship.

When I reached the headquarters building for Allegheny Supply, the people in the elevator saw me coming and held the door for me. I rushed through the lobby and into the door of the semi-full elevator.

"Thanks," I said.

One of the men holding the door was Robbie. "Um. You're welcome," he said with an awkward smile.

I smiled back at him as the door closed and the elevator began to move.

After everything with Liam, I had forgotten about Robbie. The kiss we shared was passionate and ignited feelings in me, feelings that reemerged and swirled in my chest as we stood together in the elevator. He was adorable with his glasses, perfectly-combed hair, and the cute way he glanced at me and quickly glanced away. It was totally at odds with the muscular body underneath his dress shirt and slacks. A body I remembered being pressed against in the darkness of the closet...

If Liam and I hadn't gotten together, something *definitely* could have happened between Robbie and me. *Maybe in another life*, I thought sadly as I exited the elevator on my floor.

The Operations Department was a flurry of activity this morning. I weaved in and out of my coworkers to get to my desk, dropping my bag off in my cubicle...

...And then stopped with a jerk.

On my desk, resting across the stacks of operations reports that I had printed out, was a single purple rose. A strip of paper was tied around the stem. I picked up the rose and turned the paper over.

Mon Fleur

"Arthur," I whispered as I smelled the rose. "That Frenchman is crafty."

The flower brought with it another flood of emotions related to Arthur. Like Robbie, something had ignited in me after being with Arthur in the closet. A fierce attraction had bloomed, one which I could still sense inside me as I stood in front of my desk. Another potential relationship that might have been, had things not finally blossomed with Liam.

But unlike Robbie, Arthur might be harder to let down. He seemed like the kind of guy who would be persistent to the end. *I'll cross that bridge when I come to it*, I thought as I laid the rose against my laptop screen.

It was funny how everything always happened all at once. From famine to feast all in one night.

Before my laptop could boot up, my boss John Fadringham appeared at my desk. "Can I talk to you in my office?"

There was a worried look on his face that I had never seen before. "Yeah, sure," I said as I followed him across the department.

John shut the office door behind me, then went to each window facing the department and closed the blinds. Only when we were veiled in privacy did he finally sit behind his desk and cross one leg over the other.

"John, what's going on?" I asked.

"Have you checked your email this morning?"

I frowned with alarm. "No. Why?"

"I'm really sorry about how everything went down yesterday," he said. "How Oliver was announced for the STT manager position."

"It's okay," I said truthfully. Being with Liam last night helped take away the sting more than I had expected. Like a sexy little consolation prize. My dream man instead of my dream job.

"Part of it was HR's fault," John went on. "They had the task to notify you, but somehow it slipped through the cracks. Our COO is also partly to blame. She wasn't supposed to make the announcement until next week, but they're in such a rush to get the STT project off the ground that she forced the issue publicly."

"It's fine, really," I insisted. "You don't need to give me an explanation."

John shook his head. "I'm giving you this explanation because something changed, and I don't know why. Nobody does. But for whatever reason, Oliver Edwards is out. He's no longer taking the role."

I sucked in my breath. "You mean..."

"Leslie, it's yours," John said. "You're the new manager of the Systems Transition Team."

11

Liam

Have you ever gotten everything you've ever wanted all at the same time?

I'd spent weeks lobbying for the sales liaison in the Systems Transition Team. Sucking up to the right people and putting bugs in all the right ears. Applying, interviewing, and then interviewing again with different people. I doubted I would actually *get* the position. There were a lot of applicants with more experience than me, who were smarter than me, who *deserved* it more than me. I'd applied because, hell, why not?

And then I got it. The sales liaison position was mine!

Then everything with Leslie. Asking her out, getting rejected, and then everything that happened last night. The weird jealous back-and-forth of playing seven minutes in heaven with our coworkers. Arguing with her in the closet. Then staying after everyone else had left...

It was too early to make any judgments, but I knew we were perfect for each other. We clicked emotionally and intellectually.

And physically?

Oh man. I'd dreamed—actual dreams, at night—about ripping Leslie's clothes off and fucking her on the floor of the office. Fantasized about it countless times. Her house was just as good. I couldn't wait to go out with her this weekend and do it again.

Things were almost *too* good to be true in my life.

I should have been suspicious.

After finishing all the Human Resources paperwork, I went to the third floor where the Operations Department was. The Systems Transition Team had its own section partitioned off from everything else across the hall from the rest of the department. I thought about peeking over to say hi to Leslie, but I didn't want to seem too clingy.

Maybe we can get lunch later, I thought instead.

The STT department was full of new cubicles and a big office in the corner with walls made of glass. The office was dark, and the cubicles were all empty except for the one right outside the office, which was occupied by a shriveled raisin of a woman with grey hair up in a bun typing furiously on a keyboard. The placard on her desk said Mrs. Caltrop.

"Good morning. I'm Liam Harford, the new sales liaison."

She glanced up at me and grunted.

"Am I the first one here?"

She stopped typing and gave me a withering look. "Clearly not, since I've been here for two hours."

"I meant where is everyone else? I had to sign all the HR papers, so I figured I'd be late."

Mrs. Caltrop resumed typing. "I arrived this morning to find an email from Oliver Edwards stating he had decided to turn down the position of manager of the STT. The technical and finance liaisons also failed to show up, with similarly abrupt notice. The replacement for Oliver is being hailed as we speak. Choose any desk you want."

I looked around at the empty department. "If no one else is here, should I even stick around?"

She picked up the phone and began dialing. "Whatever makes you happy."

I chose one of the cubicles halfway between the door and the manager's office and unpacked my laptop and belongings. That took all of two minutes. I'd already tied up all the loose ends from my sales job, handing off all my clients to one of the other guys. I had literally nothing to do.

Not sure what else to do, I opened *Microsoft Teams*, the company chat client. Leslie had been online for forty-five minutes, but her status was yellow. Away.

I started to send her an eggplant emoji, stopped myself, and then hastily deleted it. That probably wasn't a good idea on a company server. I pulled out my cell phone but realized I didn't have her number. *I'll need to fix that later.*

Instead, I sent her a different text on *Teams*:

Harford, Liam: Lunch later? I'm buying.

I swiveled in my chair back and forth, testing the ball bearings of the new chair. Where would we go on our date Saturday? I had two favorite Italian restaurants in Pittsburgh, one of which was a little fancier than the other. How fancy was Leslie thinking? Sure, it was a first date and I wanted to impress her, but we had known each other for half a decade. And we'd already slept together.

Man, last night was awesome.

It was almost a good thing I didn't have any actual work to do, because right then I couldn't stop thinking about Leslie. The way her lips tasted. The way her skin felt underneath my fingertips. The way she spread her legs for me, accepting my cock into her pussy like it belonged there while we rutted on the floor of her living room...

And then, as if my imagination had summoned her, Leslie walked into the room.

"Hey! I was just thinking about you." I swept my hand around. "Come to check out my new team office?"

She walked past my desk without slowing down. "I'll talk to you in a minute," she said brusquely.

I sat up straight. "Leslie? What's wrong?"

"Trust me," she said over her shoulder. "I'll explain everything soon."

"Explain *what?*"

Mrs. Caltrop stood up from her desk. "Welcome, Ms. Hill. I'm your administrative assistant. Your office is all ready for you."

Oh, I thought.

And then: *oh no.*

12

Leslie

It was too much all at once. Shock, elation, and then horror. Walking into my new team's department should have filled me with excitement, but instead I had only a dreadful feeling in my stomach.

I've already slept with one of my employees, I thought.

Mrs. Caltrop was a small woman who looked frail, but moved and spoke with the energy of someone forty years younger. "The renovations to your office were completed yesterday," she said as she led me inside. "It is quite nice."

I gazed around the room. It was a corner office, and two of the four walls were exterior windows giving me a view of downtown Pittsburgh and the Ohio River. The desk was sleek and modern. The walls facing the rest of my department—*my department!*—were floor-to-ceiling glass.

"No blinds?" I asked.

Mrs. Caltrop grunted. "It's all ESG. Electrified Switchable Glass, the same as in the C-suite offices on the fourth floor." She flipped a switch by the door and in an instant, the glass became frosted and opaque. She flipped the switch again and it returned to its transparent state.

"Woah," I said, flipping the switch myself. It was like a magic trick!

"There's another switch on the desk as well. The chair is ergonomic, but the facilities department has a variety of others in storage, so if you do not approve of that I can order a replacement."

"I'm sure this one will be fine," I said. It was a lot to take in all at once.

Mrs. Caltrop nodded. "Very good. I will bring in your paperwork."

"Paperwork?"

"All of the Human Resource documents and disclosures. There are a lot of them."

She left the office and returned to the desk right outside the door.

I gazed around the room in wonder. I'd never had my own office—always a desk or cubicle. And this office was *nice*. Much nicer than what my old boss had.

Feeling like an impostor, I put my bag down next to the desk and lowered myself into the chair. The soft seat and curved back molded to my body almost perfectly. Much better than the squeaky, uncomfortable chair at my old desk.

I sighed and allowed myself to savor it. I was the Manager of the Systems Transition Team! Sure, I was their second choice. But I wasn't going to let pride get in the way of an amazing opportunity and a huge promotion.

Mrs. Caltrop returned with a stack of documents as thick as a college textbook. She placed them heavily on the desk. "Be sure to use blue or black ink. HR is picky."

"What happened to Oliver? Why didn't he take the job?"

She shrugged. "Nobody knows for sure. The emails were sent in the middle of the night."

I frowned. "Emails, plural?"

"The technical and finance liaisons submitted their resignations as well."

"We lost two of them too?" I asked, aghast.

She nodded. "The selection committee had several candidates all vetted for the positions, including backup candidates. I can get the ball rolling on their hiring process, unless you want to review the candidates yourself..."

I had a ton of work to get started on and didn't want to waste an entire day reviewing applications and interviewing people. I shook my head. "Whoever was next in line is fine. I trust the selection committee's judgement."

Mrs. Caltrop nodded as if I had made the right choice, and left the office.

I pulled the first piece of paper off the stack of documents, found a black pen in the top drawer of the desk, and got to work on all the paperwork.

There was a lot of redundant forms from when I first started working at the company. I had to approve a background check. The company had a strict drug-free policy, so I had to consent to possibly being drug tested once a year, at the discretion of the board of directors. Then I had to fill out all new W-4 forms for taxes, and then I-9 forms for employment verification.

After that was a huge chunk of documents from legal. A twenty-page non-disclosure agreement related to any industry or commercial secrets I may learn while working at Allegheny Supply. I skimmed those pages before signing. Then there was a non-compete clause. If I left the company, I was barred from working for an industry competitor for one year, in exchange for a severance package equal to twice my yearly salary plus bonuses. I read all seventeen of those pages far more carefully to ensure there wasn't anything that jumped out as unusual.

Next was a barrage of forms related to safety and cyber security, and then I signed an IT acceptable use policy saying that all devices were only to be used for company business. The forms went on and on.

Finally I reached the good stuff: my official offer letter. I was skeptical of giving verbal acceptance of any position before seeing the salary, but it turns out that wasn't a problem.

The salary was *enormous*.

It was twice what I made as an Operations Analyst, with three times as much vacation. The benefits package was ten pages long. I had access to a higher tier of health insurance. I was bonus eligible depending on the company's yearly numbers. And part of my compensation package included company stock options up to fifty percent of my salary.

The offer also guaranteed me a management position once this role was completed, since the STT project was only temporary. One with an "equal or greater compensation package."

My eyes bulged as I read everything. I definitely didn't need to negotiate salary.

I was giddy from signing those forms that the next one, the last form in the pile, caught me off-guard.

Employee Dating Policy.

Employee off-duty conduct is generally regarded as private, as long as such conduct does not create problems within the workplace. An exception to this principle, however, is romantic or sexual relationships between supervisors and subordinates.

Any supervisor, manager, executive or other company official in a sensitive or influential position with Allegheny Supply Inc must disclose the existence of a romantic or sexual relationship with another co-worker. Disclosure may be made to the individual's immediate supervisor or the director of HR. Allegheny Supply Inc will review the circumstances to determine whether any conflict of interest exists.

It was the aspect of all of this I was trying to ignore. My new relationship with Liam. I groaned to myself as I read the rest of the form.

Matters such as hiring, firing, promotions, performance management, compensation decisions and financial transactions are examples of situations that may require reallocation of duties to avoid any actual or perceived reward or disadvantage. In some cases, other measures may be necessary, such as transfer of one or both parties to other positions or departments. If one or both parties refuse to accept a reasonable solution, such refusal will be deemed a voluntary resignation.

Failure to cooperate with Allegheny Supply Inc to resolve a conflict or problem caused by a romantic or sexual relationship between co-workers or among managers, supervisors or others in positions of authority in a mutually agreeable fashion may be deemed insubordination and result in disciplinary action up to and including termination.

At the bottom of the form was a space to disclose any existing or prior romantic relationship with coworkers.

I glanced out at the cubicles outside my office. Liam was swiveling back and forth in his chair. He saw me looking, and he gave me one of his goofy smiles.

"Shit," I muttered.

The form was clear. I was Liam's direct supervisor. It was an obvious conflict of interest.

Now what do I do?

As much as I wanted to put it off and not think about it, I had no choice but to face my options now. If I reported the relationship on the form, then I would be removed from the manager's position. *No*, I realized. They would almost certainly keep me and remove Liam. He'd lose out on a huge career opportunity because of it. Knowing Liam, he would probably say that it was fine, that he would rather date me than have some stupid job, but that was a *really* bad way to start a relationship. If things didn't work out, he would resent me for losing the job.

On the other hand, if I *didn't* report our relationship, we ran the risk of getting caught. If it came out, both of us would be fired.

The worst part was that this was all a day late. If I had gotten the job yesterday, I could have truthfully said that no current or past romantic relationship existed. But today? Liam and I had slept together *last night*. Omitting that from the form would be a lie.

But all of that was avoiding the deeper question: *should* we stop seeing each other?

My immediate reaction was *yes*, of course we had to stop. My new position changed everything. But after last night I wanted nothing more than to go on that date with Liam this Saturday, laugh and joke and learn about each other like two people just starting out together.

The thought of ending it before it truly got started made my stomach twist with pain.

Mrs. Caltrop chose that moment to walk back into my office. "How are the forms coming along? HR is breathing down my neck."

Put on the spot, I hastily checked the box that said I had no romantic relationships to disclose, then signed my name at the bottom.

"All done."

She collected the stack of forms and nodded. "You have a

meeting tomorrow with the project management coordinator to go over the timeline, budget, and expectations for the project."

"Tomorrow, good. Have we received a complete list of all the candidate software systems to evaluate? I know of two potential ones..."

Mrs. Caltrop nodded curtly. "I am pulling it all together onto a shared drive. I will have it ready within the hour."

"Excellent." She continued standing there like a soldier waiting for orders, so I said, "I'll let you know if I need anything else."

Only then did she return to her desk outside my office.

While waiting for her to send that over, I set up my laptop on the desk and opened Outlook. I had forty new emails in the last hour, all from my previous role. I began replying to them one by one, letting them know that I was no longer an operations analyst and that Bernice would be taking over my duties.

Harford, Liam: So you're the new manager after all, huh?

The message from *Teams* popped up in the corner of my screen. When I glanced up, I saw Liam smiling at me from his desk.

Not now, I told him with a gentle shake of my head. I didn't want to discuss any of our *personal* stuff on the company chat program. The last thing we needed was a paper trail.

The notification for tomorrow's meeting with the project management coordinator popped up on my calendar. I opened the attachment, which showed a prospective timeline for the project. They wanted to have a replacement software system chosen, tested, and rolled out by the end of the year. Barely more than two months away.

That's an aggressive goal, I thought.

Mrs. Caltrop poked her head into my office. "I just forwarded you the documents, Ms. Hill."

"Thank you," I replied. "Can you send Liam in to my office so I can discuss it with him?"

I watched her walk across the room to retrieve Liam. He grabbed a notepad and pencil and made his way to my office. I felt a rush of power at knowing I could make him *come* whenever I wanted—no pun intended. And although I knew this was going to be a difficult conversation, I couldn't help admire how sexy he looked in his dress shirt and well-fitting slacks.

Liam entered my office, closed the door, and then sat down in the chair across my desk. He crossed one leg over the other and regarded me like a curious painting in a museum.

"Having your secretary send me in, rather than messaging me? You're letting management go to your head, Leslie."

He smiled like it was all a joke. I wanted to smile back. But I knew this was more serious than that.

"I don't know what happened," I admitted. "Apparently Oliver changed his mind in the middle of the night."

"Same for the other two people on the team," Liam said. "Is there something about the STT that we don't know?"

"Right?"

Liam looked around the office. "These are sweet new digs. Especially the fogging glass. Good for if you ever want some privacy." He punctuated it with a wink.

"Liam, I had to fill out a relationship disclosure form."

The expression on his face shifted as quickly as the special fogging glass. "What did you say?"

"I didn't say anything. I don't know what to do. We have a problem, Liam."

"The problem is that you're extra hot sitting behind that desk."

"Stop it!" I hissed. I glanced at Mrs. Caltrop's desk. She was typing on her computer, but occasionally looked in our direction.

"Authority makes you even sexier," Liam said. "I'm serious."

"I'm serious too—stop it! I don't know how sound-proof this office is. We need to make some decisions, but we can't do it here. Meet at my place tonight?"

"If I agree, will you answer the door in a towel again?"

"Not funny!" I said. But it *was* funny. I wished I could laugh with him and talk about how ridiculous it all is. "You were never this flirty when we worked together in sales."

He spread his long arms. "What can I say? You have that affect on me."

"We'll talk about it tonight," I said emphatically. "In the meantime, we need to avoid discussing things in the office, or on *Teams*. I don't want a paper trail of conversations being read out loud at my termination."

"I doubt they ever look at chat logs."

"I agree, but better safe than sorry."

Liam cocked his head to the side. "You sound like a manager already."

"I'll take that as a compliment. Now, let's talk about what really matters. The software demos. Mrs. Caltrop put everything on a shared drive that I'm going to send to you. Installation files and documentation and everything else we need. I need you to install them and start tinkering around. Getting a feel for each product, from a sales perspective."

"You got it, Ms. Hill."

I groaned. "Oh God, please don't call me that."

He grinned widely. He was getting *far* too much pleasure out of all this.

"Keep detailed notes on the software. Pros, cons, and anything else noteworthy. That should keep you busy until the rest of the team gets here. Any questions?"

"I think I'm good." He rose from the chair. "Looking forward to working under you, Ms. Hill."

I glared at his back—while admiring his cute little butt—as he left my office.

13

Leslie

The rest of the day went by surprisingly fast. I ate lunch in my office—*my* office!—while reviewing the potential software systems we had to choose from. There were four of them, and they all seemed similar in terms of functionality and specifications. They were also well-documented. Each piece of software came with technical manuals that were all over two hundred pages long. By mid-afternoon my eyes were glazing over.

Liam knocked on the door frame of my office. I prepared to give him a look that said *keep things professional*, but it turns out I didn't need to.

"I've been testing some of the software systems on my laptop, but most of them have infrastructure requirements. A centralized server, cloud storage, and a database."

I got up from my desk and winced. "I was afraid of that. Mrs. Caltrop? When are we getting the technical liaison?"

She swiveled in her chair and pursed her lips. "Apparently their paperwork has taken longer than expected. I think HR was blindsided by the first two team members quitting abruptly, and had to scramble to put together replacement offer letters. They should be here first thing in the morning."

I nodded to Liam. "There you go. When they get here, the first thing I'll have them set up is a test environment so we can properly evaluate the new software systems."

"Sounds good, Ms. Hill."

He said it perfectly serious without any sarcasm, for Mrs. Caltrop's benefit no doubt. But I still rolled my eyes at him.

I ran out of things to do around four-thirty. Leaving early was tempting—I *was* the boss, after all—but I didn't want to set a bad example on my first day. So I surfed the internet until five, then packed up my things.

Mrs. Caltrop was still gathering her things, but Liam left the office with me. "Want to get a beer or something?" he asked me out in the hall.

"I have to go for a run."

"How many days a week do you run? Surely not *every* day..."

"Friday is a rest day," I said defensively. "See you at my place around seven, so we can discuss everything?"

"Wouldn't miss it for the world." We stepped into the elevator and watched the doors close. "Want me to bring a six-pack? I bet beer tastes great after a run."

"No beer."

"Aww come on. It has carbs and vitamins and stuff..."

"We will *only* be talking," I insisted. "Got it?"

Liam rounded on me, pushing me back against the wall of the elevator. He reached around and grabbed my ass with both hands, and grinned like he knew a secret.

"Oh I've got it alright," he said, lips a mere inch from mine.

Ugh, why does he have to be so damn handsome?

Before I could give in and kiss him, the elevator slowed down on the next floor. Liam casually pulled away until he was just standing next to me just as the door opened and three other employees walked inside.

We rode the elevator down to the lobby while pretending like nothing happened, aside from sharing a small smile.

Although it had been a pleasant walk to work in the morning, it was a chilly evening when I stepped outside the office. A cold front coming in, hinting at the end of fall and the beginning of winter. But cold weather made for fantastic running conditions, and once I got home and changed into running gear I savored the cool air on my muscles.

As I ran north-west along the Ohio River, I started thinking about what I wanted to do. Running had a way of clearing my mind of all the stimulus and extraneous information, allowing me to focus.

And the realization I immediately came to was that Liam and I needed to stop seeing each other.

Granted, we hadn't really *started* seeing each other. But we couldn't get further romantically involved while we were working on the same team. As difficult as that was to accept, there was no getting around it.

I needed to put an end to it tonight.

The realization made me sad. Like I was missing out on something that could be special. Liam was the one who got away. It felt like fate had pulled us back together... for nothing.

I wondered how he would take it. He'd probably threaten to quit the STT. I couldn't let him do that, either.

After running north-west for half an hour, I turned around and picked up the pace on the way back, channeling all of my frustration into my workout. I gave myself ten minutes to cool off, took a shower, and then changed into comfortable clothes.

The doorbell rang at six forty-five, while I was still eating my chicken salad dinner. I opened the door and began to say, "You're early..."

But it wasn't Liam.

Robbie stood on my porch, red-cheeked and with mist puffing in front of his mouth with every breath. He wore a grey peacoat over his work clothes, and had his hands in the pocket.

"Hey, um, Leslie." He adjusted his glasses and smiled weakly. "Sorry to bother you at home."

"Robbie? What are you doing here?"

"I, well, I looked for you at work today but you weren't at your desk in operations..."

I looked beyond Robbie to the street. Liam would be here any minute. "Yeah, today was a crazy day. What's up?"

Instead of asking if he could come inside, he lingered on the porch and ran a gloved hand through his hair. "I'm not good at conveying things like this. I had a great time last night. With you, and everyone else of course, but mostly you, and what we did... you know, in the closet..."

Oh no. This is the last thing I need.

"I felt a spark between us," he said in a rush. Behind his glasses, his eyes were steel-grey and intense. "And, well, I kind of like you. I mean I *do* like you. Would you want to go out with me this weekend?"

Despite the terrible timing, my stomach did a sexy backflip. Cute awkwardness aside, Robbie was *smoking* hot. A handsome nerd. Any other time, I would have absolutely gone out on a date with him. I could still feel the intense attraction for him that I felt in the closet last night.

But tonight I had to break things off with Liam. That had to be done tactfully. And there was no way I could break things off with Liam while simultaneously accepting a date with Robbie. It would crush Liam.

His feelings mattered a lot to me, I realized.

"Robbie..." I began. "I kind of like you too. And I had a *lot* of fun last night. But I can't go out with you right now."

"Oh." He swallowed a lump in his throat. "I see."

No! Stop being sad! His scowl, which he tried to cover up with an apologetic smile, made me want to wrap him in a big hug and tell him it was going to be okay.

But I needed to get rid of him quickly. If he was still here when Liam arrived, it would only complicate the already difficult task at hand.

"It's not you, it's me," I added. "Crap. I know that sounds super cliché, but it's the truth. My life got turned upside-down today, and I need to focus on myself for a little while."

"I understand," he said blandly.

Damnit. Stop being so adorably pitiful!

"I'd love to take you up on that date when things calm down," I said, desperate for him to believe me. "In a few weeks, or after the craziness of the holidays."

"But not now?"

I gave him a quick hug. His body was warm and intoxicating with the smell of cologne. "Not now. I'm not supposed to say anything until it's official, but it will all make sense next week. I've been put in charge of the Systems Transition Team."

He blinked. "The STT?" he asked, suddenly confused.

It was breaking my heart the way he was looking at me. Like a kicked puppy. I couldn't look at him anymore.

"I'm sorry Robbie. But I have to go. Goodnight."

I closed the door, then listened to his footsteps go down my walkway to his car.

"Ugh," I groaned. I couldn't believe I was going to have to let down two guys in the same night. Two guys I *liked!*

Life wasn't fair sometimes.

Liam arrived twenty minutes later, long enough for Robbie to be long gone and for me to finish the rest of my dinner. Like Robbie, he still wore his dress clothes with a thin waistcoat over the top. I let him in and took his coat.

"Thanks, Ms. Hill."

"Stop that!" I said with a worn-out laugh. "Seriously, you're killing me!"

I draped his coat over a dining room chair, and when I turned around Liam was right there. He wrapped his arms around me and pulled me close, like a fisherman reeling in his catch.

"Stop that, too," I said with less heat in my voice.

"What if I don't want to?" he said in a deep, satisfied voice. "I spent five years looking at you in the office and thinking about kissing you. Now that I've had a taste, I want to do nothing *but* kiss you. It was torture sitting at my desk all day, watching you in your office."

He kissed me softly, and I let him. Because I wanted him as much as he wanted me. And that's what made this so tough.

I stopped kissing him long enough to ask, "You were watching me today?"

"Mmm hmm. And thinking about you."

I sighed as he kissed my neck. "Thinking about what?"

"All kinds of stuff," he rumbled, vibrating the words into my collarbone. "The things I want to do to you."

"I'm listening."

His hand gripped the back of my neck possessively as he tasted my neck. "I'd rather show you."

It would have been so easy to give in. We both wanted it desperately.

Somehow, my better self won.

I put a hand on his chest and pushed him away. "Liam, we have to talk about what happened today. We have a major problem."

He sighed and pulled away, then sat on the edge of the couch. "Alright. Let's talk."

I sat next to him and prepared to say what I had been rehearsing. "Yesterday, things were simple. We could do whatever we wanted. Today that changed. Now I'm your manager."

"I know. I was there." He grinned seductively. "The fact that you're my boss makes it fun. Forbidden. I was serious when I said you were super hot sitting behind the desk."

"I had to sign a relationship disclosure today," I insisted. "Not only that, I *lied* on my disclosure by claiming I had no romantic relationships with anyone in the company. This is serious."

"Why should a corporation dictate who we can and can't sleep with?" Liam replied easily. "We can keep it a secret. Nobody has to know."

"Right, because secrets are so easy to keep?" I shot back. "Someone would find out. Plus, it would be different if you were in a different department. But you *literally* work for me now. That's a huge conflict of interest. And before you make a joke about sleeping with the boss, think about how serious this is. Our careers are on the line."

Liam's cavalier attitude slowly faded away. "What are you saying, then? We can't see each other? Last night was a one-time thing?"

"It's the only way."

He grimaced, then nodded. For a split second I thought he was going to agree with me and make this easy.

"I can't accept that," he said instead. "Forget the STT. I'll put in my resignation tomorrow."

I sighed. "I was afraid you would say that."

He put his hand on my leg. "You think I'm going to roll over because of a paycheck? It's just a job, Leslie. I can go back to sales, or get another job somewhere else. I care too much about you to let you slip away because of one project."

Boy did I want to listen to him. To let him quit so we could be together.

"That's too much pressure on a relationship," I said. "I'll always be thinking about how you sacrificed your job. It would taint everything we did. What if I want to dump your ass in a month?"

He scoffed. "Come on. You wouldn't dump me around the holidays. I'd last at *least* two months."

He meant it as a joke. Just some lighthearted self-deprecating humor. But to me, it was a eureka moment. If I was a cartoon, a lightbulb would have appeared above my head.

"Two months," I said. "That's how long the goal timeline is for the STT project."

Liam grunted. "Two months to do the entire thing? That's aggressive."

I waved it off. "My point is that the STT is *temporary*. Selecting a solution, testing it, and then rolling it out to the entire company. Once all that is done, the maintenance tasks for the new system will be handed over to the Operations Department."

His eyes widened. "And then the STT will be rolled into a different department."

I bobbed my head up and down. "I won't be your boss after that. You'll get the enormous career benefit from being on the STT project, and then we could date afterwards. The best of both worlds."

He chewed the inside of his lip. "See, there's just one problem. I don't think I can keep my hands off you in the meantime." His hand slid up my thigh.

I laughed and slapped it away. "You'll have to try. For two months, I think you can manage." I touched his cheek and looked into his eyes. "All joking aside, this is our best option. Two months, then we can be together. Do it for me, Liam."

Despite his jokes, I could see how much of an internal struggle it was for him. It endeared me to him more than he would ever know.

"If it's the only way... Alright. Two months." He ran his fingers through my hair, then gave them a gentle squeeze. "But only if you give me something really good to tide me over."

He kissed me hard, and I moaned with relief at his acceptance and at my own desire building within my loins. "Yesterday I wasn't your boss, but today I am..."

"You've already lied on the disclosure form," he said as he pushed me back onto the couch. "One more time won't hurt."

As he covered me with his lean, muscular body, I gave in to the last shred of resistance I possessed and wrapped my legs around him.

14

Leslie

Liam was asleep, but I still lay awake in the darkness of my bedroom. Watching him breathe. The lines of the muscles in his back stood out deliciously as his shoulder blades rose and fell with each breath. Silent. Peaceful.

Perfect.

I didn't intend for anything to happen tonight, I told myself while watching him. I really had invited him over so we could hash everything out and put things on hold. But that was one hell of a last hurrah! The way Liam carried me into the bedroom over his shoulder, tore my clothes off, and buried his face between my legs. The way I'd pushed him down and sucked his cock while running my hands up his chiseled chest. The hard, pounding way he'd fucked me, both of us coming within a minute because we were so desperate for one another. And then round two, much slower and passionate, true lovemaking that had lasted for hours and hours...

I shivered. As good as it had been, *this* had to be the last time. At least until the project was over.

That was probably a good thing. Now I had a really juicy incentive to meet our project timeline goals. He was the piece of chocolate cake at the end of the race.

Yet as I watched him sleep, I knew it would be difficult to keep our hands off each other for two months. Probably even longer than that. It would be easier once our team began the real work, though. Between the STT project and the marathon in December, I would have my hands full. No time for hanky panky.

I eventually fell asleep and dreamed wonderful dreams, but Liam wasn't the only one in them. First it was the two of us in bed together, and then I blinked and I was back in the closet with Robbie, kissing passionately in the darkness, and in a blink Robbie became Arthur and it was his fingers running up my skirt and parting my pussy lips, touching me in just the right way that I moaned loudly, and he spoke beautiful French to me while his fingers circled my clit...

I woke to the smell of bacon. Liam was in the kitchen, and to my surprise he was completely naked.

What else was a girl supposed to do besides walk up and smack him loudly on his butt?

Liam yelped, then grinned down at me. "Excuse me, Ms. Hill, but that's workplace harassment."

"Tough not to smack that ass when it's right here in my kitchen, begging to be smacked." I wrapped my arms around him and pressed myself against his warm body. "I'm pretty sure having a penis this close to my scrambled eggs is a health code violation."

He snorted. "It's probably a health code violation to put my penis *directly* into your mouth, too."

I giggled. "Then there's grease from the bacon to worry about..."

"I'm very careful."

"There's a chef's apron in the drawer."

"I'll remember that next time," he replied.

I sighed into his skin. "Last night *was* the last time."

He removed the egg pan from the burner and twisted around to take me in his arms. "Last time until the project is over, you mean."

"Right. But I'm serious. We can't fool around for the next two months. Not while I'm your manager. Tell me you understand."

His face drew serious. "I agree. And I understand."

"You said you agreed last night, too," I pointed out.

His smile returned. "What can I say? You were irresistible."

"We worked together in sales for years, and you resisted temptation just fine," I said.

He reached down and squeezed my ass with both hands. "That was before I had a taste of this. Now I'm addicted."

I kissed him on the lips. "Shut up and make me breakfast."

"Yes ma'am, Ms. Hill."

Our embrace devolved into a series of play-slaps as I insisted he stop calling me that.

We enjoyed breakfast together, and then he left to get ready for work. By then I realized I was running late. I scrambled to shower, change, put makeup on, and head out the door.

Despite arriving to work ten minutes later than I had hoped, I felt pretty darn good. It was Friday, and I was getting the rest of my team today. Having two other people in the office would subdue our own sexual tension. Once we all began on the real work together, it would be easier for Liam and I to act professionally.

I got out of the elevator on the third floor and walked to my department. Down the hall, someone poked their head out of a doorway. Robbie, I realized as he stepped out and began walking toward me.

"Leslie!" he waved.

Crap. He's embarrassed about showing up at my door last night. And apologizing here was just pouring salt on the wound.

He strode toward me. "Hey. Do you have a minute to, um, talk about..."

I waved him off as I reached the doorway to my team's room.

"Forget about it, Robbie. It's not a big deal. But I have to run."

"Leslie, wait..."

I went into my office and hoped he wouldn't follow me. Thankfully, he did not.

"Running late this morning?" Mrs. Caltrop asked.

"I had a long morning," I said. "I won't make a habit of it. Where is everybody?"

Mrs. Caltrop took my coat and said, "I scheduled our first team meeting for eight o'clock. Everyone should be waiting in conference room 303."

"We could have just held the meeting in here," I said, gesturing around our team room.

"The conference room has a projector, and I have a PowerPoint presentation for us all."

"Alright," I said, "let's not keep them waiting."

I dropped off my laptop bag next to her desk, and glanced inside my office.

I frowned.

"Mrs. Caltrop?" I asked. "What is that on my desk?"

She snorted contemptuously. "That was here when I arrived this morning."

Sitting on my desk was a glass vase holding two dozen orange roses. I approached and plucked the note out of the arrangement, which was inside an envelope that was still sealed.

I had a feeling I knew what it would say before I even opened it.

An auburn rose cannot compare
To the blinding beauty of your hair
With graceful smile, you do lure

My heart to you, petite mon fleur

"Arthur," I whispered. The roses and poem made me gush like a teenager, but I hastily shoved those emotions deep down inside. This was an office, and I was a manager now. Getting flowers from a coworker was a little too bold, even if we did work in different departments.

And I didn't have the emotional bandwidth to think about that this morning.

"Do you know who they are from?" Mrs. Caltrop asked as we walked to the meeting down the hall.

"A secret admirer," I said.

"Something tells me it's not so secret," she said bluntly. "I blushed like that when I got asked to prom by the quarterback. A lot has changed in the fifty years since then, but not the look on your face."

I looked sideways at her. "It's someone I just met. They work here."

"A new romance?"

"Hardly," I said. "We flirted at a party planning meeting the other night."

"He must be handsome to make you blush that much."

"He is," I admitted. "He's very smooth, and he knows it too. And he has the most wonderful French accent."

Mrs. Caltrop jerked her head toward me. "Arthur Durand?"

I winced and looked around to make sure nobody else had heard. "Yes. Why?"

We reached conference room 303, where my three employees were waiting. I gawked when I saw who they were.

"*That* is why," Mrs. Caltrop whispered.

15

Leslie

Arthur was indeed one of the two new members of my team. His three-piece suit was charcoal grey today, with a crimson pocket square that matched his tie. The biggest smile in the world appeared on his beautiful face when I appeared in the doorway.

"Good morning!" he greeted. "It is a beautiful day, is it not?"

But I wasn't just reeling from Arthur's presence in the room. The third member of my team, seated between Arthur and Liam, was also familiar to me. Robbie smiled awkwardly when I turned my gaze on him, and blinked behind his rectangular glasses.

"Hey, um, Leslie," he said. "Or should I call you Ms. Hill?"

"Ms. Hill has a nice ring to it," Arthur chimed in. "You are our manager, so such respect is deserved, yes?"

That shook me out of my frozen state. "*Please* do not call me that," I said with a self-deprecating laugh. "Leslie will do. For all of you." I gave Liam a pointed look.

"Whatever you prefer," Liam said smoothly. The only evidence that we had slept together last night was the half-smile on his face and the gleam in his eyes. "Running late this morning?"

I set my laptop down at the head of the six-person conference table and ignored the question. "I think we can get started. I'd like to welcome you all to the Systems Transition Team."

Mrs. Caltrop cleared her throat. "Why don't we go around the room and introduce ourselves? To make sure we all know one another."

Oh, we know each other alright," I thought. "That's a good idea. Arthur, why don't you start?"

"My pleasure," he said. His French accent made the word *pleasure* sound twice as dirty as if anyone else had said it. He stood up and half-bowed to the room. "I am Arthur Durand. I have worked in the finance department for two years. Before that, I worked for the World Bank in New York City. I am delighted to be part of this team."

"I bet the World Bank was a lot more exciting than a Pittsburgh construction supplier," Liam said.

Arthur shrugged amicably. "My definition of exciting may be different than yours. Banking is boring. Numbers and accounts. Construction is the dream of the new world! Building and expanding! This is the essence of what it means to be American, yes?"

"I hadn't thought of it like that," Liam said. "Welcome to the team."

They shook hands, the man I had slept with last night and the man who had sent me flowers this morning. It caused an uncomfortable—and yet exciting—tingle in my stomach.

Robbie stood up next. He cleared his throat twice before speaking. "Robert Godwin, but everyone calls me Robbie. That is, you all can call me Robbie, if you want. I'm a technical guy. I mean, I work with computers, which is what I'll be doing on this project. I've only been with Allegheny Supply full-time for a year, but I was an intern here for two years while in college."

He quickly sat back down.

Liam stood after that. "My name's Liam Harford." He gave a little wave, even though we were all sitting within a few feet of each other. "My background is in sales. In fact, Leslie and I worked together in sales when we first started at Allegheny. I'm glad she's the manager of the STT instead of Oliver Edwards. Trust me—there's nobody better prepared for this role than her."

He smiled and sat back down.

"Thanks for the vote of confidence," I said as I stood. "I'm Leslie Hill, and like Liam said I started out in sales. For the past two years I've been working in operations, which gives me a balanced view of the company's workings. I'm excited to work on this project, and delighted to have such a great team."

It felt strange addressing them from a managerial standpoint. I wasn't sure if that was because we had all fooled around together to varying degrees, or if I would have been the same with any three subordinates.

"Are there any questions before we get started?" I asked.

"This is a very important project with major implications for the company," Arthur said with a smile. "Will we be working *long* hours?"

I ignored the innuendo. "Maybe. Not at first, but once we get into a groove we might be working overtime. Now, I understand all three of you are salary, so there's no overtime pay, but I'm told there are bonus incentives for completing the project on time. I have a meeting with the project management team later to discuss those timelines."

Robbie raised his hand. "Liam mentioned it a minute ago, but do you know what happened to Oliver Edwards? Why was he fired? Not that, uh, he would have been better than you. I don't mean that. But it seems weird for him to be removed a day after taking the position…"

"That's a good question, and one I'm curious about too," I explained. "I do know that he wasn't *removed*. He quit, along with the original finance and technical liaisons. If I learn anything more about the circumstances surrounding that, I will let you know. Any other questions?"

The three of them shook their heads.

"Now, to the meeting itself. Mrs. Caltrop..."

The projector clicked on and the beginning of a PowerPoint slide appeared on the wall.

"As you know, the STT was formed to choose a replacement software solution for the company. There are four primary candidates we will be reviewing..."

The meeting went smoother once we discussed the *actual* work that needed to be done. We talked about general goals, and some of the first steps required. I told Robbie that we needed to get a test environment set up for evaluating the software, and he immediately began writing down everything he would need to do: setting up virtual machines on a dedicated network separate from our production environment. Servers and databases and other things that I didn't understand.

"Once all that is up, I can start evaluating the software," Liam said.

Arthur would handle the financial side of things. Both the costs associated with the STT and the eventual selection, such as infrastructure fees and licensing costs for the software itself. All of that would need to be evaluated and compared, because one piece of software charged a flat fee per company, whereas another company charged per computer.

"There will be operations losses as well," Arthur said while stroking his chin. "When Allegheny's two thousand employees migrate from one software to the next. A learning curve, yes? Shall I model this as well?"

"If you have time, absolutely," I said. "We can't ignore the growing pains of new software, especially since it will affect the company's bottom line. Good thinking."

"But of course." He smiled seductively at me.

I quickly looked down at my laptop. That smile could melt

even the coldest heart. I tried not to let it affect me for the rest of the meeting, but it wasn't easy.

"This was a great start," I said as we began to leave. "Everyone has their action items to work on. If there's any confusion, please let me know."

When we exited the conference room, instead of turning left to go back to our office I turned right to head to the bathrooms. Robbie caught up to me before I reached them.

"Hey, um, Leslie. I tried to warn you earlier. When you first got to the office this morning..."

I laughed. "I should have listened. I thought you were going to apologize for showing up at my door last night, which was why I avoided you."

His steel eyes blinked behind his glasses. "Um. Well. Now that you mention it... I do want to apologize."

"Robbie..."

"I completely misread our time in the closet," he said in a rush. "It was just a game, a silly game, and I made things weird. I hope that won't affect our professional relationship."

I sighed and put a hand on his arm. "Oh Robbie, you didn't misread anything." I lowered my voice as someone passed by us in the hall. "There was definitely a spark between us that night. I felt it too. And you're a *really* good kisser."

He glanced around nervously like someone might overhear. "Really?"

"Really. If things were different..." I shook my head. "It doesn't matter now. I'm your manager, so we have to keep things professional."

"Yeah. Of course."

He kept standing there, staring at me with that dorky—and intensely handsome—gaze. "I'm going to go to the bathroom now, okay?"

His jaw dropped and he realized we were standing in front of the women's room. "Yeah. Go ahead. I mean, do whatever you want, I'll... I'll be back at my desk."

I laughed to myself as he rushed away.

When I got back from the bathroom, Liam and Robbie were sitting in their cubicles. Arthur was sitting on the edge of Mrs. Caltrop's desk, chatting her up. She was looking at him like he was Frank Sinatra, and she gave a start when I appeared.

"I was just telling Mr. Durand here that flowers for a manager are inappropriate," she said, flustered. "People could get the wrong idea."

Arthur cocked his head and pretended to be confused. "I give flowers to everyone. They are a symbol of friendship, yes?" He snapped his fingers. "I see. Perhaps you are jealous, and desire flowers of your own."

She turned to me. "Mr. Durand also wishes to have a private meeting with you. I told him your calendar is busy this morning, and he can schedule something for this afternoon, or tomorrow."

"Schedule? Who must schedule? I simply wish a few moments of my manager's time. It would take longer to create the meeting than the actual discussion, I assure you."

Mrs. Caltrop looked at me for an answer.

"Alright, if it's quick," I said.

Arthur slid off Mrs. Caltrop's desk and walked right into my office. He flicked the switch inside the door, changing the glass partitions from translucent to fogged.

"That man," Mrs. Caltrop whispered to me, "Is far too attractive and charming for his own good."

"You're not wrong."

I went inside my office and closed the door behind me. Arthur was examining the view out the window of the Pittsburgh skyline. I considered switching the windows back to translucent, but decided to keep things private. Just in case.

"How can I help you, Arthur?" I asked evenly.

He turned toward me slowly and crossed his arms over his chest. "I wished to tell you that you will be a wonderful manager, Leslie. You have the proper mindset and demeanor. I am certain."

I wanted to point out that he barely knew me, but I also didn't want to extend the conversation any longer than it needed to be. "I hope so," I said.

He gestured. "Did you like the flowers?"

"They are very nice," I said. "But Mrs. Caltrop is right. No more flowers. The one you put on my desk yesterday was fine, but now that I'm your manager we can't have even the *appearance* of impropriety."

"Impropriety," he repeated, tasting the word. "What does this word mean?"

"It means, like, inappropriate. What we do may be scrutinized. There's a conflict of interest."

"Conflict? Interest? Leslie, the only thing I am interested in is you."

The words were intoxicating as they left his lips and hung in the air, fragrant like fine wine. He took a step toward me. It would have been incredibly easy to hold my ground and see what he intended to do, but I made myself step back and reach out a hand to stop him.

"I'm serious, Arthur. I had to sign a relationship disclosure form."

"Relationship? Words are words, and feelings are feelings, Leslie. Whatever you call it, I like you very much."

"I'm your manager."

He grinned slyly. "That is what makes it fun, yes? I like powerful women."

Christ, he's right. The fact that I was his manager did make it more sexy. Because it was forbidden.

"I have to get ready for this project management meeting," I said. "Unless you need anything else..."

"I will also be ready, *mon fleur*," he said. "For when you are ready."

He approached, and this time I didn't move. I just held my breath. Arthur brought his face close to mine. Just an inch away, until I could see the folded lines in his hazel colored irises. I wanted him to kiss me right then, to throw caution to the wind and do something naughty in the privacy of my office...

He brought up his hand to caress my cheek, and then moved past me, leaving me standing in my office alone.

16

Leslie

I spent a few minutes recovering from my impromptu meeting with Arthur before going to the project management meeting. The project manager was named Jen, and she jumped right into all the high-level information about my new Systems Transition Team.

The budget was, for all intents and purposes, unlimited. That surprised me until I saw the timeline expectations. We had until the end of the year to deliver the final software solution to the company. They wanted to start fresh on the first of the year, so our deadline was December 31.

"The Board of Directors is firm on this date," Jen said cheerfully. "There's no wiggle room for delay."

I stared at her Gantt chart on her laptop screen, which was a timeline of each step of the process. "That's only nine weeks."

"I know, right?" Jen laughed lightly. "Oliver Edwards was similarly surprised when I sent him the presentation outline earlier this week."

I guess that explains why he quit. He probably took one look at the project and *nope'd* out of the whole thing.

When the project management meeting was over, I spent the rest of the day growing more and more anxious about the entire thing.

110

Wondering if the systems transition was even possible in such a short period of time.

Was I being selected as a patsy, to take the fall for its failure?

Liam poked his head in my office at a quarter to five. "Want to get a beer after work?"

I glanced beyond him at Mrs. Caltrop, who may or may not have been eavesdropping. "I'll pass. Thanks though."

"Come on. It's your rest day, right? No run scheduled?"

I smiled. "No, but I have my weekly long run tomorrow. Need to get to bed early, with no alcohol."

Liam shoved his hands in his pockets and gave me that special half-smile of his. "One beer won't kill you. I was thinking all of us on the team could go."

"Goodnight, Liam."

He lingered a moment longer, but didn't push it further. But I did watch him talk to Arthur and Robbie, and the three of them left the office together to get that beer.

I wonder what they'll talk about.

I ended up staying in the office until my windows darkened around seven. Even when I finally packed away my laptop and drove home, I ended up opening my laptop on the couch and working some more. Going over each step in the Gantt chart, assigning tasks to members of my team, and creating checkpoints in Outlook to make sure I was on track with things in the next two months.

Nine weeks. How was I going to pull it off?

When I finally put away my laptop and crawled into bed, my mind drifted to my other problem: the three sexy men now working under me. I could still smell Liam's scent on the pillow and in the threads of my comforter. I wrapped it around myself and breathed deep, wishing he was here with me. Holding me close and telling me that the project was going to be okay.

Then there was Arthur. Sexy, smooth, and dedicated to seducing me. Heck, he'd already seduced me in my closet a few nights ago. Even though I had been with Liam since then, the memory of the way Arthur touched me that night, worshiping me with his mouth and fingers and purring French accent...

It made me rethink everything I was doing.

At least Robbie is easy to manage. At worst, he was a little awkward around me, but he seemed to respect the boundary between a manager and her subordinate. Which was good, because he was still incredibly adorable in a dorky kind of way.

Three different men with three varying degrees of romantic interest in me. And all of them now working for me.

What had I gotten myself into?

But all of them *did* like me. More than just like, in fact. Arthur was practically courting me like a French noble who wanted to make me a princess. If I just thought about it for a moment, the things we could do in my office with the windows fogged and the door locked...

I shook off my fantasy. If I was a male manager with three female subordinates, this would be the biggest scandal of the company's history. I couldn't let that happen to me, both because it was wrong and because it would destroy my career.

Just two months until the project is over. Then I can do whatever I want.

My alarm went off at five, and after hitting snooze once I managed to pull myself from my bed. A quick breakfast of steel-cut oats, fruit, and a protein shake, and then I was out the door and driving west to Raccoon Creek State Park. Although I did my weekday runs by myself, on Saturdays I joined a larger running group all training for the same race. They set out water stops on the trail and had pacers, and overall it was easier to run for three hours when you were around other people than when you were alone.

It was *still* dark outside as I parked the car and joined the group standing around stretching by the trailhead. I looked around for some of the people I knew, but it was dark and I didn't see anyone.

Then my gaze passed over someone who was already watching me. Someone I recognized.

Robbie put his hands up as I approached. "I've been coming to these for two months. I promise I'm not stalking you. Not that I would stalk *anyone*, I mean, but you know..."

"It's alright," I said with a chuckle. "I did take you for a fitness guy. Small world, huh?"

He blinked behind his glasses. "Why did you take me for a fitness guy?"

Now it was my turn to sputter uncomfortably. "Oh, I mean, you look like you work out. You're not scrawny like most of the computer geeks I've ever known. Not that I've been looking at you, but when we were in the closet at my place I could tell..."

I sighed and closed my eyes. "Can we start over?"

He stuck out his hand. "Hey Leslie. Fancy seeing you here."

I shook it. "You too. Training for the Allegheny Marathon?"

Before he could answer, the run coordinator started barking out instructions to everyone. "We've got water stops placed at miles four and eight, and nutrition at eight. For those of you training for the half-marathon, turn around is at the first water stop. Those of you training for the full keep going until you see the sign. Myself and the other coaches will be out there if anyone needs anything. Let's do this!"

We started jogging in a big cluster, but then began to spread out after the first minute. Robbie was in the group about fifty feet ahead of me. From behind, it was impossible not to admire him. He was wearing tight compression shorts, like triathlon shorts that stopped just above the knee and hugged every part of his strong legs and tight little butt. He had long-sleeve Under Armor on top, which also fit him snugly and showed off the expanding and contracting muscles of his upper back and arms. Unlike the other runners out here who had the thinner build of a long-distance runner, Robbie was thick with muscle.

Jacked, I thought.

I watched him for the first two miles, then realized that our paces were almost identical. So I increased my stride to catch up with him.

"Ten minute pace?" I asked as I fell in beside him.

"Ten and ten seconds, actually," he said. "But close enough."

I did the mental math in my head. "You aiming for a four-and-a-half hour marathon, then?"

Robbie bobbed his head. "That's the plan. My personal record is four thirty-six, so it should be a doable goal."

"Oh, so this isn't your first?"

"Third. First time doing Allegheny, though. I'm hoping the cold weather helps me run faster. I ran the Pittsburgh Marathon back in May and the temperature was in the nineties. People were passing out from heat stroke."

"Yeesh."

He glanced over at me. "So this'll be your first one?"

"First and only, probably."

"Why do you say that?"

"My ex got me into running," I confessed. "I was already halfway through training when we broke up, so I figured I'd finish. A bucket list item."

"Nothing wrong with that," Robbie said. "But you might change your mind. There's no feeling quite like crossing the finish line."

"And then collapsing because I'm too weak to stand?" I said with a grin.

Robbie laughed. He had a great laugh, and I realized it was the first time I'd heard it. He was normally too awkward to let out anything but an uncomfortable chuckle. But he was totally natural now. Too busy jogging along, focusing on our stride and breathing, to think about anything else. It was nice.

"Yeah, it will hurt a *lot*," Robbie admitted. "You'll probably limp around the office for a week. But then you'll forget all about the pain and search for the next one to sign up for."

"Let's get through this one first," I replied.

We ran together for a while, then I drifted ahead. When I was thirty feet in front of him it suddenly occurred to me that he was probably staring at my ass, the way I'd been staring at his. Which was fine, because my ass looked *good* in leggings.

I stopped at mile four to refill my water bottle, and he caught up to me in time to continue running together. We chatted some more, and then were quiet for a while. That was fine—there was only so much you could talk about during a three hour run, and just being next to someone else helped the time go by faster.

"I think we have a good team," Robbie said. "For the Systems Transition, I mean."

"We do," I agreed. "Liam is fantastic at what he does, and so far I like what I see from you and Arthur. Did you guys go out for beer last night?"

"Yes," Robbie said after a brief pause.

I waited for him to elaborate, but he remained strangely quiet. "What'd you three talk about?"

"Oh, you know. A little bit of everything. Getting to know each other."

"Did you talk about your terrible manager at all?"

I meant it as a joke, but Robbie winced. "We talked about you a little."

"You think I'm terrible?" I blurted out.

"What? No!" Robbie replied. "I didn't mean it like that. I just meant we talked about *you*."

I tensed. Had they shared what happened in the closet, and

what Liam and I did when everyone else left? I had already told Liam that I kissed Arthur and Robbie in the closet, but the others didn't know anything, as far as I could see.

Why am I so concerned about that? It wasn't that I was afraid of seeming like a slut, fooling around with three men in the same night. I didn't even care that I was their manager and they might not look at me the same way. No, I cared for a deeper, more primal reason.

I don't want them to stop having feelings for me.

"Any concerns about me running the team?" I asked calmly.

Robbie laughed it off. "No, nothing like that."

"Then what about me did you discuss?"

I could tell I was making Robbie feel awkward. My curiosity was stronger than my sympathy, though. I stared at him while we ran until he relented.

"Just... you, in general. How you and Liam worked together a long time, and always had a thing for one another but never had a chance to date."

My foot caught on a rock and I stumbled, but caught myself. "Liam said that?"

"More or less. We all agreed that..." His cheeks blushed even deeper.

"What?"

"We agreed you're cute. I know I would have had a crush on you if we worked together, too."

We're working together now, I thought. But that probably would have made him fall with discomfort, so instead I asked, "What did Arthur say?"

Robbie tried to look relaxed, but I could tell he was putting up a wall. "Nothing, really."

I decided not to push it further than that. "I'm glad you three went out. Next time maybe I'll join you."

"Yeah, that would be great. Team-building."

As we reached the final mile, Robbie began to speed up. Lots of training plans involved a "fast finish," which meant running the last mile or several miles at a much faster pace than the rest of the training run. I hadn't done any before, but I felt good this morning so I lengthened my stride to keep up with him. I watched the current pace on my watch increase to nine minutes per mile, then eight and a half.

By the time the end of the trail appeared in the distance, we were both at an all-out sprint. Somehow I managed to match him stride for stride, and we finished as if it was an Olympic race.

"I got you by half a foot!" I gasped as we staggered to a stop. I tripped, and Robbie threw an arm around me to keep me upright.

"No way. Where's the photo finish?" Robbie insisted.

We laughed and joked while holding onto each other for support. It reminded me of that night in the closet, feeling his hard, strong body against mine. It made me want to do more than just kiss...

I made myself let go of him. "You want to get some lunch after this?" I found myself asking.

His eyes brightened up, but then he frowned. "I actually have plans, so I have to go."

"Oh, okay."

"Probably for the best since you're, um, my boss and all. Right?"

"Yeah, totally," I said aloofly. "It was good running with you."

"You too." Robbie gave a wave and walked to his car.

I felt immensely disappointed that he had turned me down. I had meant it as a totally platonic lunch invitation, but it felt the same as if I had mustered the courage to ask my crush out and they had said no. A pit in the bottom of my stomach.

Over by the cars, Robbie was stripping off his Under Armor. His tattoo sleeves glistened in the late morning sunlight, and his entire body was packed with beautiful muscle. Then he pulled on a new shirt, covering it all up.

I sighed and wondered what had gotten into me as he drove away.

17

Robbie

"Stupid," I cursed myself as I drove away from the trailhead. "Stupid, Robbie. Fucking *idiot*."

She'd asked me out to lunch. I'd been fantasizing about that for the past two days, and when the opportunity arose I declined without thinking about it. It was true that I did have plans this afternoon, but it was something that could have waited until tomorrow.

I groaned in misery in my car.

Deep down, I knew declining was for the best. It was already tough enough fighting the crush I had on her, which was growing every day. Going to lunch with her, no matter how innocent it was, would have made things harder. I was the kind of guy who fell *hard* for women. Even spending the last few hours running with her was enough to crank up my crush from a seven to a ten.

Plus, she was a career-focused woman. She would never date one of her employees, even if we were perfect for each other.

Which I think we are.

Of course, Liam and Arthur thought the same thing. The conversation we'd had last night over beers proved that they both had enormous crushes on her too. I couldn't blame them. Especially Liam, since he'd known her for so long.

And the other thing we had all discussed about her...

I shook it off. There was no way that would work. And since it was impossible, there was no point in even *thinking* about it.

I went home, showered and changed clothes, and then drove back to the office. It was quiet and empty on a Saturday, which was just how I liked it. I wanted to get a head start on setting up the test environments for the project, so Liam could hit the ground running on Monday or Tuesday. I wanted this project to go smoothly.

Not just for my own career. I wanted it to go well so Leslie would think highly of me.

No matter what happened, I didn't want to fail her. Even if it meant working weekends until the project was done.

"I'm going to do everything I can to help her succeed," I told myself as I sat down and got to work.

18

Leslie

I walked into the office Monday morning to a giant bouquet of flowers.

But they weren't for me.

"Look at you!" I exclaimed to Mrs. Caltrop. An enormous vase filled with all manner of colorful flowers now took up a large section of her desk. "I guess you're the one with a secret admirer today, huh?"

She beamed at me. "Not so secret."

I turned around to see what she was looking at. Arthur was sitting on the edge of his cubicle, arms crossed over his chest while grinning at us. I couldn't help but laugh. He was smooth, alright.

The day went surprisingly well. Miraculously, Robbie got the test environment all set up and running by mid-morning, even though he had originally said it would take a full week. When I excitedly told him he was amazing, he blushed three shades of red underneath his glasses.

The rest of the week was a blur. With the test environment up, Liam was able to begin evaluating the software itself. On Wednesday, he showed me the first candidate software at his desk. There were lots of new features compared to our old software. It was overwhelming.

While Liam did that, Arthur chugged along on the financials. He was a one-man project team: he scheduled meetings with the software companies to discuss details and pricing, and even hammered them in areas where the pricing was not to his liking. Throughout the week I heard, "This is not to my satisfaction," spoken in his French accent, and every time it made me smile. He was clearly good at his job.

On Thursday we had another party planning committee meeting, but this time we held it in the office instead of my house. Considering what happened last time, that was probably for the best. We spent the meeting nailing down specific vendors for the holiday party. Charletta and Beth took charge of the meeting and did most of the work, which I thanked them for as we finished up.

"We don't mind," Charletta said. "We know how busy you are on the Systems Transition Team."

"Everybody knows!" Beth added.

I smiled at them, but on the inside I was thinking, *ugh, more pressure.*

Beth waited until Charletta left and then saddled up next to me. "Hey, I want to run something by you. I'm thinking of doing the charity auction idea we discussed in the first meeting. Where people bid for a dance with volunteers."

"Oh, right," I said when I remembered. "I thought it was a good idea. Especially the name, *the naughty list.* I think that's cute."

Beth grimaced. "Charletta still doesn't agree."

I leaned in and whispered, "Well then she doesn't need to know, does she?"

Beth giggled and made a note on her notepad. "Can I count you in to be bid on?"

I gave a start. "Me? Oh no!"

"It's just for a dance!"

"I'll think about it," I said as we left. "Ask me again in a month."

During the Saturday group run Robbie and I stuck together again. We chatted about anything and everything, sort of like how first dates usually went. He'd graduated from Pitt with a degree in Information Systems, and would have gotten his Master's Degree if not for having the job lined up at Allegheny Supply.

"I figured it was better to get a head start on my career," he explained. "I'm only twenty-three. I can always go back to get my Master's whenever I want."

"For sure. I've always considered that, myself."

"Yeah? Why didn't you?"

I shrugged. "I like what I do. I haven't felt the need to go back to academia."

"Maybe if the economy goes to crap and we lose our jobs," Robbie suggested.

"Exactly!"

When our run was over, I took a chance and asked if he wanted to get lunch again. After a moment of hesitation he agreed, and we went to a little cafe on the west end of the city and ordered BLT sandwiches and hot chocolate to warm our bodies after the cold run. He ate quickly and said he had to leave, though he wouldn't tell me where he was going.

The week after that was spent with more software evaluations. Each prospective software needed its own test environment, and Robbie was ahead of schedule getting the environment ready for the second piece of software. Liam spent all Monday installing the software and testing it, and then Tuesday we sat down to go over it together.

"I like the interface on this one more than the one last week," I said.

"It's more intuitive," Liam agreed. He leaned close to me to move the mouse. "That's partly because it's so similar to our old software, but with updated features."

I scribbled on my notepad. "I didn't think of it, but that's something we should take into account. The ease of training for the rest of the company. We could buy the best software in the world, but it would be useless if our people can't figure out how to use it."

Liam leaned closer to use both hands to alt-tab into another window, which showed his own notes about the software. "Way ahead of you, Ms. Hill."

I glared daggers at him. "If you call me that one more time, I'm going to fire you and do the evaluations myself. And I'm only *half* joking."

He bit his lip nervously, then devolved into laughter. I couldn't help but giggle myself.

I glanced at my watch. It was just after noon, and everyone else had already left for lunch. We were alone in the office, huddled around Liam's cubicle together.

"We have a good team here," I told him. "Things seem to be going well with the project."

Liam started to say something, then stopped himself. "Yeah."

I blinked. "What is it?"

"No, I agree," he said.

I gave him a look. "I've known you long enough to know when you're avoiding saying something."

He sighed and turned his emerald eyes onto me. "It hasn't been easy seeing you every day, Leslie."

My stomach did a backflip at the change of subject. "I know. It's been tough for me, too."

He put his hand on my knee, which was bare beneath my skirt. His voice was intense with emotion as he whispered.

"I can't stop thinking about you. I want to wrap you in my arms. Feel your lips on mine. I dream of tasting your sweet pussy again. Licking every inch of your body until you shiver and tremble and moan..."

His hand slid up my skirt.

"Liam..."

"I want to fuck you so badly," he growled with an evil smile. "I want to bury my cock deep inside you until you scream."

I wanted the same thing, I realized. He was giving voice to my own inner thoughts and fantasies. But we couldn't do it now. We had to wait.

I grabbed his arm just before his fingers touched my panties. "You're not making this easy."

"Neither are you." He glanced around to verify we were alone. "For all of us."

"What do you mean?"

"I see how the others look at you, too. Robbie, and Arthur. It's the same way I looked at you for three years when we worked together."

"I... I don't know what you mean," I replied.

Liam smiled and shook his head. "It's alright. I don't blame them. We *all* have feelings for you, and you did kiss them in the closet that night at your house. And then the other night when the three of us got beers..."

He trailed off like he didn't want to say it.

"What? Tell me!" I insisted.

"Let's just say that we all understand," he said carefully. "It's going to be a long two months until this project is done, and we all have a strong incentive to finish on time."

Before he could elaborate, Mrs. Caltrop returned to the office with her lunch. We both scooched our chairs a little farther apart, but she still made a disapproving noise as she walked by us.

It's going to be a long two months indeed.

The rest of the week went like that. Everyone was focused on their tasks, though I did notice Robbie and Arthur stealing glances at me when I was in my office. Robbie always quickly looked away, embarrassed, but Arthur embraced it by smiling devilishly whenever I caught him.

On Friday I went into the cafeteria to retrieve my lunch from the fridge, and found the place a mess. People were setting up decorations: Jack-o-lanterns were arranged in the corner, and fake spiderwebs were being strung from the ceiling. Two men walked past me carrying a keg of beer between them.

"I forgot all about the Halloween party," I said when I got back to my team.

"They were making noise all morning," Robbie muttered. "That's why I put headphones on."

"Is anyone going?" I asked.

"But of course!" Arthur exclaimed. "Who does not love an opportunity to dress up in costume? It is all so exciting!"

Robbie shrugged. "I'm not big on parties."

"Says the guy who volunteered for the party planning committee," I pointed out.

"I'll probably make an appearance," Liam said casually. "I always like to see who else goes, and what they're wearing. There are usually good costumes."

"*Sexy* costumes?" Arthur said, waggling his eyebrows.

Liam grinned. "I didn't say that."

"What about you?" Arthur asked me.

"Probably not. I have a lot of work to do—I have to give a status update to the Board of Directors on Monday."

"Surely you can enjoy one or two or *six* drinks before getting back to work," Arthur said.

"I don't have a costume, either."

"The *Party Surplus* store down the street has lots of costumes.

Although they're all promiscuous. Sexy maid, sexy cat, sexy police officer..."

Arthur gestured. "You could go as you are now. As a sexy manager. Simply open one or two of the buttons of your blouse, and *voila*!"

I narrowed my eyes at him. "That's a borderline inappropriate thing to say to your manager."

Arthur clutched his chest like he had been shot. "You mistake me, Leslie. I am merely offering helpful suggestions to your situation!"

Inappropriateness aside, his compliment did make me smile for the rest of the day. I considered the party all afternoon. It was a lot of fun last year, and the year before that. Finally I ducked out of the office early to run down to the store and pick out a costume. When I got back, everyone else had left.

I fogged the windows of my office and changed into my costume. That was a lot easier than changing in the bathroom. Having my own office certainly had its perks.

"We'll see what happens tonight," I told myself as I touched up my makeup.

19

Arthur

I was a man with a deep, profound love of women.

To be clear: that was not metaphorical. I *loved* women. The mere idea of them as the fairer sex, beautiful and mysterious and dangerous. Stronger than men in many ways, and yet also a graceful cradle to bear human life. I appreciated every woman I had ever met, whether short or tall, skinny or voluptuous, for every woman deserved to be admired and appreciated and *desired*.

Yet I had never desired a woman as much as this.

Leslie was something special. Like the rare *edelweiss* flower, only found high in the Alps where the air was thin and the trek dangerous. Leslie was such a flower. Beautiful. Precious. Desired by many.

I very much wanted to show her how desired she was. To treat her the way she deserved.

To treat her like a *woman*.

Alas, she was now my manager. The seven minutes of heaven

we had shared in her coat closet was not the *hors d'oeuvre* I had expected before a more delicious meal—it was merely a tease. A morsel at the end of the night as the restaurant shut its doors in my face, closed for the time being.

This despaired me greatly.

Like the great divas of old Paris, I wished to throw myself upon my bed and hide from the world until my pain receded. Instead, I maneuvered myself in the office as if nothing was wrong, smiling and joking and pretending to be my normal self.

No one would know how painfully I desired Leslie. Not until this project was complete.

I went home to change into my costume, and arrived thirty minutes after the party began. A man such as myself did not arrive on time. One must be fashionably late, so as to make as grand an entrance as one was able.

I strode inside the cafeteria, whose lights had been turned down low and was pumping music gently from a disc jockey in the corner. Several women looked at me as I entered, a reaction to which I was accustomed. I knew the effect I had on American women. I was exotic and charming. This was unsurprising, as I worked diligently to appear as such. Flowers and smiles and gentle caresses at precisely the right moment. Such things went a long way toward making a woman feel like a *woman*.

Plenty of such coworkers approached me and complimented my costume. I smiled and said all the right words of thanks, but my heart ached on the inside, for the woman I desired was nowhere to be seen. She must not have come to the party tonight.

My sadness was immense as I went to the bar to drown my sorrows in wine, as men before me had done for centuries.

Liam joined me as I waited for my glass. "That is a nice bullfighter costume," I said amicably.

He spread his arms. "Actually, I'm Zorro. From the movies?"

"Ah, yes of course," I said, although I knew not of this Zorro. "Leslie is not here?"

Liam grimaced behind his mask. "Doesn't look like it."

"A great shame."

"Yep." Liam looked around the party and said, casually, "She's special."

"Indeed she is."

Liam was very pointedly not looking at me. "What we discussed the other night... I understand."

"Do you?" I asked.

Now he looked at me. "Honestly? Yeah. I get it, since I feel the same way about her. If you and Robbie want to make moves on her after the project is done, you're welcome to it. Just know that I will be doing the same."

I raised my glass of wine. "May the best man win, yes?"

Liam raised his beer. "Cheers to that. But whoever does win..." His eyes grew intense. "As I said, Leslie is special. She's not like the other women I've known. No matter what, she must be treated the way she deserves."

I gave a flourishing bow. "Liam, I know of no other way to treat a woman. Especially Leslie. You have my word."

Liam seemed satisfied with that. Like it was the assurance he had come here to get from me. He drank the rest of his beer and said, "Enjoy the rest of the party."

I watched him leave the cafeteria, then lingered while sipping on my wine. It was not *bad* wine, but it was not quite good, either. I considered flirting with many of the other women at the party tonight who I knew, but that did not interest me. They were minnows, and Leslie was a powerful and dangerous shark. Hunting the minnows was not worth the trouble.

I was preparing to leave the party when she arrived.

My gaze was drawn to her instantly. Her red hair was pulled up and tied with white lace, which matched the lace of her costume. It was a French maid outfit that showed a glorious amount of cleavage. The bodice hugged her tightly and was tied up the front with string. It flared out at the waist in a fanfare of white ruffles, and beneath that she wore dark stockings that were clipped to garters.

Her mere presence filled me with happiness, but the sight of her drew a gasp from my lips.

I must have her, I decided then and there. Even if it cost me my job. Nothing else mattered to me.

You will be mine, mon fleur, I thought as I greeted her.

20

Leslie

Although I was confident in my own skin back in my office, the moment I stepped into the Halloween party I felt self-conscious. Lots of people looked in my direction as I entered in my French maid outfit. A million self-doubts flew through my head.

This dress is too provocative.

I'm a manager now, so I should set an example.

I'm not attractive enough to pull this off.

My fears were diminished when I saw other women wearing sexy outfits too, some *much* more revealing than mine. That was a relief. But as I looked around, I didn't see Liam anywhere. Had I arrived too late? He said he was only making an appearance, so he might have left by now. I was hoping to bury the hatchet after what he had told me earlier in the week. How he couldn't stop thinking about me.

Then I saw Arthur over by the bar. He gave me a friendly little wave and raised a glass of wine, inviting me to join him.

I almost didn't recognize him. He was dressed as the Phantom of the Opera, with a full tuxedo and a white mask covering half of his face, and his dirty-blond hair slicked back. The outfit was complete with a cape that was draped over his entire body and hung to the floor.

He flourished the cape and gave me a formal bow as I approached. "*Mon fleur*, I am overjoyed to see you!"

I smirked. "Isn't the Phantom supposed to be hidden down in the catacombs?"

"Tsk tsk," he replied. "He appears for the masquerade party at the beginning of the second act! And so I am here." He nodded. "And so you are also here, and dressed like a stereotypical French maid!"

I curtsied. "It's not too stereotypical, is it? You're not offended?"

He made a disgusted noise. "I am quite the opposite of offended. Such a sight has stirred something within me, endearing me to you even further."

I wasn't sure how to take that, except that it was all wonderfully charming, so I said, "Thank you," and ordered a glass of wine from the bar.

"And you wear the costume perfectly!" He leaned close enough for me to smell his exotic cologne. "The other women at this party should leave in disgrace, for they cannot compare to your beauty."

I blushed and said, "I'm not sure I would call this *beauty*. It's a little sluttier than I am usually comfortable wearing."

"Nonsense. You appear quite confident in your body, as you should." He clinked his wine glass to mine. "I am happy you came."

"Me too," I said, and I meant it even though Liam wasn't here. "So, how are the financials coming?"

He wagged a finger in front of my face. "No no no. Leslie, it is Friday night! There shall be no discussion of work this night. Tell me of yourself instead, yes?"

I laughed and said, "What do you want to know?"

We spent the next half hour chatting about my past. Where I grew up, went to college, and why I started working for Allegheny Supply. After two glasses of wine, I found myself opening up to Arthur and talking almost non-stop. It was easy–he seemed to be a great listener. I felt comfortable talking to him.

"I've been talking a while," I said. "Tell me about *you,* Arthur."

He grinned behind his Phantom mask. "What would you like to know?"

"Tell me about your childhood. You grew up in France?"

"In Cambrai," he said happily. "A small city north-east of Paris."

"Near Belgium?" I asked. "My geography is bad."

"Quite so! I lived ten kilometers from the border. My father was the groundskeeper for a vineyard..."

I listened intently as Arthur discussed his childhood. When he was very young he was too poor to be sent to school, and had to help his father working on the vineyard instead. He did not receive any formal education until he was twelve years old, and then had to play catch-up on everything he had missed.

"I was teased relentlessly by the other children, for I could not read or write," he said.

My heart broke for him. "That's terrible, Arthur!"

But he only smiled. "Indeed, but it pushed me to work hard and learn on my own. I did not have hobbies or recreational time to myself. From the moment I woke to the instant I fell asleep, I spent all of my time studying. And it was a great success! By the time I finished primary school, I was not only caught up to the other students, but I had a greater appreciation for my education. I went to university, thrived there, and graduated with my degree."

"Still though," I said. "To not know how to read or write until you were thirteen..."

"I would not have it any other way!" he said happily. "It made me the man I am today, and I take nothing for granted in life. May we all be so lucky."

"You have such a positive outlook on everything," I said.

"How else could I be?"

"If it were me, I would have felt sorry for myself," I replied. "Being teased would have probably crushed my spirit."

He rubbed my forearm. "Surely not, Leslie. A woman of your strength would have persevered through such things. I am certain of it."

I smiled. "Thanks for the vote of confidence. Then you moved here?"

"Three years ago, yes." He spread his arms. "I love the idea of America! Open spaces and new beginnings. You are all such industrious people. I wanted to be part of it. And so I came to New York to work for the World Bank." He waved a hand dismissively. "That bored me, so then I moved to Pittsburgh. Far more industrious people, with their blue necks."

"You mean blue-collar," I said with a laugh.

Arthur frowned. "This is what I said, yes."

"Well, I'm glad you're here Arthur. And I'm glad you're working on my team."

"As am I!" He put his glass down. "I am going to the bathroom. I would very much like you to promise that you will still be here when I return. Yes?"

"I'll be here."

He grinned, then left the cafeteria, flourishing his cape for people as he went.

I ordered another wine from the bar and smiled to myself. Arthur was quite the character. Based on the way he dressed in perfectly-tailored three-piece suits, I never would have guessed that he came from a poor family. It made everything about him more impressive. His confidence was hard-won, rather than inherited.

It makes him sexier, too.

Arthur returned. "Another glass of wine for the manager who

insists she has to work tonight?"

"I'm not sure any more work is getting done," I admitted. I frowned at my glass. "But the wine isn't very good. We'll need to choose a different vendor for the holiday party."

Arthur cocked his head. "What type of wine do you prefer?"

"Cab Sauv," I said.

Arthur took my hand. "Come with me!"

"Where are we going?" I asked as he pulled me across the room.

"We are going on an adventure to save you from a mediocre vintage!"

I felt a thrill as he led me out of the cafeteria and down the hall. Through the building we hurried until we reached our little department. Arthur flicked on the lights and brought me to his cubicle, then opened the bottom drawer in his desk. He pulled out a dark bottle with a crimson label.

"Voila!" he said smugly. "I have saved this for a special occasion."

I gawked at the bottle of Cabernet Sauvignon. "A hidden bottle of red wine in your desk? That's the most stereotypically French thing I've ever seen. Do you have cheese, too?"

"I have no cheese, baguettes, or croissants, I am afraid," he said with an ominous tone. "But if the red wine is not enough to please you..."

"No! It's great!"

"Excellent!" He fished a bottle opener out of his drawer—yet another hilariously stereotypical surprise—and removed the cork. Then he smacked his forehead. "Ahh! I have forgotten glasses." He handed me the bottle. "Do not move, for I shall return with..."

He trailed off as I took a long pull straight from the bottle. I made a satisfied noise when I was done with my sip. "Who needs glasses?"

Arthur looked like I had punched a kitten. "This offends me greatly."

I giggled. "Too bad. More wine for me..."

He playfully snatched the bottle from me, hesitated, and then drank from the end. He smacked his lips when he was done and considered the act.

"It is better in a glass, for it needs to breathe. But I suppose this is still acceptable."

"Good!" I grabbed the bottle and took another sip.

Arthur leaned on his cubicle and smiled at me. "How are you able to do it?"

"Do what?"

"Manage three handsome men without succumbing to temptation. Were the roles reversed..." He spread his hands as if that explained that.

I blushed. *He's a direct one, isn't he?* "It's not always easy, I have to admit."

"Such as with Liam?" Arthur asked. "You two have a, ahh, *history*, we should say?"

"Something like that," I replied carefully. "It does make things difficult."

I was feeling warm and free from the wine, as relaxed as I had been since taking this position. So when Arthur put his hand on my leg, I didn't flinch away or think about inappropriateness. I enjoyed it for what it was.

Something *naughty*.

"And now?" Arthur asked softly. "Does this make your job difficult as well?"

"Maybe it does," I said.

"In my language, *maybe* is just *yes* in different underwear." Arthur's warm hand slid up my leg until it reached the edge of my costume skirt. "What underwear do you have on, Leslie?"

What are we doing? whispered a voice in my head. But I wanted nothing more than to give in right now. To let loose. Arthur's handsome face was looking at me like I was the most beautiful woman in the world.

I bit my lip. "Would you like to see?"

Arthur answered without hesitation. "Very much so, *mon fleur.*"

21

Leslie

Arthur ripped off his Phantom mask and crushed his lips against mine in a deep kiss. Our hands were on each other instantly, his in my hair and on my back, and mine along his neck and cheek, feeling the bumps where he had shaved. His mouth tasted tangy from the wine as we kissed, his tongue pushing into my mouth in a French kiss the way it had in the closet of my house those weeks ago, but we were in the darkness there, and here I could see every hard line in Arthur's beautiful face as he kissed me passionately.

I realized I had wanted him desperately since that night. To go further than just touching. I needed to feel him inside me.

As his hand slid up my skirt, I pushed his lips away. "Let's go into my office and fog the windows."

Arthur's dirty-blond hair swayed as he shook his head. "I must have you here." Another kiss. "Without delay."

I squeaked as he picked me up and set me down on the edge of his desk, then kicked his chair, sending it rolling across the floor toward Mrs. Caltrop's office. The walls of the cubicle weren't high—we were in plain sight to anyone who poked their head in the room.

"Someone might see us," I whispered.

Arthur's smile was sly. "That is what makes it exciting, yes?"

His hands deftly ran up my legs, found my thong, and pulled it off. Then he knelt between my legs and buried his head underneath my skirt.

I gasped as his tongue ran up my pussy lips, tasting me. There on his desk he devoured me like it was all he had ever wanted to do. He used his fingers to pull apart my pussy and then jammed his rigid tongue deep inside, then moved his head back and forth, tongue-fucking me while his thumb pressed on my clit.

I craned my head back and savored how it felt, being eaten out here at work. In the room where I was their manager. There was something so deliciously *naughty* about it all. It made me feel powerful in a way that simple managerial duties did not.

I grabbed a handful of his hair and guided him back and forth while he tongued my pussy. Muting my moans was difficult because the pleasure was intense, and I found myself holding my breath as his fingers and tongue went to town on my lady-parts...

Suddenly there were voices in the hallway, just outside the door. I twisted to look over my shoulder just as a head appeared in the doorway.

It was John Fadringham, my boss from the Operations Department. He was dressed like a cowboy. He blinked when he saw me. "Leslie!"

John could only see my upper body—everything below my waist was blocked by the walls of the cubicle. Which meant he couldn't see Arthur.

Unless he came into the room...

"John!" I said in greeting. I gripped Arthur's hair tightly to make him stop, but he kept going, driving his tongue deeper into my pussy.

"I was just heading to the party," John said, still lingering in the doorway. "I usually don't enjoy them, but Tanya convinced me to make an appearance this year. You coming?"

Arthur hummed with silent laughter between my legs, adding a pleasing vibration to my clit while he ate me out. "I just came from there. Taking a breather—I'm not feeling good."

John frowned. "Do you need any help? Some water..." He began walking toward us.

"No!" I yelped. "I think I might have the flu. Forgot to get my shot this year."

John froze in place twenty feet away. "Oh no. You don't look good—your face is all red."

Arthur's tongue began swirling around my clit, heightening my ecstasy a few notches and driving me closer to an orgasm. I managed to keep my voice level as I said, "Yeah, I'm about to drive home. You go on up to the party and have fun though, okay?"

"Hope you're feeling better," he said, gesturing around the room. "The Systems Transition Team looks great. I hope the project goes well for your career."

He disappeared through the doorway. A few seconds later, I was unable to contain the pressure building in my loins. I gripped Arthur's hair tightly and let out a soft moan as waves of pleasure crashed over me. He kept his face pressed hard against my pussy until I finally came down from my high.

Arthur was grinning when he stood up between my legs. "I love how you taste, Leslie. As sweet as I imagined."

I pulled him toward me and kissed him, tasting the combination of my juices and the wine on his lips. "I want you."

He stepped back and removed his cape with a flourish, then allowed it to drift to the floor. He gazed at me lustily while unbuttoning his pants. I slid off the edge and turned around, bending over the desk. If anyone walked in now, they would only see him and not me.

The suave Frenchman made a noise deep within his throat as he lifted my skirt. "I have imagined this and only this since meeting you, *mon fleur.*"

His cock was as hard as steel as he buried it in my pussy. We moaned together at the moment of joining, and then he gripped my waist and fucked me from behind in long, smooth strokes.

"Your cock feel so good," I moaned softly.

"*J'aime ta chatte,*" Arthur replied. He put a hand between my shoulders and pushed me lower, pressing my face into the keyboard and raising my ass higher.

We were really doing it. We were having sex in the office where we worked. Someone could walk in *right now.*

"Fuck me," I begged. "Fuck me harder, please, *harder...*"

Arthur's cock pounded me from behind, our skin slapping together like a snare drum. I closed my eyes and savored the way he filled all of me, every single nerve ending on fire with ecstasy.

Then I felt something *different.*

His hand palmed my ass cheek, squeezing gently, and then his thumb rested against my rear entrance. His thumb felt wet, like he had coated it with saliva for lubrication. Then it pressed against me, sliding into my asshole.

"Oh," I moaned in surprise.

"*Aimez-vous?*" he whispered. "Do you like that?"

I'd never had a guy do that before. My first impulse was to say no. But his thumb was an inch inside of me, and it felt so... so...

So *good.*

"Yes," I breathed.

His thumb went deeper, hitting new nerve endings I didn't even know I had. "*Oui?*"

"Yes," I repeated, pushing my hips back against his cock and thumb. "Oh yes, fuck me like that, right there please *fuck me* Arthur..."

He drilled me harder and harder while keeping his thumb inside my back-door. All of it together—finally giving in to Arthur, having sex in my office, and having a finger in my ass—mixed together into a naughty, taboo experience that filled me with ecstasy in a way that normal sex never had.

While the Halloween party raged down the hall, we fucked and moaned and came together in his cubicle, and nobody knew except us.

22

Leslie

"So," Arthur said casually. "What do you think of the wine?"

We were sitting on the floor with our backs against his desk where nobody could see us, passing the bottle of wine back and forth. Arthur's handsome face regarded me with warmth and satisfaction.

"It's good," I said, taking a sip and passing it back. "Not as good as the company, though."

He took a sip and grinned widely. "I very much agree."

Arthur kissed me, sharing the tangy taste of wine from his lips. Our tongues swirled together, wet and warm and reminded me of how it had swirled around my pussy and clit just moments before.

"You seemed to enjoy it," he said. "The extra finger, yes?"

I blushed. Doing it in the heat of the moment was different than talking about it after. "Maybe."

"Which, as I have established, means *yes*," he said happily. "Have you not done this thing before?"

"First time," I admitted sheepishly. "Is that something... Do other women enjoy..."

Arthur shrugged casually. "Some women enjoy this, some do not."

I nodded as I considered that. I had never understood the appeal of anal sex—why do that when there was a perfectly good vagina *right there?*—but after experiencing this I was beginning to rethink my position.

There's a big difference between a finger and a dick, I thought. But the idea sent a tingle of excitement through my body.

Arthur wrapped an arm around me and kissed my hair. "I am very happy this thing happened, Leslie."

"Me too."

Yet as the pleasure of the act wore off, the reality of what had happened began to sink in. Arthur and I had just had sex at work. I was his superior, and he was my subordinate. If anyone found out, I would lose my job. My career would be ruined. What if someone had seen us leave the Halloween party together? Did security cameras in the hall catch us holding hands and coming into here together? Was there evidence of the deed sitting on a server somewhere downstairs, like a bomb waiting to go off and destroy my career?

My anxiety must have been obvious because Arthur began rubbing my shoulders and making shushing noises. "Leslie, *mon fleur*. Do not worry. Love is natural, and unavoidable between two people with chemistry such as ourselves."

"If we get caught, I'll lose my job," I said. Panic was quickly growing inside me, like water flooding a room.

Arthur kept rubbing my shoulders. "No one will ever know. If you are accused, I will deny everything." His face changed. "No, of course I have not made sweet love to Mademoiselle Hill! Our relationship is purely professional. She is my boss, and I am her employee, and there is nothing more to discuss!"

His enthusiasm made me laugh, and my anxiety drained away. "You're sweet, you know that?"

"I am not sweet," he said simply. "I am merely French. It is in our *blood*."

As he smiled at me and rubbed my shoulders, I could tell that what had just happened wasn't merely physical. I was intensely attracted to *all* of him. His charming personality, his intellect, his emotional support.

And sure, his beautiful body fucking me in all the right ways.

"Thank you, Arthur," I whispered. "For everything."

He kissed me softly on the lips, this time without tongue. "Think nothing of it, *mon fleur.*"

We cuddled together against his desk, then left separately so as not to arouse any suspicion.

I went home and showered, and when I came out of the bathroom I had two text messages on my phone:

Liam: I missed you at the party.

Liam: Correction: you missed me. I looked fine as hell in my Zorro costume.

Me: Sorry I missed it! I showed up half an hour after it started. Had to run out and get a costume

Liam: Ah, so you were fashionably late, as Arthur calls it. To make a grand entrance. Did you see his costume?

I winced. Was he mentioning Arthur because he knew something, or was it a total coincidence?

Me: I did—he plays quite the Phantom

Liam: Did he sweep you off your feet?

Liam: He told me he was going to carry you down to

his catacombs and play you the music of the night. Whatever that means.

Me: It's a Phantom of the Opera reference!

Liam: Never seen it

Me: And here I thought you were classy. Sad to see I'm wrong.

Liam: I make up for it in other ways

Liam: Anyways, sorry I missed you. Sweet dreams, Leslie.

Me: Goodnight Liam

I smiled, and was grateful that he didn't push me for an answer about Arthur. I didn't want to have to lie to him.

But as I went to bed, I wondered what I was going to do about this. I'd put a hold on doing anything with Liam because I was his manager... and then I'd turned around and had sex with Arthur anyways. And although I had deep, long-seeded feelings for Liam that were sprouting fresh and were incredibly exciting, I felt an intense attraction for Arthur as well. The way I felt about both men was similar and totally different, all at the same time.

I woke up early for my Saturday long run feeling as confused as ever. Every fourth week of training was a lighter day, and today we only had a ten mile run scheduled. Robbie smiled and chatted me up while we stretched, but I wasn't in the mood to talk much today.

As we ran down the trail in a group, I couldn't help but feel guilty about Liam. We weren't exclusive. In fact, we weren't technically dating. But having sex with Arthur felt like I was betraying some unspoken agreement between us. I wondered how I would feel if Liam started dating a girl in another department.

Jealous, that's for sure.

Yet Liam hadn't been jealous when he learned that I had kissed Robbie in the closet at my house, and had done *more* than kissing with Arthur. Was he fine with that because it was just a silly game? Is that what made it different than a proactive romantic coupling?

Regardless, Arthur felt amazing last night. All the stress of the week had melted away at his touch. Even the upcoming meeting I had with the Board of Directors on Monday no longer filled me with crippling fear.

"Shit," I muttered.

"What?" Robbie asked.

"Nothing. I meant to get some work done last night but got sidetracked."

"By the Halloween party?"

"Yep, the party," I replied. "I have the meeting with the Board of Directors on Monday, and I still have to finish my presentation."

Robbie hesitated. "Are you, um, going to go into the office today to work on it?"

"Heck no. I'll work on it at home, underneath a heated blanket."

Robbie chuckled and gazed up at the sky. "It's getting colder, isn't it? Before long, we'll be running through snow."

"Please don't remind me."

I darted to the right to avoid a pothole in the path, and suddenly my calf seized up. I winced and hopped on my other foot, slowing to a stop on the edge of the path.

"Cramp," I said. "This is what I get for drinking the night before my long run."

Robbie stopped with me. "You going to be okay?"

"I'm fine." I waved him on. "You go ahead, I'll catch up."

"We're not far from the parking lot. Want, um, a piggy-back ride?"

"I'd love one," I said sarcastically. I didn't think he was being serious. But then Robbie crouched in front of me.

"I'll, uh, carry you. I don't mind."

I laughed when I realized he was serious. "You're not going to use this against me later, are you?"

"I might poke fun," he admitted. "But only a little. I promise."

He backed up until he was like a frog crouched between my legs, and finally I gave in and rested my chest on his back. He scooped up my legs under each arm and stood up, carrying me like a backpack with my arms around his chest. I bobbed gently as he began to jog.

"I can't go very fast," he admitted. "But let me know when your cramp is gone."

In truth, my cramp was already fading. But being pressed against Robbie's warm back was comforting and nice. I could feel the muscles in his lower back flexing with each stride, rubbing against me in a way that would have made me blush if not for my already-rosy cheeks.

With my face practically touching the back of his head, I was close enough to see every detail. The curl of his ear underneath his beanie. The line where the back of his hair had been shaved. The little follicles of brown farther down his neck, where his Under Armor shirt pressed tightly against the muscles in his shoulder.

I frowned. "Did you get a haircut?"

I felt Robbie tense underneath me. "Yesterday after work."

"Let me see." While still clinging to him, I reached up and removed his beanie. I could see it more clearly now: the sides of his head were shaved short, with a larger flop of hair on top. It reminded me of the way David Beckham looked about fifteen years ago.

"It looks good," I said while running my fingernails across the shaved part on the side. "I love how a man's hair feels right after getting a shave. It's so short and firm!"

"Heh, yeah, I bet it feels good," he said.

I realized I was caressing his hair a little *too* much, and stopped myself awkwardly. "I think my cramp is better," I said.

Robbie lowered me to the ground, and watched while I shook out my leg and tried a test jog. I nodded.

"About a quarter mile to go," Robbie said.

I'm giving all of my employees mixed signals, I thought as we finished the run together.

23

Robbie

Leslie is giving me mixed signals, I thought as we finished the run.

I had thought my piggy-back offer was cute. Helping a friend along while their leg cramped, so she didn't have to sit around in the cold while waiting for it to go away. Sure, I had selfish motivations—wanting to feel her sexy body pressed against mine. But the offer and act itself was relatively innocent.

But running her hands through my hair? Caressing my head with the tips of her fingernails? That was about as sensual as it got. I *loved* when a girl did that. It was my biggest weakness. If I was a dog, I would have started kicking my leg and panting.

Thankfully, she was behind me and couldn't see the hard-on pressing against my compression shorts.

"Feel like lunch?" I asked when we finished.

Leslie glanced at her watch. "Too early for me, since it was a short day."

Stupid. It was still only nine-thirty. I should have asked her out to *brunch,* not lunch. This was why I was always single.

"Yeah, um," I said, "maybe instead we could..."

"I've got to get working on that presentation. Rain check, alright?" She grinned.

"Sure. Next time."

"See you Monday!"

I watched her walk back to her car. It was tough not to stare. She had her red hair pulled back in a ponytail, which swayed with every step. Her perfect hourglass figure was accentuated by the tight running clothes, and her hips swayed as much as her ponytail. She was gorgeous. An absolute smokeshow.

And my boss.

I waited until she drove off to get in my car, then went home to change. I'd rented the studio apartment in downtown Pittsburgh because I told myself I was going to be going out a lot, doing more social things with other people. In reality, I didn't do much socializing at all. I didn't like skimming Tinder for dates, and I was awful at picking up women. All of my interactions with Leslie proved that.

But she noticed my haircut. She couldn't have made me happier if she had asked me out on a date.

Even though it was Saturday and the office was deserted, I still felt like I had to dress in a shirt and tie. The heat in the office was cranked up, though, so I allowed myself one luxury: I rolled up my sleeves. Visible tattoos were against company policy on the weekdays.

I turned on the lights in our team office. There was an empty bottle of wine on Arthur's desk, but aside from that it was exactly how I'd left it yesterday. I'd enjoyed working here for the past two weeks. As an IT geek, most of my job usually entailed fixing things that broke. Replacing dead hard drives and installing computer monitors. It got boring. It was monotonous, with no real benchmark for success.

But on the Systems Transition Team, I was building something new. Setting up test environments so Liam could evaluate the software candidates, and then I would eventually be setting up and configuring the production servers for whichever software we chose. I was doing something vital to the company's success. That meant more to me than a thousand repaired laptops.

Which was why I didn't mind coming in on the weekends to get a head start on my work. Liam didn't need the next server and database installed until Tuesday, but I wanted to get it done early in case he needed it early. Putting in the extra effort that made a project go from *good* to *great*.

Yet as I sat down at my desk and began remotely-connecting to servers, I knew that wasn't my real motivation. I wanted to impress Leslie. I wanted her to see how good I was at my job. I wanted her to think I was smart, and capable, and everything else.

I wanted her to *like* me.

I was thinking about all of that when her voice suddenly cut through the silent Saturday atmosphere.

"Robbie?"

I spun around in my cubicle to see her standing in the doorway. She wore jeans and a t-shirt underneath her coat, too casual for the office.

"Hey Leslie." I felt embarrassed that she had caught me, but then a thrill went up in my chest at the thought of her learning how hard of a worker I was. How dedicated I was to the project.

Instead, her face twisted in confusion. "What the hell are you *doing* here?"

"Oh," I stammered. "I, um, I decided to come in... What are you doing?"

She pointed. "I forgot that I left my laptop in my office." Her scowl deepened with distrust. "Did you know that I left it here? At the trail, you asked if I was coming into the office today. Did you come in so that you could run into me like this?"

Oh no. Leslie had the wrong impression. She thought I had orchestrated all of this! My chest turned cold and my heart raced with embarrassment as my excuses poured out of me.

"I've been coming in every weekend. I mean, last weekend, and the one before that. To get, um, ahead in the work. Setting up the test environments for Liam. It's a lot of work, and I didn't want to be the bottleneck. The STT project is important, especially for you since you're, you know, the manager of it, and I wanted to do everything in, um, my power to make sure it's a success, so *you* are a success. So I've been coming in. Just on Saturdays. Not Sundays. I promise."

Her scowl hadn't shifted a single degree. "Why didn't you tell me?"

"I didn't want anyone to know," I quickly said. "Liam and Arthur would think I'm an overachiever, trying to one-up them. Or maybe you would all think that I'm not good enough to finish the work in a normal weekday. I wanted you to be, I don't know, impressed by me. I wanted you to know you can trust me to work hard."

She walked toward me like an angry boss who was about to fire someone. I steeled myself for her anger, which was still plainly visible on her beautiful face. Seeing her upset with me felt like the worst punishment in the world, and made me feel like I had failed everything I had been trying to achieve.

Leslie stopped in front of me and gazed up at me, her eyes as fiery as her hair. And then she did the last thing I expected.

She kissed me.

24

Leslie

I didn't know I'd left my laptop at the office. I was frustrated to have to drive back to the office when all I wanted to do was curl up on my couch underneath a heated blanket with the Board of Directors presentation I needed to review.

Seeing Robbie already there and dressed up was a shock to my system. I'm not proud to admit that I reacted with anger and suspicion. And Robbie, the poor sexy puppy-dog of a man, recoiled from my anger and spilled his guts about everything.

It was like a knot was being untied in my gut. He'd been working weekends to help get ahead of everything. To keep Liam from being delayed, and to keep the project running smoothly and ahead of schedule.

It was so selfless that I wanted to cry.

Instead, I kissed him.

It was one of those reactions that was totally automatic. One moment I was glaring up at the hard lines of his handsome face, and the next I was sticking my tongue in his mouth and wrapping my arms around him. And in those moments, I was transported back to that night in the closet at my house. My feelings for Robbie, new and fresh and vulnerable, returned like a flood of water from a dam bursting. A dam whose foundation had been cracking for weeks. He wrapped me in his strong arms, arms covered with delicious tattoos, and held me against his body like he needed every part of me touching his at that moment or he would literally die.

There was something so forbidden about it, so tantalizingly *naughty* about making out with him in the office, that was familiar. Because of course we were only a few feet from where Arthur and I had gotten down and dirty last night.

But right then, with Robbie's warm lips on mine? I didn't care one bit.

Robbie was the one to stop the kiss first. He gazed down at me with satisfaction in his eyes. And confusion.

"I thought we, um, said we couldn't do this," he said quietly.

"I know," I said with a sigh. "We shouldn't."

"Well. Um. We sort of *are*."

I grabbed his tie and used it like a leash to pull his lips back down to mine. "You really have been coming in to work on the servers for Liam?"

He scratched the back of his head. "I guess, yeah."

"You didn't have to do that," I said. "We're not at the point in the timeline where we need to be working on weekends."

Robbie shrugged. "I know. But I don't have a lot of other things going on. And I wanted to make sure I wasn't the bottleneck in the project."

"That's not what you said," I pointed out. "You said you wanted the project to be a success, so that *I* would be a success."

"I meant all of us," he quickly clarified. "You, me, Liam, Arthur. If the project does well, it will be good for, uh, all of us."

I could tell he was covering now. Embarrassed that he had revealed how much he cared about my professional success in the project. So I decided not to call him out on it again.

I glanced around, and caught sight of the bottle of wine still on Arthur's desk. Empty, with red lipstick around the end where my lips had been. *That's not the only place my lips were last night.*

And it all crashed down on me at once. Everything I'd done. Lying on the relationship disclosure form. Sleeping with Liam that night, after he was already on my team. Sneaking away from the Halloween party last night to fuck Arthur. And now kissing Robbie here in the office...

It was all so sexy in a forbidden, secret way.

But it was also dangerous. And that terrified me.

What am I doing?

"I have to go," I said, rushing into my office to retrieve my laptop. "Please don't feel like you have to work today."

"I want to..."

"I'll see you on Monday," I said as I fled the office.

*

I felt like an idiot as I rushed home. Of course Robbie had been working extra hours, rather than pulling miracles out of his hat with the servers. I should have seen it before now, especially considering how he always had plans on Saturday afternoons but would never tell me what they were. All this time, he had been in the office.

Helping me.

I got home and opened my laptop to review the Board of Directors presentation, but my eyes scanned the screen without really absorbing it. All I could think about were the three men working on my team. Sleeping with Arthur last night had released a knot of tension in my stomach. And the kiss with Robbie today left me feeling as giddy as a schoolgirl who had finally kissed her crush.

It's stupid, whispered my conscience. *You're going to get fired if you keep doing this.*

But as I thought about it, I realized it was already too late. I had crossed the Rubicon. There was no undoing what had already happened. I had been with all of them to some degree. Did it matter if I *kept* doing it now? If we were discovered, the punishment would be the same if I slept with them once or a hundred times.

The only risk was that continuing to break the office romance rules meant a greater risk of getting caught. But somehow that made my feelings for the three of them feel even *stronger*.

Was I really that cliché? Wanting what was forbidden to me *because* it was forbidden?

I focused on the presentation for a little while, then opened up *Teams*. Robbie's name had a little green icon next to it, indicating that he was online.

Hill, Leslie: I thought I told you not to work

Godwin, Robbie: I'm not working.

Godwin, Robbie: Okay yeah, I still am. But only because I'm in a groove.

Hill, Leslie: It's kind of rude to ignore a direct order from your boss. If this was the Marines, I'd make you do push-ups.

Godwin, Robbie: Technically, you didn't give a direct order. You said "Please don't feel like you have to work."

Godwin, Robbie: I know I don't *have* to work. I *want* to.

Hill, Leslie: Technicalities won't help you here. It's Saturday, Robbie. Go home.

Godwin, Robbie: I will.

Godwin, Robbie: When I wrap up what I'm working on with this server build ;-)

His dedication, even after being discovered, was endearing. He'd kept it a secret because he wanted to help the team, but didn't care about getting credit for the extra work. I'd never seen such selflessness in the workplace.

Hill, Leslie: I'm sorry I kissed you

I waited for his response, which took long enough for me to get up, grab a glass of water, and sit back down. The icon indicated he was typing. *It's probably a full page of text*, I thought as I waited, growing more anxious by the second.

But when he finally responded, it was underwhelming.

Godwin, Robbie: Don't be sorry. I'm glad you kissed me. I'm just confused.

Hill, Leslie: Me too.

I closed out of *Teams* to keep from getting distracted—and to keep me from saying too much to him.

25

Leslie

Despite my distractions and swirling maelstrom of internal emotions, I was able to spend the rest of the weekend reviewing the presentation for the Board of Directors to the point that I had it memorized. I practiced my presentation in front of the mirror until every sentence was smooth and confident.

Then on Monday morning I ignored the smiles and greetings from my male subordinates and invited Mrs. Caltrop into my office, where I practiced the presentation some more in front of her and listened to her feedback.

Finally it was time for the presentation itself. As I left my office, Robbie smiled reassuringly. Arthur gave me a secret little wink. Liam flashed me a big thumbs-up, and said, "Go get 'em."

I carried my laptop up one flight of stairs to the fourth floor. Aside from the huge offices around the outer walls and the big conference room in one corner, the entire floor was an open design without any partitions dividing it into smaller departments or teams. There were only a dozen or so individual cubicles spread out in the space. This was where the holiday party would be next month. All they had to do was clear away the cubicles and there was enough space here to house hundreds—if not thousands—of Allegheny Supply employees and their families.

I passed massive offices on my way to the conference room, and all of the titles began with *Chief*. Chief Financial Officer. Chief Technology Officer. Chief Operation Officer. Chief Marketing Officer.

Every title I passed ratcheted up my anxiety another notch.

The boardroom in the corner had the door closed, and someone was already speaking inside. I was early, so I sat in a chair outside and picked at lint on my pencil skirt. Waiting was always my least favorite part of any activity.

Eventually, the door opened and a sharp looking man in a suit exited in a hurry. "Impossible demands..." he muttered under his breath while making a bee-line for the elevator.

I rose, smoothed out my skirt, and walked inside.

The boardroom was dominated by a single gargantuan table, oval-shaped like the Eye of Sauron. Built into the table were microphones and internet jacks. The table could hold at least forty people, but presently it was only occupied by seven—six men and one woman. The seven of them were eating bowls of salad from a catering tray in the corner. None of them looked in my direction.

I cleared my throat. "My name is Leslie Hill. I'm here for the presentation...?"

The woman seated closest to us—Katherine Chandrakhan, the Chief Operating Officer—frowned at me like I had given the wrong answer in a spelling bee. "*Everyone* who has come here today is giving a presentation, Ms. Hill. Can you please elaborate on *which* project you will be updating us?"

They don't even know my name. That was simultaneously disheartening and relieving. "The Systems Transition Team. To select the new sales software for the company..."

"Ahh, yes, please come in!" said the man at the head of the table, which felt like it was a football field away from me. "There's a video jack down at that end, go ahead and plug your laptop in. We're just finishing up our lunch, so don't mind us."

"You're welcome to some food, if you're hungry," Katherine added.

Food is the last thing I want right now. Standing in front of these powerful people who could end my career with the snap of their fingers, I would probably throw up anything I tried to eat.

I set up my laptop to the video and internet connections, and opened PowerPoint. The presentation appeared on the screen on the wall, just like it was supposed to. I breathed a sigh of relief that there would be no technical issues.

"Whenever you are ready, Ms. Hill. We are all very excited to hear about your team's progress."

My team. The three men downstairs, all of whom I was romantically involved with, to one degree or another. I felt my pulse race at the thought, with the irrational fear that the Board of Directors would be able to sense what was going on just from the look on my face.

I clicked the spacebar on my laptop to start the slideshow. "As I said, my name is Leslie Hill. I'm the manager of the Systems Transition Team." I clicked the spacebar again to go to the next slide. "Some background on me. I started working for Allegheny Supply five years ago, beginning in the sales department before moving on to..."

"Excuse me," Katherine interrupted. "This is a project update presentation, not a job interview. Do you mind skipping to the status update?"

"We are all very busy, as I am sure you are," said one of the other directors in an orange tie.

"Yes, of course." I tapped the spacebar and watched the slides skip ahead. "Shoot, I went too far. Um. How do I go back... Here we go. The project status."

I took a deep breath and tried to collect myself. All that practice for nothing.

"Here is the revised timeline based on our progress thus far. As you can see, I had to trim some of the steps along the way. The test environment requirements have been reduced by three days thanks to the dedicated work of Robbie Godwin, our technical liaison. He's a rock star."

An intrusive image popped into my head, Robbie's face close to mine as he wrapped me close and kissed me.

"Because of this, the evaluation of the candidate software is ahead of schedule," I went on. "We have reviewed two candidate softwares thus far, both of which meet our needs adequately. Liam Harford, the sales liaison, is spear-heading this."

Another memory invaded my head: Liam lowering me to the floor of my house, half on the kitchen tile and half on the living room rug, spreading my legs and touching my wet pussy before entering me...

I switched slides and smiled proudly. "Based on our current estimates, we should meet the deadline required. It might be tight during the installation and implementation phases near the end, but I can confidently say that we will do everything in our power to have it ready on December thirty-first."

As I said the rehearsed line, I felt like a gymnast who had stuck her landing. I was telling the Board of Directors what they wanted to hear. They should have been pleased.

Instead, they all shared looks among themselves.

I blinked. "Is there something wrong?"

"It's just that..." Katherine trailed off to glance at the man at the head of the table, who nodded once. "It's just that this is the *old* deadline."

"Haven't you met with Jen?" the man with the orange tie asked.

"Jen and I met two weeks ago," I said carefully. "We have another biweekly meeting tomorrow to review what I've shown you."

"That explains it," Katherine said to the man next to her. "A scheduling SNAFU."

"Should have met with Jen before giving us the presentation," he agreed. "I will speak with her admin to make sure it doesn't happen again."

I stood at the front of the room awkwardly. "I don't understand. Has something changed?" I felt a wave of hopefulness. "Has our deadline been extended?"

Once again, everyone in the room shared glances. I was beginning to feel like an outcast being ignored by the cheerleaders.

"December thirty-first is not ideal," Katherine finally said to me. "I am out of the office that week, for New Year's."

Orange-tie nodded. "Christmas is on a Wednesday this year, so I've taken that whole week off."

"With so many of us out of the office, we need the new software roll-out completed by the Friday before the holiday," Katherine said firmly. "The twentieth."

I gave a start. "*December* twentieth?" I gestured at the slide. "I don't... Our timeline is already extremely tight. Losing nearly two weeks is... it's..."

I was at a total loss for words. If the seven people around the table weren't so powerful, I would have told them bluntly that they were crazy.

Instead, I collected myself and said, "That is an extremely aggressive deadline. Even if we work nights and weekends, I don't see how we could adequately meet that date..."

The man at the end of the table waved a hand. "You seem like a motivated young manager. I'm sure you'll find a way to make it all come together. If you don't, you'll be on Santa's naughty list!"

He chuckled at his own joke, and a few others smiled. But Katherine and two other directors were staring intently at me. Letting me know they were serious.

"If there is nothing else...?" the orange-tie man said. "We have two more presentations before I have to get on a plane to Boston."

Katherine rose and opened the door. "You can come in and set up," she said to whoever was waiting next. Already the group was shifting their attention away from me, the STT, and their impossible deadline.

With nothing else to do, I gathered my laptop and fled the room.

Liam

"How long has she been in the meeting?" Arthur asked.

"Not long," I replied. "Her presentation should last an hour."

Arthur rolled up his jacket sleeve to look at his watch. His *expensive* watch. Based on that and the clothes he wore, I got the impression that the Frenchman had expensive tastes in all of his endeavors.

"I hope it goes well," he said.

"You sound doubtful. Do you not trust Leslie?"

He shrugged in the most stereotypically French manner I had ever seen. "I trust Leslie with all of my being. It is the men and women on the fourth floor I do not trust."

Something in the way he described Leslie tugged at my heart and made me a *little* jealous. "Leslie told me she saw you at the Halloween party."

Arthur's smile was quick and easy. "Indeed she did, and I saw her as well."

"Did anything happen?" I asked.

Arthur shrugged once more. "We had fun."

I pursed my lips and did not push it any further. We had all agreed last Friday to share with each other everything that happened. *Everything*. But Arthur wasn't revealing something. And I wasn't sure if I wanted to know what it was.

I had respected Leslie's wishes up to this point. I teased her and flirted a healthy amount, but overall I was holding myself back from truly pursuing her. Giving her space until the project was over.

But now that it felt like she and Arthur had done something together at the Halloween party...

Leslie's high heels announced her entrance before she appeared in the doorway. "That was quick," I said.

"How did it go?" Robbie asked hopefully.

Leslie didn't slow down as she walked past our cubicles. "It went fine. We'll go over it in the team meeting this afternoon."

She marched into her office, closed the door, and fogged the windows.

I shared a look with Arthur and Robbie. No matter what she said, it did *not* go well. I pulled up *Teams* and waited for her name to change from red to green.

Harford, Liam: Okay, how did it really go?

Hill, Leslie: It was fine

Harford, Liam: The expression on your face said otherwise

Harford, Liam: Seriously, what

happened? Are they unhappy with our progress?

Hill, Leslie: It had nothing to do with our current progress. They're just adding more stress on me.

I pulled out my phone and switched to text messages.

Me: You know what always makes me feel better when I'm stressed?

I added a gif of someone thrusting in the air.

Leslie: Alright, I'll admit that made me laugh.

Me: Imagine how good I could make you feel if we pretended that I didn't work for you.

Me: Just for a day.

Leslie: You're incorrigible!

Me: That's only because I've been thinking about you.

Me: A *lot*.

Leslie: Is that so?

Me: As a matter of fact, I'm thinking about you right now. The things I want to do to you when this project is complete.

Me: *Filthy* things.

Leslie: I'm listening.

Me: Nope. If I have to wait until the project is over, so do you.

For a long time, she didn't respond. I put my phone down and returned to working on my software evaluation. A few minutes later she finally sent another text.

Leslie: I wish you were fucking me right now.

God *damn*. That was not what I was expecting Leslie to write. I felt myself growing hard at the thought.

I glanced at the office, whose windows were still fogged. Arthur and Robbie were chatting about server and database licensing costs, totally oblivious.

Me: That would be a lot more fun than software evaluations.

Leslie: What would you do to me if you could?

Me: You're going to have to use your imagination. I'm going to torture you the way you're always torturing me, walking around with your sexy self ;-)

Leslie: I want to wrap my lips around your throbbing cock and feel you cum down my throat.

I grinned when I saw the text. We had agreed not to do anything together... But sexting didn't count, right? It probably did since it was still a manager and employee acting inappropriate together, but for now it felt like a totally reasonable loophole.

Me: You're getting me hard.
Leslie: How hard?

I pulled up the camera app on my phone. Mrs. Caltrop's view was blocked by her monitor, and Arthur and Robbie still had their heads together. I spread my legs underneath my desk, then adjusted myself. The outline of my long cock pressed against the fabric of my pants, extending down one thigh halfway to my knee.

I snapped a photo and sent it to Leslie before I could change my mind.

She didn't respond immediately. She didn't respond at all, in fact. I began to second-guess what I had done, if I had somehow crossed a line in our sexual stalemate. All the while, she remained in her office with the windows fogged.

Finally a meeting invite popped up on my calendar.

SUBJECT: Status update
TIME: Monday, November 4, 1:00 PM-1:30 PM
LOCATION: Leslie's Office

Oh shit. Was she serious?

There was no way she was serious.

I spent a minute waiting for my erection to go away before gathering my notepad and pen. Mrs. Caltrop glanced at me as I walked by but said nothing. I opened the office door. Leslie was seated behind the desk, looking busy.

"Close the door," she said. And in a lower voice, "And lock it."

I obeyed, twisting the lock as slowly as I could so it wouldn't make any noise.

"Leslie..." I began as I approached her desk. She was wearing a tight pencil skirt, and a dark blouse that didn't show any cleavage but still hinted at the fullness of her breasts underneath. Classy but sexy at the same time.

And she was looking at me like I was the glass of wine she needed at the end of the day.

"I liked your text, with the photo," she began, still seated. "Do you send that to all your bosses?"

I grinned. "Just the gorgeous ones." I made myself take a deep breath. "As much as I enjoy teasing and flirting in the office, though..."

Leslie grabbed the bar underneath her chair and the whole thing suddenly dropped a foot. "I love the chair they got me for my office. So many more options than the old one I had."

"As exciting as this is..."

"I want you to fuck my mouth," she said, pursing her lips together. She'd put on lipstick since the meeting, and her lips were a delicious shade of cherry red.

"You want me to *what?*" I blurted out.

She grinned like the devil. "Come stick that cock down your boss's throat. Before she changes her mind."

I realized that's why she had lowered her chair—she was now at the perfect height. And the way she was looking at me, this beautiful redhead with full lips and a come-fuck-me gaze?

There was no way I could say no to *that*.

I rounded the desk and unzipped my pants. Part of me still thought this was all a trick, that she was going to stop at the last minute and yell, "Gotcha!" and tell me that this was what I deserved for teasing *her* with my text. But as soon as I pulled my long prick out of my pants, she grabbed hold of the shaft and pulled me toward her, guiding me into her mouth.

She opened wide enough to take my girth with ease, even though I knew I was wider than most men. Her red lips wrapped around my shaft, and she gazed up at me through her eyelashes while pushing farther down, and farther, and *farther*, until I felt my cock reach the back of her throat. And she never gagged.

"Oh my God," I moaned as her lips remained tight around my base, her nose pressing into my pubic hair. "I didn't know you could do that!"

She pulled back slowly, ending with a kiss on my tip. "You never asked," she said, smiling sweetly. "Now, like I said. *Fuck my mouth.*"

I cradled her head in my hands and thrust back inside her mouth. She moaned deeply as I filled her completely again, ending with her lips wrapped tightly around my base. Making my cock completely disappear inside her mouth and throat.

Looking down at her? It was the hottest thing I'd ever seen in my life.

Even though it felt incredible, I was hesitant to go any harder. So Leslie grabbed my ass with both hands and urged me on. I obliged her, gripping her silky auburn hair in my fingers and pushing her head down on my cock while I thrust up inside her, face-fucking her like she wanted. Her moans deepened around my dick, a chorus of pleasure that mirrored my own.

All the while, our coworkers were just on the other side of the glass. Mrs. Caltrop outside the door, and Arthur and Robbie over in the cubicles. The fear of getting caught added urgency to my strokes, demanding that we finish our lewd and forbidden act before anyone found out. Before we were discovered. That made it even sexier than it would have been if we were in the privacy of our own home.

Soon I was pumping her face like there was no tomorrow. Shoving my cock as deep into her throat as I could, feeling the soft tissue of her mouth rubbing against my tip with each frenzied thrust. She hiked up her skirt and rubbed her pussy frantically, like she was already nearing her climax. I wasn't going to last long, myself.

"Leslie," I moaned softly, still cognizant of the people just outside the office. "I'm... close..."

She pulled back long enough to say, "Come down my throat. I *need* you, Liam."

I grabbed a handful of her hair tightly and shoved her back down on my shaft, giving her the final thrusts as I raced toward the finish line. Like a good girl, she kept her lips wrapped tight the entire time.

I wanted to scream at the top of my lungs, to roar like no man had ever roared before, but I managed to choke on my gasps of ecstasy as I began to come. With both hands firmly on the back of her head I held her down on my cock, giving her every last inch of me. She moaned with me, deep in her throat where I was shooting my massive load, and it raised my climax even higher as I filled her with every drop of love that I had.

27

Leslie

It was exactly what I had needed.

All the stress of the workday had risen within me, like pressure building in a volcano. The hours I spent preparing for my presentation. Not getting a chance to go over most of it with the board. And then their sudden and inexplicable changing of the deadline, cutting off nearly two weeks of time we needed to complete the project.

After all of that? I needed sexual release more than I needed anything in my life.

Liam's text had sent me over the edge. As soon as it came across my phone, I began touching myself and imagining his body on top of mine, smothering me with kisses while fucking away the stress. My climax had come quickly, but it was a forced orgasm rather than one that came slowly and naturally.

So I decided to call Liam into my office and help *him* out. Because that turned me on far more than just a photograph, or a memory.

There were a lot of types of lovemaking. Slow and gentle. Hard and fast. Slow but *rough*. All of them had their place, but sometimes a girl just needed to be manhandled.

I loved it when a man took charge, and Liam was no exception. After a little urging, he was grabbing my head and using me like his dirty little sex kitten in a way that I needed after the day I'd had. I was practically orgasming the moment his cock hit the back of my throat. When he finally filled that throat with his come, holding me down on him forcefully? It shot me over the edge in a much deeper way than could ever come from a sext message.

I gazed up at him while he came. Drinking in the way his face twisted with pleasure so intense it almost looked like pain.

Knowing that I could bring such a response from Liam, or any man, made me feel more powerful than just some manager at a supply company.

"Leslie," he gasped as he finally pulled his cock out of my mouth. "Holy fuck…"

I sighed and kissed the tip of his penis, carrying away the tiny glob of come still there. "That was *exactly* what I needed."

He cupped my chin and tilted my head up so he could kiss me deeply. "You must have had one hell of a meeting with the board."

I groaned. "Why'd you have to bring that up after distracting me?"

"Sorry. But seriously, what happened?"

Before I could answer, a knock came on my office door. Liam and I shared a frightened look before we scrambled to make ourselves look presentable. I ran to unlock and open the door.

Mrs. Caltrop was waiting outside. "You just received a last-minute meeting invite from Jen."

I gritted my teeth. "*Now* she schedules it. Thanks for letting me know." I stepped aside and held the door for Liam. "Thank *you* for the software update."

"My pleasure."

We shared a private smile as he left. *It was my pleasure, too.*

I was starving and hadn't eaten lunch yet, but I was ready to give Jen a piece of my mind for not notifying me about the STT deadline change. But the perky project management coordinator only laughed and waved a hand when I reached her office.

"The board can be such a *pain*, can't they? Yours isn't the only project where they've abruptly changed deadlines, or canceled them altogether!"

I closed the door to her office and sat down. "It just seems that their reasons for the deadline change aren't legitimate. They—"

Jen cut me off with another rueful chuckle. "It always seems like the board is as fickle as the weather, doesn't it! But we have to remember that they're looking at the bigger picture, while us grunts are down in the trenches. We have to trust their strategic vision."

She was so aloof about all of it that I wanted to shake her until she stopped smiling. "But the thing is... The timeline was already extremely aggressive. The new deadline is impossible to meet. That's not an exaggeration—there's no way to hit each of the project milestones in the time allotted. Not even working weekends."

Jen pursed her lips. She probably believed it made her look thoughtful. "Not meeting the deadline would be very unfortunate. The Systems Transition Team is probably the most important project in the company right now."

It doesn't seem that way, based on how much attention they paid to my presentation. "All the more reason to make sure it's done right. I want to go back to them with a revised proposal. We need to—"

"Woah woah woah," Jen said with another condescending laugh. "The board has set the deadline. It's now your job to meet it—even if it means rolling up your sleeves and doing some of the grunt work!"

"You've seen the project chart," I protested. "Heck, you created the outline for me. I've already trimmed days off all the tasks I can. How else am I supposed to meet this deadline?"

"I'm sure you'll find a way!" Jen said happily. "Just make sure you meet that deadline—it would be *super* bad for your career if you have to give the board bad news!"

I groaned as I went back to my office.

I spent the early afternoon going over the project timeline again. Even if I forced my team to work seven days a week, we wouldn't finish before Christmas. I began to consider crazy options, like cutting the entire week of deployment testing. We could push out the software to everyone's computer and just *hope* everything worked, right?

But of course, that was a recipe for disaster. Rolling out a solution with bugs and errors was far worse than missing a deadline.

I was going to fail everyone. It would hamstring my career, and the careers of my team. And the worst part was that it wasn't even my fault.

With no solution available on the project timeline, I gazed out my office window at the three handsome men working diligently at their cubicles.

And once again, the same question I had been asking myself lately scrambled its way to the front of my brain: *what the hell am I doing?*

It was one thing to sleep with Liam when we had barely started working together. It crossed a line, but it was *close* to that line. Then there was kissing Robbie in the office on Saturday. It was only a kiss, though, and nobody was around. Arthur and I had sneaked down here during the Halloween party and had sex, which was all sorts of risque and dangerous, but at least everyone was off at the party.

But *this*? What Liam and I had just done?

Bringing him into my office during business hours?

Fooling around with Mrs. Caltrop right outside? With Arthur and Robbie sitting at their cubicles nearby?

I was getting too reckless. Whatever had come over me, I needed to stop. Before I went too far and we got caught.

But as I wallowed in self-pity, I began to wonder... did it really matter?

The project timeline was barely doable before, but now it was literally impossible. And the board—and smiling Jen—didn't seem to care.

The project was going to be a failure. *I* would be a failure. And then I'd probably lose my job.

So if I was going to lose my job regardless, did it truly matter what I did with my subordinates? Did we need to hold ourselves back, or could we throw caution to the wind and do whatever we wanted?

My phone vibrated on my desk.

Liam: That was amazing. But also totally unexpected.

Liam: But did I mention amazing? Because it was amazing.

Me: You started it by texting me a picture of your hard-on!

Liam: I was only teasing you. I didn't know it would whip you into a sex-demanding frenzy!

Me: But it was amazing, right?

Liam: Totally amazing. I probably didn't mention that already, but it was DEFINITELY amazing.

Liam: Next time I'll return the favor.

Next time.

I daydreamed about that until our scheduled team meeting with everyone. We held it in the office this time, gathering chairs around the open space between Mrs. Caltrop's desk and the other cubicles.

I spent a few minutes relaying how the Board of Directors meeting had gone. Mrs. Caltrop remained as stone-faced as ever, but my three employees' faces all grew grim.

"December twentieth is, um, impossible." Robbie removed his glasses and cleaned them on his dress shirt. "And to be clear, I am not exaggerating. It is *literally* impossible, even if I completed every one of my checkpoint tasks in a row with no gap-time in between."

"Surely we can find a way to make this work," Arthur said in his easy, smiling manner. "I would be happy to work late, if it would help. The others would as well, yes?"

"That's the thing," Liam said with a frustrated gesture. "I have a list of testing practices ten pages long. I have to perform them on each candidate software. Some of them are long—including bundling batches of sales orders at the end of the day, sending them to the database, and ensuring they propagate up to the cloud backup after three days. There's a whole page of steps like that. I can't just *work late* to complete them. We have to literally wait for the system to process the sales orders naturally."

Liam jabbed a finger in the air. "And that's not all! Not only do we have to test this while evaluating which software to buy, but we have to repeat those same steps in a test environment prior to the rollout. And then repeat them *again* in production."

The smile disappeared from Arthur's face. Somehow, he was even more handsome when he was scowling. "I see."

"Yes, um." Robbie cleared his throat. "I have a significant amount of work in each of those steps as well. Technical evaluations using Wireshark to ensure our network can handle the bandwidth." He shook his head at me. "These are steps that cannot be rushed, or skipped."

"I told them the new deadline was impossible," I said with a sigh. "They didn't seem to want to listen. They were more concerned with having it done before they broke for Christmas and New Year's."

"Leslie," Arthur said softly. "What are we going to do?"

He didn't ask what *I* was going to do. He asked what *we* were going to do. It was a small comfort, but it meant a lot to me right then.

"I don't know," I admitted.

Mrs. Caltrop, who had been silent this whole time, stood up. "I've been on projects with tighter deadlines than this one, and you four are as sharp as anyone in this company. I'm going to get some coffee, and we're going to go through the timeline and list of checkpoints and figure out how we can hit December twentieth with time to spare. Who else wants coffee?"

"I would absolutely *love* an espresso," Arthur said.

Mrs. Caltrop gave him a level stare. "The options in the Allegheny Supply break room are caffeinated and decaffeinated."

Arthur smiled widely. "Caffeinated would be divine, *merci beaucoup.*"

As soon as she was out of our team's workspace, Liam turned to me and said, "While we're all here, alone, I want to talk about something more important."

"More important than the project?"

"I want to talk about us." Liam swung his finger in a circle. "*All* of us."

I tensed. "I, uh, don't think we have anything to talk about." I gave him a pointed stare, but he ignored it.

"Do not be alarmed Leslie," Arthur said smoothly. "We discussed this thing last week, when we went out for beers."

"You *what?*"

"All of us, um, like you," Robbie said. He crossed his arms over his chest, which made his dress shirt tighten and gave me a view of the tattoos peeking out at his wrists. "We like you a lot."

"We know it's weird, but we're all sort of a team," Liam told me. "So it's not as weird as it might be. And we know you're busy. We're *all* busy with the project, obviously."

"Too busy for a steady relationship, yes?" Arthur added.

I didn't know how I felt about the three of them talking about this bluntly, in the open. "I don't understand what you're saying."

"We do not mind dueling for your affection," Arthur said.

Robbie shook his head. "Not *dueling*, Arthur. Just competing."

Arthur frowned with confusion. "This is what I said. Dueling."

"Dueling involves pistols and death," Liam replied.

"Oh. I did not mean this. I am a lover, not a fighter," Arthur said with a grin.

Liam waved it off. "Forget it. What matters is that we're all *competing* for your love, Leslie. To whatever degree you think is acceptable. Then, when the project is over and we all have more time, you can choose one of us."

"*Choose* one of you?" I sputtered.

"The most charming and attractive one, of course," Arthur said smugly. "I hope you will not break their hearts too badly." He winked at me.

"I think she'll choose the one she has known the longest," Liam replied.

Robbie looked back and forth between them. "Or she will choose the... um... well, I don't know."

The thought of choosing one of them at the end of the project made me feel queasy. They were acting like this was a season of *The Bachelorette*, and I was going to hand roses out to whoever I liked the most.

I shook my head in amazement. "You are all forgetting that I'm your manager." I lowered my voice. "We can't talk about this here! What if someone overhears?"

"We just wanted to let you know where we stood," Liam said gently. "Better to have all the cards on the table rather than playing a guessing game with your feelings."

"Now we have a plan," Arthur said happily.

I gestured at the computer screen with the project timeline. "We don't even have a plan for how we're going to meet our new deadline, let alone a plan for anything else! We..."

I trailed off as Mrs. Caltrop returned with two cups of coffee. She stopped a few feet away and frowned.

"What did I miss?"

I closed my laptop and shoved it under my arm. "Our meeting is over. I need some time to think."

"But Leslie..." Robbie began.

"We'll discuss the project in the morning," I said as I practically ran out of the office.

28

Leslie

I took the stairs down to the first floor because I didn't want one of the guys trying to catch up to me while I waited for the elevator. But in the lobby I came face to face with someone else.

"Leslie!" John Fadringham exclaimed. He looked like he was on his way out for the day. "How are you feeling? After the party?"

It took me a moment to remember the excuse I had given him when he saw me in the office—that I thought I had the flu. "Oh, um, yeah, I ended up going home. But I feel much better now."

He smiled warmly. "We didn't get to chat when you started your new role, because everything happened so fast. But I wanted to tell you that I'm proud of you. I know you're going to do great things for the company."

It was all so nice, and warm, and unexpected, and comforting having a caring boss again.

I started tearing up.

John's face went deathly white. "Leslie, oh no! I didn't mean to make you cry!"

I shook my head and said, "No, it's not you, it's me, and this new position..."

He put a comforting hand on my back and led me to the coffee shop next door. By the time we sat down I was blubbering and telling him about everything that had happened with the STT and the impossible deadline.

John listened quietly until I was done. "I suppose this is why the original manager, Oliver Edwards, abruptly quit."

"Apparently."

He put his hand on mine. "I'm so sorry Leslie. I really am." He paused and added, "Have I ever told you the story of when I first became the manager of the Operations Department?"

I shook my head.

"I was older than you—in my late thirties. Experienced, but still green around the ears. This was back in the nineties. The company was flying by the seat of its pants back then. Sales orders written on napkins, invoices going months without billing, rebates and credits issued without anyone checking the work. The wild west days of supply. Back then, operations was only three people, and none of them cared much about their job. I was promoted to manager of the team, and the president of the company told me I needed to increase our gross profit by four percent. Four!"

I gasped. Since I had worked in operations, our goal was always two percent savings on gross profit. And even *that* was difficult.

"The next year was the longest of my life," John admitted. "I knew that the goal was impossible to meet. I even talked to people in competing companies to get a feel for things, and they all told me the same thing! But I didn't give up. I fired two of the operations analysts and hired my own team. We created new processes for reviewing and organizing manufacturer's rebates. Same for the process for reviewing customer credits. By the end of the year, we had saved *seven percent* on gross."

"Seven!"

He nodded proudly. "Sure, the company was a mess back then. It would be impossible to get seven percent on gross today because everything runs more smoothly. But the point is that even though I believed the goal couldn't be met, I worked as hard as I could as if it *was* possible." He jabbed a finger at me from across the table. "You're one of the hardest workers I've ever seen. One of the smartest, too. I know you'll be able to come out ahead of all of this, and impress the board at the end."

I smiled. "I don't have a year to figure it out. I have less than two months."

"What about hiring more people?" he suggested. "I heard the budget for the STT is unlimited."

"Our problems aren't manpower-related. The project tasks are mostly sequential. Evaluate the software, buy the software, install the software, test the software, deploy the software. We can't just hire ten new people and have them work on steps out of order."

He patted my hand. "I recommended you for that position because I knew you were the best candidate, Leslie. I'm sure you'll figure it out soon enough."

"I hope so. But keep my old position open just in case I need to come back?"

He smiled warmly. "We'll cross that bridge if we come to it. But there will always be a place for you on my team, Leslie."

Even though his advice was overly simplistic, it made me feel a little better by the time I got home. I always thrived when I had a manager who I knew cared about me, and my career. Now, my manager was the entire Board of Directors. I didn't feel like I had that mentor guiding me.

Maybe I'm not cut out to be a manager.

I pulled out my laptop when I got home and reviewed the project timeline again. A solution didn't magically jump out at me, so I closed my laptop and considered going for my afternoon run. When I failed to muster the motivation for that, I changed into sweatpants and curled up underneath a heated blanket to watch TV.

I'm failing at the project. I'm failing to prepare for the marathon. I'm a failure at everything.

I was in a dark place. The only thing missing was a pint of ice cream. I also didn't care.

Since I didn't want to think about the project, I turned my thoughts to the three men working under me. Had they really come right out and said that they didn't mind vying for my love? I'd been sort of seeing each of them at the same time, dancing around the subject, and they just bluntly discussed it out in the open. And apparently they had discussed it when they went out for beers the other week, too.

Before, I thought the end of the project would be a relief because I wouldn't have to hold back my feelings. I could do whatever I wanted. But now that they said I would have to choose one of them? I was beginning to dread it.

How could I make such a decision? A week ago it was Liam by a mile, but now...

Arthur was so charming and smooth. I couldn't stop thinking about the way he went down on me in the office while I sat on his desk, and then bent me over and fucked me with my face on the keyboard. And what he did with his finger, sticking it in my ass... That was a whole different realm of sexiness that I had never explored, and now was excited to try.

Then there was Robbie. He was incredibly sweet, and sexy in a dorky kind of way. We had only kissed—once in my closet, and again in the office this past weekend—but somehow that just made me desire him more. If he was that good of a kisser, how good of a lover would he be? I was eager to find out.

Choosing between the two of them would have been excruciating. But then when you threw Liam into the mix, with our history and the way our bodies melded together perfectly, a chemistry that could not be faked...

Yeah. I was *definitely* dreading having to make that choice.

I was on my third hour of binging Netflix when the doorbell rang.

I groaned as I tossed aside my blanket and went to the door. I had no idea which one of them was at my door. I also didn't know which of them I *wanted* to be at my door.

So it was a shock when I opened it to find the three of them standing there.

"*Bonsoir, mon fleur,*" Arthur said, taking my hand and kissing the palm. He strode into my house without an invitation.

"We need to talk," Liam told me. He didn't kiss my hand, but he patted my shoulder reassuringly.

Robbie looked nervous, and barely made eye contact as he slipped inside.

I closed the door and rounded on them. "I'm sorry, but I don't have the emotional energy to talk about dating you and making choices and everything else, alright?"

The three of them had brought their laptops, and were setting them up on my kitchen table. "Oh, we're not here for that," Liam said.

"Then what the hell are you guys doing?"

"We want to, um, talk about the project," Robbie said. "And the deadline. The new one, I mean. December twentieth."

Arthur patted the chair next to him. "Come, Leslie. Sit. We have much to discuss."

I joined them and frowned at the laptop screen. "How did you get a copy of the overall project timeline?" Up until that point I had only showed them the overview, not the detailed version with each checkpoint.

Liam grinned. "Arthur sweet-talked your admin assistant."

Arthur gave us a confused look. "What is this *sweet talk*? I merely gave Madam Caltrop the delight of my exquisite presence until she gave me what I wished."

"We have changes," Robbie said. "To the timeline."

Liam turned his laptop around and pointed. "First of all, we scrap the remaining software candidates. The first two are good enough to choose from, and we will make a decision *tomorrow* based on the information we have. That saves me a week."

Robbie adjusted his glasses. "Not needing to create those test environments would save me several days as well."

"But we have the representatives from the four software candidates coming in next week to give their formal pitches," I said.

Liam made a karate-chop motion. "Forget them. We'll cancel them all."

My mind was still foggy as I began to process that we were having this meeting now. "Those were scheduled by Jen weeks ago. The CEO of InterLync Systems is coming on-site himself."

"Doesn't matter," Liam said bluntly. "With this new deadline, we're performing triage."

Arthur grinned. "*Triage.* This word comes from the French word *trier*, which means *to sort*. Baron Dominique Jean Larrey, the Surgeon in Chief to Napoleon Bonaparte, used it to decide which of the wounded could be saved and which should be abandoned."

"Let's save the history lessons for another time," Liam said.

"What? I am merely sharing with you English-speakers the beauty of the French language."

"Skipping the other software evaluations frees up a significant portion of my time," Robbie said. "I can get a jump on the production environment. The server build, creating the distribution points, the new database and storage, plus configuring the cloud backups."

"And I can begin negotiating with the software company for licensing," Arthur added.

I chewed the inside of my lip as I considered that. "But if they know that we've canceled our meetings with the other software pitches, then won't it be more difficult to negotiate pricing? We won't be able to leverage the other companies against the one we choose."

Arthur gave a dismissive wave. "*Mon fleur*, leave such concerns to me. I will begin negotiating our licensing costs tomorrow."

I turned my attention to the new timeline on Liam's laptop. "Even if we make these changes, we're still finishing after December twentieth," I pointed out.

"Um. We can cut our infrastructure testing from three days to one," Robbie said. "Not ideal, of course, since any problems in production take three times as long to fix compared to a test environment, but necessary given the circumstances."

"We can also work late at night," Liam added. "And weekends."

"Which Robbie has already been doing, apparently," I said with a smirk.

"I think our computer-inclined friend has been trying to impress your heart, yes?"

Robbie blushed.

"The numbers work," Liam said, returning us to the topic at hand. "This whole situation sucks, but this new timeline gets us to the finish line before December twentieth."

"In time for the holiday party!" Arthur said.

I mentally chopped off parts of the timeline and adjusted the entire project. We didn't have any wiggle room, but it could work.

It really could work!

"This is amazing," I said. "Really. You three worked on this together?"

"Spent the last three hours hammering out which steps we could remove," Liam said proudly.

"Send me a copy of the new timeline so I can consider it?"

Arthur's fingers flew over his laptop. "*Voila*! It is done."

They stood and gathered their things. I prepared for them to change the subject back to *them*, and my relationships with them, but they surprised me by walking straight to the door.

"We're going to find a way to get this done," Liam said confidently as he left.

Arthur bowed formally and kissed my hand again. "Until the morning, *mon fleur*."

Robbie gave me an awkward little smile. "Goodnight, Leslie."

I watched them walk down my sidewalk together, simultaneously relieved and confused.

With renewed enthusiasm, I brewed a cup of coffee and began reviewing the timeline again. Mapping out every process on a calendar, breaking them down to the individual *days* that they had to be complete. We had no wiggle room, so it all had to work.

When I walked into the office the next morning, I wore a huge smile on my face. "Alright," I told my three employees and Mrs. Caltrop. "Let's do this."

29

Leslie

The next few weeks were rough.

We started arriving to work early. First at seven, then closer to six. We met every morning for ten minutes to review what steps we needed to complete that day, to ensure no part of the timeline slipped at all.

We worked all morning, then had food delivered so we could work through lunch. The afternoons were survived only through perseverance and several pots of strong coffee. Mrs. Caltrop solved that problem by stealing one of the coffee brewers out of the break room and putting it on the fourth cubicle that nobody was using. Time spent walking to the break room was time that could be better spent.

The only luxury I allowed myself was slipping out around five o'clock for my afternoon run. Just half an hour to an hour, then I changed in the gym downstairs and returned to work by six.

I had dinners delivered to the office for everyone. Pasta. Chinese food. Pizza. Thai. Nobody was picky, which helped us avoid arguments when it was time for me to order dinner. I expensed it all to my manager's account. If Jen told me that I had an essentially unlimited budget, then by God I was going to make use of it.

We usually worked until ten. Eleven sometimes, when we had

the energy. Then the four of us crawled home, got what sleep we could, and woke up early to do it all over again the next day.

The grueling hours would have caused dissent in the ranks in any other team, but my guys never complained. They were machines focused on a single purpose. They stayed enthusiastic and positive, even when it was late at night and everyone was fantasizing about the comforts of their own bed.

It helped that as hard as we worked, we also *played* hard.

It started with Liam. One Wednesday he followed me home in his car and parked it behind mine in the driveway. He didn't say a word as he followed me to my front door, came inside, and helped me take off my coat.

And then he carried me into the kitchen and fucked me on the countertop until we had knocked all the pots and pans to the ground and had made a mess neither of us wanted to clean up.

The next day it was Arthur who made eyes at me. Winking throughout the day, and grinning at me through my office windows. Making love to me with nothing but his eyes in that charming way of his.

That evening, when I came back from my jog around downtown Pittsburgh, he was in the lobby chatting with someone from the Finance department. As I passed him, I gave him my own little wink and an inviting look as I went into the company gym.

The gym was divided into two rooms: one for free weights, and another for cardio equipment. Instead of two gendered locker rooms, there were five executive locker rooms with individual showers. I walked to one of them and paused at the door, waiting to see if Arthur would follow.

When he walked into the gym, I grinned widely at him and went inside the locker room, leaving the door open.

By the time he entered, I was already nude and in the shower, lathering myself with body wash. Arthur locked the door and then slowly, deliberately, undressed himself. I watched with anticipation as he removed his blazer, hanging it on the peg on the wall, and then removed his tie. Next he unbuttoned and removed his vest, then slowly unbuttoned his dress shirt. One button at a time, slow enough to make me quiver with anticipation in the shower as the darkly handsome French man undressed.

Soon I was touching myself while enjoying the show. Arthur had a way of making every small act seem erotic, but the way he undressed was like whipped cream on top of a milkshake. He unlaced his dress shoes and removed his socks. He carefully folded his pants over the chair in the corner, and then did the same with his tight briefs.

Only then, when he was totally nude, did he join me in the shower.

My engine was warm and ready to go by the time his lips touched mine. His hands ran over my body, helping lather me with the soapy body wash covering my skin. I leaned into him and ground my pussy into his thigh, eager to feel his skin on mine.

With a rough, commanding hand, Arthur spun me around and bent me over. I gasped and readied myself for his cock, but then it was his face burying into my pussy from behind, tongue swirling and licking all around.

And then, to my surprise, his tongue moved up my pussy... and flicked across my asshole. I tensed at first, then relaxed as he licked me faster, giving me a rimjob in the executive shower. It was sexy and pleasurable in a completely different way, especially when he pressed his tongue deep against my back door and wriggled it around inside, moaning as if it was the thing he desired more than anything.

When he finally rose and shoved his cock in me from behind, I was craving him. He fucked me like that, and soon added a wet finger to my ass. I had been waiting for this, and hoping for it the way he had done last time, so I pressed my hips back against him to let him know what I wanted.

Two of my holes filled at the same time. Even though one of them was just his finger, it made me wonder...

"I'd been fantasizing about you," I moaned in the shower.

"*Est-ce vrai?*" he groaned back at me. "Is this true?"

"I've been dreaming about you playing with my ass," I said. The dirty talk drove him to fuck me harder, and I said the words I'd been thinking about since the night in the office. "Do you want to... fuck my ass?"

Arthur moaned loudly, and shoved his finger deeper inside of me. I could feel it against my inner walls, pressing against his cock with each thrust, driving me wild.

"I do not think so, now," he said. "I will do this with you another time. When we can go slow and relax."

I was disappointed, but his throbbing cock made me forget all about it.

"Does this disappoint you?" he asked.

"Only a little, but now I'm looking forward to it." I gazed back at him, slick with water that covered his muscular form and made his muscles pop. "Now fuck me like we have a project to get back to."

He grinned lustily. "*Oui, mon fleur.*"

Our cries of passion echoed off the tiled walls as he did just that, and then we got dressed and went back to work as if nothing had happened at all.

The weeks went like that: sneaking time with Arthur and Liam wherever we could, when we had the energy to spare. Only Robbie respected our distance, though I caught him looking at me throughout the day. I wondered what was going on behind those glasses. What he was thinking.

We skipped the holiday party planning committee. Thankfully Beth and Charletta understood why, and they seemed to have everything under control.

"We should switch places," Beth teased me when I told her that we wouldn't be able to help with the planning. "Charletta isn't very fun. It's not fair that you have all the sexy men to yourself!"

If only you knew how true that was, I thought.

"Oh!" Beth suddenly added. "But I did convince her to do the singles auction. *The naughty list.*"

"That's great! How'd you convince her?"

Beth leaned in conspiratorially. "She's going to be one of the singles people bid on. I think she needs the ego-boost."

"Good, then she can take *my* place," I said. "I think that will be a blast!"

"I think so too!" she said.

The next day, Arthur marched into our office like Napoleon entering Moscow. "I come bearing wonderful news. I have completed the contract negotiations with InterLync Systems!"

"That's fantastic!" I said as I came out of my office. "Do you have the final pricing hammered out?"

He handed me a stack of documents. I skimmed the pages until I found the number I wanted.

"Twenty-five dollars a month, per client?" I said. "That's hardly more than what we're paying now, for our crappy old software!"

Arthur beamed. "Did I not tell you I would do this?"

I wrapped him in a big hug. "This is awesome! I thought for sure we would be paying twice this for the new system."

"I take back everything I've ever said about you," Liam announced as he shook Arthur's hand. "You're not just a pretty Frenchman."

Arthur's grin widened. "Of course, I am also this thing. But I am far *more* than just this, yes?"

We cheered and celebrated the momentary victory. It was a major milestone passed.

We might just be able to pull this off after all, I thought.

30

Leslie

On the Saturday before Thanksgiving, I woke up for my long run and was greeted with a surprising image.

Snow.

Outside my bedroom window, illuminated by the street light, was a steady stream of snow. Big, heavy flakes that fell straight down without being affected by the wind. A silent winter landscape that made me feel nice and cozy inside my home.

But I would be even cozier in my bed. And I was exhausted from the relentless work in the office. And the thought of going out in the freezing weather to run twenty miles did not appeal to me one bit. As important as the marathon had seemed a few weeks ago, now it was several notches lower on my priority list.

I turned my alarm off and crawled back in bed.

The next thing I knew, my doorbell was ringing. I threw off my warm cocoon of blankets and went to the window. It was a brighter shade of grey outside now, and the snow was still steadily falling. Somewhere behind the frigid wall of clouds the sun was up.

And there was a handsome, bundled man gazing up at my window and waving.

I opened my window. "Robbie! What are you doing?"

"I'm, uh, making you wake up!" he shouted back. "You missed the run this morning."

"It's cold!" I protested. "And snowy! And my bed is *warm*."

He disappeared under my porch and the doorbell rang two more times.

Groaning, I went downstairs and opened the front door. He was wearing long black running pants and several layers underneath a windbreaker. A knitted cap covered his head and ears, and his glasses were fogging every time he let out a puffy exhale.

Before I could ask what he wanted, he marched past me and took charge of the situation in my kitchen. Dumping yesterday's coffee out of my pot and filling the tank with water to brew another pot. Then he pulled a skillet off my hanging rack and put it on the stove, and turned the burner on.

"Go upstairs and do your morning routine," he commanded. "Shower, put deodorant on, pray to the running gods. Whatever you normally do before a long run."

"It's already eight o'clock," I said. "We need to get to the office."

The skillet sizzled as he added a slice of butter to it. "The office can wait. Go get ready for our run."

"Are you making yourself breakfast?"

He grinned bashfully at me. "I'm, uh, making *you* breakfast. Seriously, go get ready. Pretend that I'm the boss and you're my employee. If you're not downstairs in five minutes, you're fired."

I laughed, but he looked like he was dead serious. I scrambled upstairs to get ready.

He had a fried egg sandwich waiting on a plate when I came downstairs. "You only had American cheese, so I hope this is good enough."

I sat down and took a bite out of the sandwich. I made a happy noise as I chewed the delicious food. "What other kind of cheese does one put on a breakfast sandwich?"

Robbie blinked behind his glasses. "Cheddar. Swiss. Monterey jack is always good. Seriously, you've only ever had American cheese?"

"Just on a breakfast sandwich," I replied in an affronted tone. "Don't be a cheese snob. That's Arthur's job."

We both laughed at the expense of our French colleague.

I sipped coffee and said, "I've got to admit. I kind of like this side of you."

"What side?"

"You stormed in here and took charge. It's hot when a guy is assertive." I flinched. "Not that you're not hot normally. Since you're kind of shy and quiet."

He blushed, proving my point. "Today and next week are the final two long runs before the marathon. They're the most important ones. I couldn't let you skip out on them like a wimp."

I stuck my tongue out at him.

My car was covered in six inches of snow, so I rode with Robbie to the park. Most of the runners were just finishing up as we got started, but coach told us he would leave the water jugs out for us.

The trail was packed down from all the other runners, giving us a mostly-clear path to run on. As we started running, I allowed myself to veer off the path to crunch through the snow. Feeling it compress underneath my shoes.

"Despite freezing my tushy off, I love running in the snow," I said. "It feels like winter!"

"I'm glad you like it, since we will, you know, be out here for several hours."

"You've run a bunch of marathons before, so tell me something," I said. "Why does our marathon training plan have us only doing twenty miles? Why don't we get up to twenty-six in training?"

"Long runs are risky," Robbie explained. "Especially for someone who has never run this much in one day. Once you get above, say, fifteen miles in a run, your risk of injury skyrockets. So most training plans will end at a twenty-miler or two, before tapering off."

"But what about the last six miles?"

"Six-point-two," he corrected. "And they're not really necessary. If you can run twenty miles, you can run a full marathon."

"That remains to be seen," I said doubtfully.

He smiled sideways at me. "I know you'll crush it on race day. Well, let me clarify that. I know you'll crush it on race day once you've completed today's run. So, you're welcome."

"Don't break your arm patting yourself on the back there, Romeo," I teased.

We fell into a groove as we ran down the trail. With the snow falling silently around us through the trees, it was an incredibly peaceful morning. It helped me zone out and allow my body to take over. One foot in front of the other, inhaling and exhaling every third step like coach had taught me.

To make it easier to set up water stops, our route was five miles out, then turning around and running five miles back. Then doing the whole thing over again. As we returned to the starting point for the ten mile mark, it took *all* of my willpower to make myself turn around and go back out on the trail. It would have been so easy to grab Robbie's keys and go sit in the warm car while he finished the run.

But for some reason, I didn't want Robbie to tease me for quitting halfway. As we ran along, side by side, I realized it was something deeper than that. I cared what Robbie thought about me. I didn't want to disappoint him.

If he drove to my house and made me breakfast because he

believed in me, then surely I could believe in myself.

I was running on fumes by the time we reached the final mile. Robbie wanted to do a fast mile to end it, but I told him I didn't have the energy and insisted he go on ahead without me. Instead, he slowed down and stayed by my side all the way to the end. I was glad he did, because that kept me from stopping to walk.

Robbie cheered when we reached the parking lot, and gave me an enthusiastic high-five. I could tell his adrenaline was pumping. "How's it feel completing your first twenty-miler?"

"My hamstrings are tight, my fingers are cold, and I've been daydreaming about pizza since mile seventeen. But I actually feel pretty darn good."

Everyone else had already left—even the coaches. Robbie's car was the only one in the parking lot. My feet crunched on the snow-covered pavement as we walked to the car and began stretching.

"Hey," I said softly while doing a hamstring stretch. "I really appreciate that you came all the way to my house and forced me to wake up. I needed that push this morning."

Robbie smiled weakly, then gave a cute little shrug. "I know the marathon is important to you. After all the training you've put in, it would be a shame to miss the last few long runs because you have tunnel vision at work. You've been working your butt off in the office, too. Seven days a week. It's important to get out and clear your head."

"All of us have been working hard," I said. "Not just me."

He smiled. "Yeah, well, I care more about your health than the others. I'm glad you let me bully you out of bed."

Not only was his sentiment incredibly sweet, but he was adorable standing there in the snow with huge flakes landing on his shoulders and beanie, cheeks red from the cold rather than his normal blushing manner. He didn't just want to make me happy in a shallow way—he wanted me to succeed in the things I cared about. It was easy for a guy to shower a girl with compliments and flowers, and to say whatever they thought was necessary to get in the girl's pants. It was a lot harder to be the jerk who made the girl get out of bed and go run twenty miles in the snow.

It was there in the parking lot, with snow drifting down all around us, that I kissed him.

His lips were warm and tasted like the last cup of lime Gatorade we'd had. He kissed me back hesitantly.

"What was that for?" he asked.

I rested my head against his chest. "For everything."

"What about our, well, you know, the *team*. You're my manager and whatnot. We're breaking company policy."

I shook my head. "Robbie, I don't care about that anymore. If something is meant to be, then it will be."

Something changed in his eyes when I said that. Hope appeared, and his resistance dropped away like a magician's curtain. He kissed me this time, harder and more needy than before.

"I've thought about this since the office last weekend," he whispered. "Since we spent seven minutes in your closet when we first met."

"Me too," I gasped as we made out some more.

Soon Robbie was unlocking his car and opening the back door. He pushed me down into the back seat, then crawled on top of me, our lips magically finding each other again as if it was impossible for them to be apart. Robbie's hands slid over my body, searching for my sensitive places, rubbing me through my running tights.

"I'm all sweaty," I protested. "Sweaty and gross."

He grinned. "Me too. We can be gross together."

The door closed and we stripped off our clothes, totally comfortable in each other's grossness. The chill in the air made me shiver when I removed my underwear, but then Robbie's body sank between my legs and covered me with warmth.

"Right there," I moaned, reaching down to touch his throbbing dick and guide it into my pussy.

He groaned as he filled me, and I wrapped my legs around him tightly.

Robbie went slow, kissing me tenderly while fucking me. Taking his time, pacing himself as if it was a marathon rather than a sprint. Our combined body heat kept us warm and fogged the windows like we were Rose and Jack on the Titanic. Robbie cupped my face while pressing his lips against mine, and I could see the love in his eyes. I knew from the way he looked at me and held me that he cared deeply about me. This was more than just sex.

There in the parking lot, in the middle of a snow storm, we made love until our bodies were even more exhausted than they were from our run.

*

We drove back to my place and showered together. Unlike the sex-filled shower I'd shared with Arthur at work, showering with Robbie was a sensual affair. He lathered me up with body wash and cleaned my body, holding me in his arms from behind while rubbing my neck, arms, and breasts. He planted gentle kisses on my skin as he worked every inch of my skin. When I was totally clean I returned the favor, lathering my hands and touching every inch of *his* body. I ran my hands up and down his back, appreciating the thick muscles there. Next was his arms, covering the dark ink with bubbly soap. Then I coated the globes of his ass with the lather, giving them a playful squeeze. I cleaned his penis too, circling underneath his shaft, stroking him gently with soap, even reaching farther to clean his balls.

It was a pleasant vulnerability with him in the shower. More intimate than sex.

"Don't get dressed yet," Robbie said as we dried off.

I narrowed my eyes at him. "As much as I'd like to have a cool-down session, we need to get to the office."

"It's not that," he promised. "Come here."

He led me into my bedroom and made me lie face-down on the bed. He found a bottle of lotion in the bathroom and then stood over me while squirting a dollop into his palm. Then he ran his hands over my body again, but this time with more pressure. Digging his fingers into my muscles and kneading out the knots.

I hissed as he rubbed his palm into the back of my thigh. "That hurts just a tiny bit."

He chuckled. "It's a sports massage. The pain is how you know it's working because it's stimulating extra blood flow to your muscles. But trust me, you'll be thanking me later when your legs aren't as achy."

"Sounds like I'm just trading future pain for *present* pain," I grumbled.

"Don't be a baby."

I twisted around to look up at him. His tattooed arms were bulging as he worked on my body. "That's no way to speak to your manager."

"Right now, you're *not* my manager," he said. Then he blushed, and his confidence disappeared a fraction. "You're, um, only a woman right now. A woman with a beautiful body."

"Your manager enjoys these compliments," I said as I relaxed back into the bed.

After the massage, we got dressed and drove to work together. We were quiet, but it was a *content* quiet rather than an awkward one.

At least, until Robbie drove into the parking garage and stopped the car. "You have feelings for them, don't you?" he asked suddenly.

There was no need to clarify who he meant. "Yes."

He sighed. "I was afraid of that."

I put a hand on his leg. "I have feelings for *all* of you. It's complicated, I know. Even if I wasn't your manager, this would be a big mess. Honestly, I don't know what I'm going to do when our project is over, Robbie. I've been trying not to think about it since I have to focus on the STT project, but... I just don't know."

It felt good to admit it to someone, even if it was one of the guys themselves. I'd gotten myself into a mess and had no easy way out. Saying so out loud relieved a little of the pressure.

Robbie squeezed my hand and smiled down at me. "Leslie. I don't know what you're going to do either. But, well, I don't care."

I gave a start. "You don't?"

"I'm happy with you." His voice was thick with emotion, and his eyes shimmered behind his glasses. "I'll take any part of you I can get, even if it's temporary. Even if it means losing our jobs if we get caught. And when we come to it, I'll respect whatever choice you make."

He gave my hand a final squeeze, and then got out of the car.

I don't want to have to make that choice, I thought as I followed him into the building.

31

Arthur

"*C'est moi,*" I said confidently to Liam in the other cubicle. "It is I who will win her heart in the end."

The office was quiet on the Saturday, especially with just the two of us working together. But we had gotten a lot of work done. Liam may appear to be a shaggy-haired loafer, but he worked quite hard when he must.

Liam glared over at me. "You may be exotic, but I'm the all-American boy next door. She and I have been flirting with each other for years before finally getting together."

I scoffed. "You say this as if it is a positive thing. It took you half a decade to convince her to sleep with you—how impressive! Fifteen more years and perhaps you two will be married."

Liam shrugged. He was very good at shrugging and pretending as if things did not bother him.

"We have a history."

"My encyclopedia has a history," I shot back. "That does not mean it knows how to properly make love to a woman."

Liam laughed. Despite our little rivalry over Leslie, I liked the man. He was a joy to work with, and had an endearing attitude about work and life. I hoped to share many beers with him in time.

"You sound worried," Liam said while typing on his keyboard.

"Me? Worried?" I scoffed again. "You are mistaken."

Liam glanced at me. "I'm just saying, you seem awfully preoccupied with my relationship with Leslie."

"This is the incorrect word. You do not have a *relationship* with Leslie. You have a fling." I patted my chest. "What we have is *love*. A deep connection in our very souls, like Romeo and Juliet."

"You know they died, right? Murder-suicide isn't the happy ending you may think it is."

"My love will follow Leslie beyond the grave," I said confidently.

Liam stopped typing and swiveled his chair around to face me. Our banter had been friendly and lighthearted up to this point. Now Liam appeared serious.

"You've always had a reputation for being a flirt," Liam said. "You're the ladies man of the office. Everyone kind of has a crush on you, and you love the notoriety."

I spread my hands. "Thank you for the compliments, my friend."

"But," Liam pointed out, "you never seem to date anyone for very long. Brianna says you two dated for a month. Ashley over in the Transportation Department says you dumped her after three weeks. *Your* relationships never last, because *they're* just flings. You get bored with a girl and then move on, every single time without fail."

I sat very still in my chair. "You have gone behind my back and spoken to these women? Why would you do this thing?"

Liam was usually an easy-going guy. Rarely was he

confrontational. But now his eyes stared daggers into me, bringing with them a warning and a threat.

"Don't screw around with her. She's not like the others girls, who you can date for a few weeks and then toss aside. If you're serious about her with all your talk of souls and undying love, then great. But if this is just some game to you..."

Liam shook his head slowly.

He did not say anything more. He did not need to. I heard the threat underneath his words, and knew that he was completely serious.

It is not just a game, I thought as I returned to my work. *Leslie is far more than that.*

She and Robbie arrived in the office in the early afternoon. We had expected this because of their marathon training run. But what I had not expected was the way they smiled at each other as they entered, blushing together like they had a new secret to keep. Like they were *hiding* something.

Robbie smiled widely as he fell into his cubicle. "How'd the morning go?" he asked casually.

"Liam and I did much work together," I said. "Did you and Leslie have a good *workout?*"

Robbie was facing his computer, but I could see the smile tugging on the skin of his neck. "It was, um, good. Yep."

"Surprised you went running in the snow," Liam said. "I would've stayed in bed."

Robbie shrugged casually. "We motivated each other." He was still grinning as he pulled out his laptop and connected it to the docking station.

Liam glanced at me, and it looked like he was thinking the same thing: *we have a new competitor.*

I gazed at Leslie in her office. I would need to ramp up my strategy with her.

I will have her, I thought eagerly. *When this is all done, she will choose me.*

32

Leslie

I felt fine for the rest of Saturday, although I was a little tired. But Sunday morning I woke up feeling like a boxer had spent all night using my legs as punching bags.

"Yeah, twenty-milers really hurt," Robbie agreed when I arrived in the office and complained about it. I was limping across the room toward my office.

"If I'm this achy now, I can't imagine how I would have been without your massage."

Liam spun around in his chair. "Massage?"

Arthur leaped from his chair like a soldier ready for battle. "*Mon fleur*, I will give you a massage so relaxing that you fall asleep in your chair."

"It was a *sports* massage," I clarified. "It actually hurt while he was doing it."

Arthur smiled devilishly. "Oh. If you want it to hurt a little bit, I can do this as well."

I stuck my tongue out at him and went into my office.

Now that Arthur had signed the contract with InterLync, we could begin building the production environment to their specifications. Robbie was focused on that for the next two weeks while Liam began working on writing the software documentation that would help the employees of our company transition to the new software. Since Arthur came from the accounting department and had no experience using the sales software, he was the guinea pig for Liam's documentation to make sure it was simple and easy to understand.

The snow fell outside our office almost every day, a sign that winter truly was here. In a scene reminiscent of our days in sales together, we fought over control of the thermostat to our little area. Every time I walked past it, I cranked it up to seventy-three degrees. Whenever Liam walked by, he discreetly turned it down to sixty-eight. It became a silly game between us, neither of us saying a word about it to the other—just constantly yo-yo'ing the temperature up and down.

Until the building manager sent an email to all the managers complaining about the strain on the heating units. Then we grudgingly agreed to compromise at seventy degrees.

On the Wednesday before Thanksgiving, the CEO sent out a company-wide email that everyone could leave at noon. Our team ignored it and kept working until five o'clock, when I finally called it.

"Tomorrow is a holiday, and we've earned a day off," I announced to everyone. "Enjoy Thanksgiving."

"We don't *need* the day off," Liam protested. "We still have work to do."

"I, um, do not mind coming in," Robbie added.

I shook my head. "Too bad. I'm telling the security guard downstairs not to let any of you in the building. Enjoy the day off and come back fresh on Friday."

Arthur lingered while the others packed up. "Got any plans tonight?" I asked casually.

"I am cooking a beautiful woman dinner," he told me. I felt a pang of jealousy before he smiled, and I realized he was talking about me. "An old family recipe from France."

"How can I say no to that?"

He arrived at my place with a sack full of groceries. He gave me a kiss on the cheek and went straight to my kitchen to begin prep work.

"Go treat yourself to a long, relaxing bath," he told me. "I will have dinner ready in an hour."

"I don't mind helping," I offered.

He waggled a finger in front of my face. "No no no. I am making dinner for *you*, and I need no assistance. The only thing I need is for you to get very clean. Do this for me and I will give you a very special treat later." He gave me a wink.

A tingle of excitement went up my spine at what he was implying. If it was what I *thought* it was...

When I got out of the bath, the house was filled with a savory smell. Arthur was stirring green beans in a pan, but there was something baking in the oven. He cut a striking figure as he maneuvered around the kitchen—he'd removed his suit jacket, but still wore the vest underneath and had rolled up his sleeves. His face was strained with concentration.

"What are you making me?" I asked.

He bent down, eyed the oven window, and then pulled out a baking dish. "Chicken cordon rouge," he announced proudly.

I frowned. "Isn't it supposed to be cordon *bleu*?"

"No no no," he said while returning to his green beans. "In French, cordon bleu means *blue ribbon*. First place, yes? My family recipe is red ribbon. Second place."

I crossed my arms over my chest and smiled. "I'm not sure I want to settle for a second-place dish."

He sprinkled salt and pepper over the green beans, picked one up with his bare finger, and plopped it in his mouth. He frowned while chewing, then nodded with satisfaction.

"This is an old family recipe," he explained. "From the war. My great-grandmother did not have any ham, but our neighbor raised cows for slaughter. So she used thinly-sliced beef instead."

My mouth watered at the thought. "That sounds delicious."

Arthur shrugged casually. "Yet you say second place is not good enough, so perhaps I throw this in the trash..."

I shoved him playfully.

He began prepping two plates. "You made a *lot* of green beans," I said as I stared at the huge pan piled high with them. "I hope you are not expecting me to eat half of those."

"They are good as leftovers," he replied simply.

He pulled out the dining room chair for me, then pushed it in like a proper gentleman. Then, as if he was a waiter in a fancy restaurant, he uncorked a bottle of wine, poured two glasses, and then served the plates of food.

"*Bon Appétit!*"

Arthur sipped the wine and didn't touch his plate—he was watching me expectantly. I picked up my knife and fork and cut into the spiral of food before me. It was rolled into itself like a cinnamon roll, but with chicken and beef and cheese instead. I bit into a morsel, savoring the crunch of the crusty outer layer.

Against my will, I made a noise very close to an orgasm. "Arthur! This is amazing!"

Only then did he pick up his knife and fork. "But of course. It is family recipe, as I said."

I tore into the food like a starving woman. It was easy to forget that we had been eating take-out for every lunch and dinner for the past few weeks. Finally tasting a home-cooked meal was a wonderful change of pace. I had two helpings of the chicken, and could have eaten a third. The green beans were covered with butter and delicious as well—even though there were enough left over to feed an army.

"I love to cook," Arthur explained while finishing his own

plate. "And it is an even greater pleasure to cook for one as lovely as you."

I beamed at him while sipping my wine. "What's for dessert?"

He shrugged. "Something special. But it is not food."

He took me by the hand and led me into the bedroom, then removed my clothes slowly. He kissed me sensually, and ate me out until I was moaning and clutching a handful of his dirty-blond hair. While his mouth focused on my clit his index and middle fingers glided in and out of my pussy, twisting as he went in a way that stimulated all of my nerve endings.

Everything below my waist was tingly and numb after I came. Arthur kissed me on the lips, then undressed himself at the foot of the bed while I watched. He stood before me like a French god, muscular frame glistening in the soft light of my bedside lamp.

And then he retrieved something out of his pants on the floor. A small bottle of lubricant.

I bit my lip and tensed with anticipation. "I don't know if I can handle this."

"Then I shall go slow," he reassured me while coating his cock with lube. "And if you do not enjoy it, we will stop, yes?"

I hope I enjoy it, I thought. I'd been fantasizing about it for so long with Arthur that I was beginning to doubt if it could live up to the hype.

Arthur pulled my legs down to the edge of the bed, then put a pillow underneath my lower back. He approached and rubbed my clit with his thumb, sending new shivers of pleasure through my body.

His fingers found my tight little backdoor. He rubbed them in a circle, coating me with the lube that glistened on his rock-hard cock. Then he pressed the tip of his cock against my asshole, and I felt my tight ring give underneath the pressure of his manhood.

"Oh!" I yelped as it slid right inside. The lube was doing its job marvelously—beyond a little pressure I didn't feel much else.

"*C'est bon?*" Arthur asked. "Are you okay?"

"I'm more than okay," I breathed. "Keep going."

Arthur's handsome face was tight with concentration as he pushed himself deeper inside my ass, fucking me a little bit at a time. To my surprise, it never hurt. It felt... different. In a good way.

A *very* good way.

"Do you like it?" I asked as my own pleasure rose.

Arthur's laugh was rich. "*Mon fleur,* I like it very much." He let out a long sigh. "Your ass is so tight. *C'est très serré.*"

I moaned louder at hearing his native tongue. His cock was pressing indirectly on my pussy walls, filling my body with new and exciting ecstasy. The louder I moaned, the deeper he ventured inside my ass. It was like feeling his finger inside of me, but *better.*

"Fuck my ass," I breathed. "Oh Arthur..."

He grinned down at me while savoring the way I felt. Soon his fingers on my clit wasn't enough, and I pushed him aside so I could rub my own pussy rapidly. Arthur fucked me harder, throwing aside caution as he pounded my ass with ecstasy-filled abandon.

"Oh, *mon fleur,*" he moaned while gripping my legs and pumping my ass with his dick. "Leslie! Ohh!"

I rubbed myself faster as he began to come, and the way his beautiful face twisted with indescribable pleasure flung me over the edge. I came with Arthur as he came deep in my ass, filling my forbidden hole with his milky seed in a way that made me feel dirty and sexy and desirable all at the same time.

We slept in the next morning, which was a wonderful change of pace after waking up early for work for a month straight. I clung to Arthur's body for warmth as the snow fell outside the window, and decided that I never wanted to get out of bed again.

He made a sleepy noise and rolled over. I rolled with him, allowing him to be the big spoon as he pulled my body against his and sighed.

"The parade," he purred into my hair. "We are missing it, are we not?"

"Parades are dumb," I whispered. "They're too commercialized now. I miss the old days where there were just floats and marching bands."

"Parades still give me great joy," Arthur said defensively. "I wish to see Snoopy."

I reached to my night stand and pulled up my phone. Within seconds I had the Macy's Thanksgiving Day Parade streaming on the phone in bed. A giant inflatable Minion was currently floating across the screen, rocking back and forth with the wind.

"Much better," he said happily. "How do you feel, *mon fleur?*"

I kissed his arm. "I feel great."

"I meant..." He thrust up against my ass. "How does *this* feel? The next morning?"

"Honestly? I'm surprised at how good I feel," I said. "I'm a *little* sore, but hardly noticeable."

"Lubricant is magic," Arthur replied. "And was the experience everything you dreamed?"

"I really liked it!" I said. "It was different. And fun. I wouldn't want to do it *every* time..."

"But of course."

"...But I would love to do it again."

He kissed my hair. "I am happy. *You* make me happy, Leslie."

I sighed back into his warm, nude body. He was my own personal space heater underneath the covers. "Want to stay in bed with me all day?"

I was half-joking, half-serious. But Arthur made a sad noise. "I have plans this afternoon. A Thanksgiving potluck with friends."

"Oh," I said. My stomach twisted painfully at the pseudo-rejection. "Of course."

He twisted until he was on top of me. He smiled sadly. "I am very sorry, Leslie. I would rather stay in bed with you, of course. But I will stay for a little while longer."

He kissed me, and for a moment my sadness disappeared. But only a moment.

"I understand," I said. "I'll be right back."

I rolled out of bed and went to the bathroom, then decided to take a shower. It was silly, but suddenly I wanted to cry. I'd expected Arthur to hang out with me all day, even though we hadn't discussed it. And he had not even considered inviting me to his potluck.

Granted, bringing me along would be a bad idea if the potluck was with work people. Then I would be surrounded by strangers and unable to show any affection toward Arthur. But still, it would have been nice to at least be *invited*.

I fought down the tears in the shower, then put on some comfortable sweatpants and a sweater. Arthur was not in the bedroom, so I went downstairs and found him at the front door.

"What are you doing?" I asked.

He threw open the door. Liam and Robbie strode through with smiles on their faces.

"Happy Thanksgiving!" they said in unison.

33

Leslie

I gawked at the two men in my doorway. Liam was wearing a big antique pilgrim hat, and had an arm-full of grocery bags. Robbie was carrying a stack of laptops.

"What..." I stammered. "What is all of this?"

Liam carried the food into the kitchen. "You said that we weren't allowed in the headquarters building. But the security guard can't keep us out of your house."

I glared at Arthur. "You were a trojan horse! Letting them through the front door while I was in the shower!"

Arthur grinned widely at me. "Better the front door than the *back door*, yes?"

I blushed and giggled. Liam and Robbie didn't seem to catch the innuendo, thankfully.

I hugged Arthur. "I'm very happy that you lied to me about your plans today."

He frowned. "What lie? This is the potluck I am going to, with friends. Every word was the truth."

I hugged Liam next, then Robbie. "Why do you have a stack of laptops?" I demanded.

Robbie's eyes widened. "We, um, were going to try to get some work done."

"I told you to take the day off!"

"Yeah, yeah, you're the boss and give orders and have the power to fire us," Liam said. "But we're disobeying you today."

"We promise to get only a *little bit* of work done," Robbie told me. "Just a few things that need to be completed before tomorrow's tasks."

"Why isn't the parade on TV?" Liam asked.

"Our dear manager finds parades distasteful," Arthur said with a judging tone.

Liam stared at me. "What? You don't like floats?"

I rolled my eyes as they turned the parade on TV.

The three of them got to work turning my kitchen upside-down. Robbie boiled noodles in a pot and then cooked bacon in a skillet. Liam was on the kitchen island coating a raw turkey breast with butter and spices.

"I didn't know you were so handy around the kitchen," I told him.

"I fake it well," he said, flashing me a smile.

While the parade played on the TV, I enjoyed watching my three guys working diligently in the kitchen. Robbie was wearing a nice polo shirt today, which framed the V-shape of his torso even better than his dress shirts usually did. He drained his noodles, crumbled the bacon into them, and added a bunch of cheese. Then he poured the cheesy macaroni mixture into a casserole dish and baked it in the oven until the top was crispy and brown.

While Liam prepped the turkey and stuffing, Arthur peeled potatoes and cut them into cubes for boiling. When they were done, he added milk and several sticks of butter before mashing it all together until it was a golden-yellow color. Liam's turkey and stuffing came out of the oven about that time, and Arthur quickly reheated last night's green beans in another skillet.

"That's why you made so many green beans last night!" I said as we set the table. He beamed with pride.

"Sneaky Frenchman," Robbie said with a smile.

I realized that we had just indirectly revealed that Arthur slept over last night. But to my surprise, Liam and Robbie didn't seem to notice. Or they didn't care.

Liam raised a glass of wine as we sat down at the table. "Here's to a wonderful Thanksgiving with three people whose company I enjoy more than my family's."

We all chuckled and clinked our glasses. "Happy Thanksgiving everyone. This was a wonderful surprise. Much better than sitting around by myself."

"I can't believe you didn't have any plans," Robbie said. "When you insisted we take today off, I assumed you had plans to go somewhere."

"Honestly, I've been too busy to think about it," I admitted. "Thanksgiving kind of snuck up on me this year."

"Christmas will be here before we know it," Liam said with a smirk.

"Don't remind me. We have a lot to do before then."

"Which is why, you know, we brought our laptops," Robbie said.

I waved a hand. "Enough work talk. Let's eat."

We passed the food around the table. Soon my plate was piled high with moist turkey, fluffy mashed potatoes, and gravy. The four of us were silent for several minutes while we dug in, save for complimenting everyone on the food.

"You made fun of me for not having plans," I said while serving myself seconds. "But none of you had anywhere to be today? No family or anything?"

"The only family I have is back on the east coast," Liam said.

"*My* family is on the west coast," Arthur chimed in. "The west coast of *France*, that is! I have no one but my dear friends and colleagues to spend this day with, and no one I would *rather* be with, at that."

I squinted suspiciously. "I thought you were from Cambrai? Near Belgium, not the coast?"

"We spent summers on the coast," he said simply.

"Well look at you, mister fancy pants. What about you, Robbie?" I asked.

He shrugged while stirring mashed potatoes into green beans. "I usually do Thanksgiving with my sister in Philly, but I always feel like the odd man out. They have six kids. It's kind of a zoo." He smiled sheepishly. "I feel more welcome here, too."

I raised my glass. "You *are* more welcome here."

Just like last night, it was a fantastic change of pace to have a home-cooked meal after all the take-out we had been ordering in the office. And sharing the meal together around the table, rather than eating while working at our desks, felt nice too. We joked about parades and talked about our childhood Thanksgiving traditions. Arthur listened to it all eagerly, though he didn't contribute any stories since they didn't celebrate the holiday in France.

After dinner, I rummaged through my pantry and came up with enough ingredients to make a chocolate pie. While that baked, the boys pulled out their laptops and did some work while sitting on the couch. Not *too* much work since by that time the football game was on. Liam was from Virginia, so he was very interested in the Redskins game. This caused Arthur to declare his allegiance to the Cowboys on the spot, just to annoy Liam.

"You don't even know how the game is played," Liam pointed out.

Arthur scoffed. "I have attended no fewer than *two* American football games. My office went to a Giants game when I lived in New York. And I attended a Steelers game last year."

"Then you should *hate* the Cowboys," Liam complained.

"Why would I hate them? They are America's team, and I *love* America!" Arthur jumped up from the couch and cheered. "The valiant cow-men have touched the down! They are clearly superior to your silly Washington team!"

He high-fived Robbie, then me. When he tried to high-five Liam, Liam crossed his arms over his chest and pouted.

I enjoyed watching them all together, outside of the normal office environment. Everyone got along well, aside from a little bit of friendly teasing.

I was lucky to have such a good team.

I served pie and ice cream as the snow fell outside. It felt like a small contribution compared to the huge meal they had cooked, but they all loved the pie and Liam and Robbie went back for seconds.

We relaxed in the living room—I was seated on the couch between Liam and Robbie, while Arthur sat in the recliner. I thought about the first night we had all been together, during our first holiday party planning meeting. How we had cleared aside the coffee table and spun a wine bottle on the rug.

We could play seven minutes in heaven tonight, I thought to myself. We already had an empty bottle of wine, and the four of us were a *lot* more familiar now than we were that first time. It would be silly to play it with just one girl, but of course that made it even *more* fun for me. I began to fantasize about taking each of them inside the closet. The dirty things we could do...

But then the football game ended, and Liam stretched his arms. "Alright, I think I'm going to go home and get some extra sleep."

"Me too," Robbie said. "I'm still sore after the twenty-miler."

"I know, right?" I said, sharing a smile with him. "You three did some good work today, despite my protests. And the food was amazing."

I hugged Liam at the door. "Thanks for letting us crash here. See you tomorrow."

Robbie gave me both a hug, and then a kiss on the lips. He smiled at the two others guys after, as if he was staking a claim on me.

Not wanting to be outdone, Arthur swept me in his arms and then dipped me suddenly. I yelped as I fell to the floor, but he stopped me when I was parallel to the ground, and he held me there while gazing into my eyes.

"I had fun today." His gave me a long kiss, and then whispered, "*And* last night."

"Me too."

"Until next time, *mon fleur.*"

I watched the three of them crunch through the snow on my walkway, and wondered how I had gotten so lucky.

34

Leslie

We cruised through the next two weeks into December. All of us knew our roles at work, and our morning group meetings helped keep everyone laser-focused on what needed to be completed that day. Robbie finished building the production environment, then got started on the database connection. Liam flew through the software documentation while leaning on Arthur to point out the parts that didn't make sense. I followed-up behind everyone's work, double-checking things and making sure we weren't forgetting anything.

We were cutting corners on the production testing, but that was unavoidable. And despite that, it looked like everything was falling perfectly into place. This project might get done after all.

"You're quite the manager, dear," Mrs. Caltrop told me one morning.

I chuckled. "I don't think so. It's the three of them that are busting their butts."

But Mrs. Caltrop shook her head. "I have worked on a lot of teams in my five decades here, dear. A good manager knows how to motivate their team. Keep them in line and working hard. And I've never seen a group as motivated as this. You're the reason behind that, whether you want to admit it or not."

I thought about what she said while watching my three guys work, and I wondered if she was right.

During those two weeks I tapered for the marathon, which meant gradually cutting back on my workouts to allow my body to rest and heal before the big race.

The Friday night before the marathon, Liam and Arthur insisted that Robbie and I leave work early, and that they had things covered. Robbie and I went to an Italian restaurant for dinner to carb-load on pasta and bread, then kissed goodnight and went home.

Even though I was under my covers at eight-thirty—earlier than I'd gone to bed in probably three months—I struggled to fall asleep. I was a bundle of nerves thinking about the race, and I stared at my ceiling for what felt like hours.

Next thing I knew, my alarm was going off at four the next morning. I went through my morning routine and tried to pretend like it was any other Saturday run. Robbie picked me up and drove me down to the start.

The Allegheny Marathon ran along the Great Allegheny Passage Trail, which was a rails-to-trails route where old railroad tracks were converted to walking and biking paths. The route began in Pittsburgh and followed the river south before finishing in Buena Vista, Pennsylvania. The trail was too narrow for the route to be an out-and-back, so we were finishing in Buena Vista and then taking shuttles back to the city.

We parked in a garage and walked to the start, which was at the base of the Hot Metal Bridge in Three Rivers Heritage Park. There were hundreds—if not thousands—of people milling about, and a giant inflatable starting arch rose above the crowds. It was freezing out, in a way that felt much colder than all of my training runs.

"I'm going to grab a Gatorade to sip on while we wait, "Robbie said. "I'll be right back."

As soon as he left, my nerves began to get to me. I was surrounded by strangers, crammed into a small space like at a rock concert. It was overwhelming. Since I had been focused on the STT project for the past two months, I hadn't given this race much thought.

Even though I had completed my training runs and was physically prepared, it was clear that I wasn't *mentally* prepared. Suddenly I was terrified that I was an impostor, a wanna-be runner who didn't belong here with all these other athletes who were stronger and faster than me. My heart raced and I felt a panic attack coming on. I glanced at my watch—we still had twenty minutes before the start.

Robbie reappeared at my side, but now that I was panicked there was no stopping it. "Remember your training," he told me. "You're going to want to start faster than normal because you'll be full of adrenaline, but make yourself slow down and stick to the pace you trained at."

"Uh huh," I mumbled.

Robbie frowned. "Are you okay? Leslie, you're shaking. Are you cold?" He began rubbing my arms, warming me with the friction.

I shook my head. "No," I stammered. "I'm..."

I gasped, trying to catch my breath.

Everything was happening so fast.

I wasn't ready. I needed to go home.

I couldn't do this.

Robbie realized something was wrong. He put an arm around my body and guided me through the crowd, yelling at people to make way. We got away from the crowd and found a coffee shop near the start, but it was packed with people. I was still struggling to take a deep breath, so Robbie pushed through the coffee shop crowd until we came to a pair of double-doors that led into the neighboring restaurant. It looked like a fancy steakhouse that wasn't open. Chairs were stacked on the tables and all the lights were off.

Robbie pushed me through the empty room, away from the crowds, until we reached one of the dining rooms in the back that was completely silent. He rubbed my arms some more and made calming noises. It was warm in here, much warmer than outside.

"It's okay. It's alright, Leslie. The crowds can be overwhelming your first time."

"It's... not... that," I said as I began to regain my breath. "I'm... I'm not ready. I can't do this, Robbie. Twenty miles isn't enough training. I'm going to fail. I'm not used to running with so many people. This is colder than I'm used to. I want to go home..."

Robbie pulled me into a big hug and stroked my hair, and continued making shushing noises. Gradually I began to relax in his soothing, caring embrace.

"The cold will help you," he whispered. "Especially once you start running and your body warms up. Like coolant flowing into an engine. And everything else? That's normal. I panicked before my first marathon. Everyone does. Think of it this way. You're only competing with yourself. It's you against the twenty-six point two miles. The worst thing that could happen is you have to walk a little. Big deal. You still get a medal at the end."

His words were like a snow shovel, removing the layers of self-doubt and fear that were pressing down on me. "What if I struggle? What if I get halfway done and hate it?"

His smile was light and reassuring. "Then you learned something about yourself, and you never have to do it again."

"I don't have to do it now, either. We could go home. I could take an Uber and get back in bed..."

"Leslie," Robbie said firmly. "I'm not letting you do that. You've worked too hard training for this to quit now. You're ready. I know you are."

Before I could protest any more, he kissed me.

It was innocent at first. A calming kiss meant to reassure me. But it felt so good, and it was the distraction I needed, so I kissed him back even harder until I was pushing my tongue against his and feeling our warm lips intermingle.

I grabbed his compression pants and pulled them down. "Leslie," he said. "What are you..."

"I want you," I begged. "I *need* you, Robbie."

To my immense relief, he didn't argue. He kissed me back even harder, and then pulled down my running pants until I could kick them off. Then he pushed me against the wall and lifted one of my legs into the air, and thrust his cock up into my waiting pussy.

There in the closed restaurant Robbie made love to me, fucking me against the wall to help me forget the impending race outside. Our sexual release helped destroy all of my anxiety and panic about the marathon, and afterwards I wondered why I had been afraid at all.

"We have to go," Robbie said while we quickly dressed. "The race is starting."

"Good thing we got our *stretches* in already," I teased.

"Ha ha, very funny," Robbie said.

"It *was* funny," I replied.

We hurried through the restaurant and back outside. Music blared from the speakers at the starting line, and the huge crowd of people was flowing toward the inflatable arch. The marathon had indeed started.

Robbie grabbed my arm to stop me. "Hey, Leslie?"

"What?"

He kissed me again on the lips, and grinned behind his glasses. "Kick this marathon's ass."

I smiled widely at him as we joined the group and began running down the trail.

35

Liam

I was wearing five different layers. A compression shirt, then a long-sleeve shirt, and a pull-over on top of that. Then my heavy winter coat. Finally a scarf covered my neck and face, protecting all the exposed skin up to my eyes.

Despite all those layers, I was *freezing my balls off.*

"I am not pleased," Arthur said unhappily next to me. He was thick with as many layers as me, and kept bouncing from one foot to the other in a vain attempt to stay warm. It wasn't working.

"I know," I agreed.

"I would like to get more coffee," he said.

"I could use the caffeine too."

He shook his head. "No no no. I do not wish to drink this coffee. I wish to merely hold it in my hands and savor the warmth."

As good as that sounded, I sighed and said, "She should be finishing any minute. You don't want to miss it. Then you would have come down here for nothing."

The marathon website warned to arrive at the Buena Vista finish early because parking was scarce, so we had been up since five o'clock to make sure we got down here. We were both tired and cold.

It's worth it to be here for Leslie, I thought. *The smile on her face will be worth it.*

We watched runners trickle through the finish in twos and threes. Finally I saw someone I recognized in the distance. "There! That looks like..."

"Robbie," Arthur agreed.

Sure enough, Robbie came jogging along the trail. He looked strong as he glided through the finish, grabbed a Gatorade from the finisher's table, and then hopped the fence to get to us in the spectator's section.

"Who made you guys come down here?" he asked with a surprised smile.

"Cease talking and hug me!" Arthur said, wrapping Robbie in his arms. "We have been freezing our extremities out here waiting, so I require nothing but gratefulness from you!"

Robbie laughed and patted him on the back. "Leslie's going to be so happy to see you two."

"You did not let her win?" Arthur grunted. "How ungentlemanly of you."

"She'd hate me if I did," Robbie panted. "I stuck with her for the first sixteen, and then she let me go on ahead. She said she wanted to finish it herself."

I looked at my watch. "How much longer do you think we have?"

Robbie winced. "Tough to say. She could be right behind me, or she could be thirty minutes behind me. Honestly? It's her first marathon, and she was worked up this morning, so she's probably going to struggle these final miles..."

"There she is!" Arthur suddenly shouted.

"No way..." Robbie said.

Sure enough, the figure in the distance looked like Leslie. Black pants, pink jacket, and pink beanie covering her auburn hair. I raised the sign I had made, which said, "WORST PARADE EVER." Arthur raised his sign, which said, "GO LESLIE GO."

Leslie was clearly struggling through the final chute, leaning forward as she ran and shuffling as if she was in pain. But then her entire demeanor changed when she saw us. She stood up straight and ran harder. Her face was split in half by a massive smile. Arthur and I screamed at the top of our lungs like rock band groupies. She beamed at us as she flew across the finish line.

The finishers had to walk through a gauntlet of volunteers handing out awards and snacks. One draped a heavy medal around her neck. Then other volunteers handed out water, Gatorade, bananas, and bagels.

As we pushed through the crowd to reach her, I swelled with pride at seeing her finish. Back when we were in the Sales Department together, she was the least athletic person on our team. She playfully teased people who ran endurance races and boasted that she could never do something like that.

Yet here she was. She'd finished.

The pride I felt shocked me. I couldn't stop smiling. I was just so happy for her, and I couldn't explain why.

We finally caught up to Leslie at the end of the volunteer stations, where she was sipping a cup of hot chocolate. Her face lit up when we reached her, and she threw her arms around me and held me tight.

"You said you would be in the office today!"

I grinned like an idiot, smug that we had fooled her. "We lied."

Arthur hugged her next. "You have been leaving the office to run in the evening, and coming in late on Saturdays. We wanted to verify that you had a *legitimate* reason for doing so, and were not making it all up!"

"I can't believe you braved the cold weather for this," she said.

"Cold?" Arthur said as his teeth *literally* chittered. "It is a pleasant day, is it not?"

"You okay, buddy?" I asked Arthur. "I think he's lost all feeling in his body at this point."

Leslie and Robbie shared an emotional hug. "Thank you for everything. I needed the pep talk this morning."

Robbie blushed, and it wasn't just from the cold. "We all need a kick in the butt sometimes. Next time, you'll be the one motivating *me* before the marathon."

"Next time!" she blurted out. "I'm never running one of these again!"

As much as we would have liked to spend the day celebrating, we still had a lot of work to do. Arthur and I drove back to the office with the heat cranked all the way up in my car, and when we got into our team's office I turned the heat up to seventy-three, just like Leslie preferred.

"How did she do?" Mrs. Caltrop asked as she handed us mugs of coffee.

"She finished," I said. The mug was warm in my hands. "I don't know what her exact time was, but she looked strong."

Mrs. Caltrop smiled warmly. "I think it is so nice that you young men went out to root for her. Leslie is lucky to have such a close-knit team."

"We are the lucky ones," Arthur said with a wink.

"It is a shame that..." she began, but trailed off.

"A shame that what?" I asked.

"I was going to say it is a shame that managers cannot date their employees," she said. "You two would make a good couple."

I almost choked on my coffee. "Oh, I don't know about that,"

I said.

"Which two?" Arthur asked. "Which two would make a good couple?"

Mrs. Caltrop was focused on her computer screen as she answered. "Oh, any of you. You all mesh together so wonderfully. It reminds me of how my husband and I looked when we first met. You're always happy, always smiling, even when the stress and work levels are high."

Arthur leaned on her desk. "Madam Caltrop. You did not tell me you had a husband! What will he think of *us*?"

She leered back at him. "Don't tempt an old woman, Arthur. You wouldn't be able to handle me."

I roared with laughter at the shocked look on Arthur's face.

We settled in and got to work. We were hitting all of our project benchmarks and checkpoints, but the entire project was still being held together with duct tape and perseverance. We had *zero* wiggle room in case anything went wrong. A single hiccup would delay the project and we would miss the December twentieth deployment deadline.

A deadline that was just six days away.

Don't think about that, I told myself. *It's better to focus on the positives, not the negatives.*

Leslie and Robbie arrived in the office early in the afternoon. Both of them were wearing their marathon medals over their work clothes. We applauded as they entered, and Leslie tried to give a bow—but winced when her torso got to a forty-five degree angle.

"How do you feel?" I asked.

"My lower back is a little tight, and my legs are *really* stiff. But I feel okay." She winced as she took a few more steps. "I'm a little chafed, too."

Arthur glanced over at Mrs. Caltrop, then lowered his voice. "Tonight, I shall rub lotion into your blisters and shower them with soothing kisses."

"I hope you're serious, because I might take you up on that," she whispered back.

Leslie hobbled into her office, and I followed along. She dropped off her bag, then turned and seemed surprised to see me. "Hey. What's up?"

I took her hands in mine and squeezed them. "In the years I've known you, you have always pushed yourself in every endeavor. I'm glad to see that you're still that same determined, and even *stubborn*, woman I met five years ago. I'm so proud of you, Leslie."

She smiled, and then her eyes shimmered. "That means a lot to me, Liam. Thank you."

Not caring that Mrs. Caltrop and anyone else could see us through the glass, Leslie and I shared a long hug before we got back to work.

36

Leslie

After finishing the marathon and returning to the office, I came to a realization.

I wouldn't be able to do this without all of them.

Robbie's support was the only reason I was able to complete the marathon. Both because of his help going out for my training runs, and for calming me down on race morning. If we hadn't been together, I would have let my panic attack overwhelm me. I would have jumped back in my car and driven home, and then I would be regretting ever signing up for the stupid race.

Instead, he'd calmed me down—in a way that was both effective *and* sexy. And now I was sitting at my desk with a marathon medal around my neck, feeling like I could do anything.

And it was more than just the race. I wouldn't be able to manage this project if it weren't for their support. I would have been overwhelmed by the crushing responsibility weeks ago. I might have even quit the position, just like Oliver Edwards had the moment he saw the timeline.

Instead, we were on track to finish by the end of next week, meeting the Board of Directors' impossible deadline.

We worked late into the night until I was falling asleep at my desk. I went home and slept, and then came in the next day and we worked from seven in the morning until eleven at night. Robbie completed the database configuration on Monday, which was one of the last technical hurdles we had before Liam could begin the final production setup of the software.

Monday night was when the party planning committee met for the final time before the holiday party. I stopped by Beth's desk that afternoon just to make sure she and Charletta had everything under control, and she confidently said that they did.

"Friday night is going to be a blast!" she said excitedly. "Are you guys going to be able to come?"

"That's the plan," I said with a hopeful sigh. "Friday is the official deadline for the project. We're supposed to send out the documentation and software to all the branches in the company, and then meet with the Board of Directors on Saturday to answer any questions they have. So if all goes according to plan, we'll be at the party."

Beth let out a happy squeal. "Yay—I'm so happy to hear that! You four deserve the holiday party more than *anyone*."

"Believe me—I agree!"

Beth hesitated, then said, "Hey, I have a question. I still need volunteers at the holiday party. For the cookie decorating station, and for—"

"Assuming we get this project done, count me in for whatever you need," I said.

"Perfect! I'll email you all the details."

I met with Jen, the project management coordinator, on Tuesday to give her an update. She booked the meeting in the huge boardroom on the fourth floor, but we were the only two people invited. Yet when I arrived, I found Jen accompanied by Katherine Chandrakhan, the Chief Operating Officer.

"Thanks for meeting with us," Katherine said as I entered. "I'm just here to listen in on the progress."

"Of course, it's no problem," I said. Her presence made what would have been an easy meeting suddenly much more tense. I could feel the pressure of the impending deadline looming over us as I gave them a high-level breakdown of the project.

"I'm proud to say that we will meet Friday's deadline," I said when I reached the final slide. "My team has really busted their butts to meet it."

"That's fantastic to hear," Jen said.

Katherine tapped her pen against her notepad. "Do not count your chickens before they are hatched. The system needs to be running and flawless, so the two thousand employees of Allegheny Supply can use it immediately."

"It will be," I assured her.

She nodded, but looked unconvinced. "We have the walk-through with the board scheduled for Saturday morning. How long do you expect the walk-through to go?"

"Umm." I did some mental math. "I'll have to verify with my sales liaison, but it shouldn't take more than an hour or two."

Katherine nodded. "Very good. After that meeting I'm boarding a flight to Denver to go skiing with my family, so I certainly hope everything will go smoothly."

I bit back a laugh when I realized she was serious. *Our deadline is thanks to her vacation plans?*

"Of course," was all I said. "We'll make sure there are no delays."

On the elevator back downstairs, Jen shook her head at me. "I have to admit. I'm impressed by your team."

I leaned against the elevator wall and sighed. "Me too. I wasn't sure we could do it."

"Just make sure there are no hiccups," Jen warned. "If anything malfunctions..."

"I'm doing my best," I said with a little bit of attitude.

Jen took it in stride. "I am glad to hear it."

I got back to my desk and there was an email from Beth waiting in my inbox. Something about the thing I had volunteered for at the party on Friday. *I'll look at it later*, I thought as I began working on something else.

Thursday was when the *really* big tasks started falling into place. The new system software had a server-client relationship. That meant in addition to a centralized server and database, there was client software that needed to be installed on every computer in the company. That's what Allegheny's employees would log into when making sales or checking orders.

In a normal deployment, we would get the server up and running, verify the connection and stability of the system for a week at a pilot location, and *then* begin the software rollout to the rest of the company.

But we didn't have the luxury of time. We had to setup the server and database at the same time we deployed the client software to all two thousand computers in the company. That rollout was happening overnight on Thursday.

"It's a completely silent package," Robbie explained in my office on Thursday afternoon. He adjusted his glasses and frowned with concentration. "I have written a script that will push the installation files down to each machine, unzip them, and then install the software silently."

"Push, unzip, install," I repeated deadpan. "Sounds erotic."

Robbie chuckled, then returned to somber seriousness. "If everything works the way it should, the two thousand employees will come in Friday morning and have a new shortcut on their computer."

"How will you verify the install?" I asked. "You don't have to call every person to make sure they got it, right?"

He smiled. "Right. Every time a client installs, it sends a heartbeat signal to the main server. I will, um, be able to login to the server and see how many clients have checked-in. We usually get ninety percent on the first night, since some people turn their computers off. The remaining ten percent will trickle in after that."

"Sounds like a plan," I said. "I'll have my fingers crossed."

"Me too."

Robbie was staying late to monitor the beginning of the deployment, but the rest of us packed our things and left together at seven. Liam, Arthur, and I were quiet in the elevator until Arthur leaned over and put his lips close to my ear.

"Would you like to come over to my place tonight? I have a lovely bottle of Cabernet Sauvignon I have been saving for you."

"What are you two talking about?" Liam asked with a half-smile.

"It is none of your business," Arthur said.

"I was going to ask Leslie if she wanted to get a beer," Liam said.

Arthur snorted. "Yet you did not. And I have already extended an invitation to Leslie."

"We can all go out," I said diplomatically. "I need a drink, and I'm sure you both do too."

"I do not wish to go out," Arthur said stubbornly. He glared at Liam. "I invited Leslie back to my place for wine."

"Then I'll come too," Liam said. "Thanks for the invite, buddy."

A scowl fell over Arthur's beautiful face, but he did not protest further.

Arthur lived in a studio loft in downtown Pittsburgh, on the nineteenth floor. It was a corner loft, which meant two of the walls were floor-to-ceiling glass with a tremendous view of the city. I pressed my face against the glass and stared down at all the bright lights. The river was a dark snake through it all, with brightly-lit bridges crossing it like the rungs of a massive ladder.

"I've never seen Pittsburgh from so high!" I said. "It's so peaceful from up here."

A cork popped softly as Arthur opened a bottle of red wine. "I like it very much. Pittsburgh is a little big city."

"That's kind of a contradiction," Liam pointed out.

"No no no," Arthur said. "It is not a contradiction. There are big cities, yes? New York, Chicago, Paris, London. But then there are big cities which are not quite as large. Pittsburgh, Richmond, Portland."

"Makes sense," I said. Arthur smiled widely at me and glared at Liam.

"I guess Pittsburgh is the biggest city I've ever lived in," Liam admitted. "We lived in a D.C. suburb in Virginia, but never actually *in* a city. So Pittsburgh seems large to me."

"Perhaps you will acquire worldly experience in time," Arthur said casually. Half-teasing, half-insult. Liam only shrugged it off.

"Maybe so."

I sat on Arthur's couch, and then Liam sat next to me. Arthur turned the lights down in his apartment until everything was bathed in a soft glow, then played some gentle piano music from the speaker system in the living room. He joined us on the couch, sitting on the other side of me. We sipped our wine in an awkward silence.

"So," I said. "We're really going to meet our deadline, huh?"

"Don't jinx it," Liam said. "But yeah. If all goes well tonight, we'll be done in time for the holiday party tomorrow night."

"Have you told Santa Claus what you want for Christmas?" Arthur asked. "Or have you been a bad girl?"

I giggled. "I've been bad, but in a good way. Honestly, I haven't given Christmas much thought at all."

"I know what gift I would desire." Arthur leaned into me and kissed my shoulder. I gasped with surprise, then pleasure, as he nuzzled my neck.

Liam grunted and ran a hand through his messy hair. "Hey now. No need to be territorial."

"I brought Leslie here with the intention of making love to her." Arthur pulled my lips to his and kissed me deeply, sharing the tart taste of the wine from his tongue. "Your presence is an unfortunate obstacle, Liam, but if you are uncomfortable you may leave."

Liam didn't flinch. He put down his glass of wine and took my head in both of his hands, and kissed me passionately. Harder than Arthur, like it was a competition. I heard Arthur make a disapproving noise behind me, but I was too busy melting into Liam's mouth to care.

My chest heaved when he was done kissing me. It was strange kissing each of them in front of the other... But not as strange as I would have expected. It felt naughty. In a good way.

"You brought Leslie here tonight with sexual intentions," Liam said. He wasn't upset—he was only stating facts. "Yet we all agreed to wait until the project was over to vie for Leslie's affection."

Arthur grunted. "You say this thing to me, yet you have been with Leslie yourself! *J'accuse!*"

"He's got a point," I told Liam.

"In my defense, *you're* the one who lured me into your office."

Arthur made a choking noise. "You did this in her *office?*"

Liam narrowed his eyes. "I saw the bottle of wine left on your desk after the Halloween party. Are you going to tell me you two didn't do anything in that room? Hmm?"

Arthur's face returned to calmness. "I will not deny this, no."

"Okay, okay," I interrupted. "We have all broken the rules to some degree. With both of you, and with Robbie."

I waited for their reactions, but they didn't seem surprised. They must have already suspected.

"Well then," Arthur said. "If we are not waiting until after the project, then perhaps you should not wait to make a choice. Who do you prefer, *mon fleur?*"

"Me, or *him?*" Liam added.

They crossed their arms like two pouting children who were fighting over a toy. It was adorable. And now that all of this was out in the open, I was having fun with it. Honestly, it was more of a relief to discuss it without sneaking around.

"I have to choose now?"

"But of course," Arthur said. Liam nodded.

I took a deep breath and let it out slowly. "Then I guess I choose Robbie."

"What!" Liam exclaimed.

"*Merde,*" Arthur cursed.

I giggled. "You said I had to make a decision right now, so..."

Liam shrugged and stood up. "Well, I guess if you've made your choice then I'll leave."

"No! Wait!" I jumped up and grabbed his arm. "I was only joking. Sit back down."

He obeyed. I held his arm. An idea occurred to me, one which sent a tingle of excitement through my stomach.

But would they go for it?

"I don't like having to choose," I explained. "Not yet, at least. And I also don't want to leave both of you dissatisfied tonight. You have both worked so hard lately, you deserve a reward."

"Do we?" Arthur asked.

The best way to solve two boys fighting over a toy? Make them share it.

    I nodded. "You can do whatever you want to me tonight. Both of you."

37

Leslie

Liam and Arthur paused while my words sank in. I watched them both consider it, glancing at the other cautiously.

They're not going to go for it, I realized. *It's too weird.*

"If you two don't want to share me together..." I began.

"I would like this," Arthur quickly said.

To my surprise, Liam nodded. "Me too."

Without any other prompting, Arthur pulled me toward him and kissed me. I managed to put down my wine glass and then straddle him on the couch. He was already hard, and I could feel his cock pressing through his pants into my skirt.

While we kissed, Liam walked behind me and began undressing me. He pulled my blouse over my head, then unclasped my bra and let it fall to the side. Liam's arms wrapped around me to cup my breasts as he began planting kisses all along my back, his tongue tracing a line along my spine.

Arthur's lips moved from my mouth down my neck. He pushed Liam's hands aside and sucked on my breast, and I sighed as electricity shot through my nipple.

Liam hastily removed his pants, then grabbed a handful of my hair. He twisted my head sideways and pushed me down on his steel cock with a desire that made me moan. I sucked on his prick while Arthur's tongue ran circles around my nipple, and his hand slid down between my legs and began rubbing my already-wet pussy.

There was no way to remove the skirt without climbing off of him, and we were too lustful to waste any time doing that. I unzipped Arthur's pants and fished out his dick until it stood vertically beneath me. Arthur pulled apart my panties, and I lowered my hips, impaling myself on his throbbing cock.

"Ohhh," I moaned around Liam's dick.

"*J'aime cela*," Arthur breathed. "I love this, how you feel..."

I pulled Liam's cock out of my mouth. "Even with *him* here?"

Arthur grinned hungrily. "I do not mind any hindrance, so long as I have you."

"Gonna have to agree with my French colleague," Liam said, fingers interlacing in my hair again. "I'll take you any way I can get, Leslie."

I smiled up at him. "Then take me how you want."

His fingers pulled my hair tight, then shoved my head back onto his cock.

I rode Arthur on the couch while sucking off Liam for a while, and then we switched—Liam pulled me off Arthur, bent me over, and fucked me from behind. Arthur stayed on the couch and I bobbed my head on his cock, sucking him for all I was worth while he moaned and stroked my hair and whispered sweet French nothings at me.

Outside, the bright Pittsburgh city sprawled beneath us while we sighed and cried and fucked ourselves silly, blowing off steam from the work project that had taken up so much of our lives.

*

We slept at Arthur's that night, sharing the big bed as if it was a slumber party. I was the demarcation line between the two men in bed, partitioning things off so they never had to touch one another. But we all slept deeply, and when we woke the two men were draped across me in a tangle of nude flesh. Legs and arms and heads in every direction.

There are worse ways to wake up, I thought.

I savored the feel of their bodies against mine. Outside the window, a heavy snow was coming down. The air was so thick with it that I couldn't see any of the city below. It was like we were living in a snowy fog.

But inside Arthur's apartment, we were warm and happy and safe.

There was no peaceful morning routine, nor any nude breakfast made by Liam. I forced myself to get out of bed, gathered my things, and said goodbye to the two of them. Liam left with me, but he was going home to change, and I needed to shower and change into fresh clothes too, so we drove separate. By the time I reached the office, Liam and Arthur were just pulling into the garage as well.

"Fancy seeing you two here," I said as we walked into the lobby together.

"Quite the coincidence indeed," Arthur exclaimed. "I had a dream about you."

"Did you now?"

"Indeed." He nodded at Liam. "He was there too."

Liam grinned. "Sorry to ruin your dream with my presence."

"No no no," Arthur said, patting him on the back. "It was a welcome inclusion, to the surprise of all of us."

"Good, because I had just as much fun," he admitted. "We'll have to do it again sometime."

"But of course," Arthur replied.

"Do I have a say in it?"

They looked at each other, then shook their heads.

As we waited for the elevator, a truck pulled up to the front of the building and began unloading boxes. Tables and chairs, and other party equipment. When the elevator opened, Beth and Charletta emerged.

"I think the party arrived!" I told them happily.

Charletta sighed with relief when she saw the truck. "They are thirty minutes late, but I suppose we will have enough time. It is going to be a very long day."

"Relax, Charletta! Everything's going to be great! Did I tell you Leslie volunteered for the big event?"

Charletta blinked in surprise. "Did you? Your project is completed?"

"We're about to find out," I replied. "What big event are we talking about?"

"The one I emailed you about, silly!" Beth said. "You read the instructions, right?"

"Yeah, of course I did," I lied. "I haven't had my coffee yet."

Charletta strode past me and started barking directions at the crew unloading the truck. Beth smiled at me and said, "See you tonight!"

"What did you volunteer for?" Liam asked in the elevator.

"One of the holiday party events," I said.

Arthur's smile was bordering on laughter. "It appears you are not aware of your volunteering responsibilities."

The elevator opened on the third floor and we exited. "I need to read her email. It'll be fine. The holiday party is the *least* of my concerns today."

"Everything went smoothly last night," Liam said. "I can feel it."

We walked into our office.

Robbie jumped up from his cubicle. It was clear he hadn't left the office; his tie was loose, his sleeves were rolled up, and there was alarm in his eyes.

"Leslie," he said. "Something's wrong."

38

Robbie

On Thursday evening, I watched Leslie, Arthur, and Liam leave the office together and felt jealous. Not because the three of them were leaving together, but because they were leaving at all. I knew I had a long night ahead of me ensuring that the software deployment went smoothly.

During the day, we throttled network traffic to make sure we didn't crush our entire network. Like changing some highway lanes to HOV lanes to make sure the important sales traffic could get through. That throttling ended at eleven o'clock at night, and I saw right when the switch happened. My software deployments suddenly went from trickling out to each computer to flooding out, like the faucet had been opened all the way rather than a drip.

I watched the traffic stream across my computer screen with deep satisfaction. Within a few hours, the software would finish downloading on each device, it would unzip itself to a temporary directory on the root C: drive, and then it would install silently.

I leaned back in my chair and sighed happily. Everything was falling into place the way it should.

In a few hours I would start spot-checking individual clients to verify the install. In the meantime, I could rest my eyes. I set an alarm for midnight and crossed my arms over my chest, and my eyes were so heavy...

I woke up with a jerk and nearly fell out of my chair, but managed to steady myself against the cubicle wall. I glanced at the time on the computer:

3:31 AM

"Shit," I muttered. I'd slept longer than I meant to. I must have turned my alarm off. Still, it didn't matter as long as the computers had installed successfully. All of the file transfer windows on my screen were gone, which meant they had completed.

Good.

I logged into the new InterLync Systems server and pulled up the connection records. By now, we should see close to two thousand clients. Maybe more like eighteen-hundred for some of the slower locations.

But that's not what the server showed.

There was only one client connected to the server. My own laptop, which I had used as a test yesterday.

"No," I moaned. "No, it can't be..."

I opened the administrative tools on the server and forced it to refresh the client connection list. Still no change. Next I pulled up the server logs to verify everything there. Database connection was fine. Network connection was fine. Everything was the way it should be.

With a trembling hand on the mouse, I started checking individual clients.

The first computer I checked was at our Harrisburg location.

But it wouldn't let me connect. I opened a command prompt and ran a ping on the device, which would tell me the network connection information.

But the computer wasn't pingable.

I tried another random computer on the list.

Same thing.

A third computer. Still no response.

I was panicking by the time I pulled up the Allegheny Supply network dashboard. What greeted me was a sea of red indicators which were usually green.

The entire network was down.

For the entire company.

"What the fuck."

Adrenaline was pumping through my body as I began troubleshooting the issue. Deep down I was terrified of the project failing, and of me personally failing Leslie. We didn't have any wiggle room for problems. I had to fix this, and I had to fix it *quick*.

Over the next half hour I tracked down the problem to the individual DNS servers, which were the networking servers which gave IP addresses to individual computers. For some reason, the services on all the DNS servers were shut down. I remotely connected to one of them and immediately realized what was happening.

In the middle of the screen was a *Windows Update* box with a progress bar halfway filled. The DNS servers were being patched.

And in order to patch them, the network had to be temporarily taken down.

"Fuck," I cursed. "Fuck fuck fuck *fuck*..."

I opened *Outlook* and checked the Networking Team's shared calendar. Maintenance was scheduled for last week, but nothing was scheduled for tonight. I switched over to *Teams* and checked the two Networking Engineers that I knew, but of course they were offline right now. These patches had been scheduled ahead of time.

Fucking network guys.

"Okay, calm down," I told myself as I went to the coffee machine and started brewing a pot. "The network went down a few hours ago. My software deployment might have finished by then. The software deployed successfully, but can't talk back to the server yet. As soon as I bring the network back up, they will all check-in and everything will be fine."

Once I'd brewed some coffee, I sat down and got to work. The DNS server patches were going to take several more hours, and I didn't have that kind of time, so I began logging into each server and aborting the patches. Once the patching was halted, I had to start the networking services.

The problem was that I had to do this manually on each DNS server, and we had one per region. Eighty altogether.

I grinded through the work of bringing the network back up. It took two hours. Once it was back up, I forced our InterLync Systems server to refresh the client connections.

The results on the screen made me hang my head.

That's when Leslie, Arthur, and Liam came strolling into the office. They were laughing about something, smiling and happy.

I've failed you, was the only thought running through my head. *I've failed the woman I care about.*

I jumped up from my cubicle. "Leslie," I said in a voice barely more than a whisper. "Something's wrong."

39

Leslie

"What is it?" I demanded. "Robbie, what happened?"

His eyes were wide and he looked like he hadn't slept at all. Only when Arthur reached him and put a comforting hand on his back did Robbie finally come out of his daze.

"The network went down overnight. All the traffic was cut off."

"What do you mean, cut off?" I asked. "Did the software rollout happen or not?"

A stranger walked into our office. A scrawny guy with glasses even thicker than Robbie's.

"Victor! What happened last night?" Robbie demanded.

Victor calmly walked toward him. "I just logged in and checked the logs. It looks like all the DNS servers failed to patch…"

Robbie grabbed the man's arm and yanked him toward his cubicle. "They failed to patch because I stopped the patching. Why the hell were they patching in the first place? Patch Tuesday was *last* week!"

"Oh." Victor blinked rapidly behind his glasses, like a Vietnam prisoner trying to speak in Morse code. "Let's see. Patch Tuesday *was* last week, but Microsoft released an out-of-band security update that applied to our Windows Server 2019 builds. I deployed it last night."

"Last night? You deployed it *last night?*" Robbie was borderline yelling, and his face was red. I had never seen the IT geek so emotional before. I shared shocked glances with Arthur and Liam.

"Y-y-yes," Victor stammered. "Why, is that a problem..."

"It wasn't on the schedule!" Robbie roared. "The network maintenance schedule that shows all changes. Why wasn't it listed!"

Mrs. Caltrop walked into the room and froze at the sight of Robbie looming over the smaller IT guy.

By now, Victor was sweating profusely. "I didn't... I don't. Ahem. I didn't think it was a big deal. It wasn't a black-out period, and the security patch was critical, so..."

"Get out," Robbie said. "Get out of this office before my colleagues realize what you've done, and how you've doomed our project."

Victor needed no other urging, and rushed from the room like we were going to physically attack him. Mrs. Caltrop calming walked over to the little coffee machine area, filled a cup with hot water, and began steeping a bag of tea.

"You don't mean that, do you?" I asked Robbie nervously. "He didn't really doom our project. Did he?"

Robbie slumped into his chair and held his head in his hands. "I don't know."

"The deployment last night," Liam said. "Did it go, or not?"

Robbie shook his head. "The network went down for maintenance in the middle of the deployment. Not a single computer finished downloading the software."

The room was quiet as his words sank in.

"Okay," I said slowly. "It's seven o'clock in the morning on Friday. We have some time. You can push it now, right?"

Robbie shook his head again, still not looking up at us. "I can't believe I yelled at Victor. He's never said a mean word to anyone. And

I *screamed* at him..."

I walked over to him and gripped his shoulders. "Hey. I know you're exhausted, and this is a big wrench thrown into our schedule. But I need you to focus right now."

Mrs. Caltrop handed Robbie the cup of tea. "Drink this. It will soothe your nerves."

"If he worked all night, he might need something stronger than that," Liam said.

Mrs. Caltrop gave him an even stare. "Based on the dregs at the bottom of the pot over there, more coffee is the last thing he needs. Some tea will smooth him out."

Robbie thanked her and sipped on the murky liquid. Mrs. Caltrop watched him closely, then nodded to me.

"You can push the software to the computers right now, can't you?" I asked.

Robbie took a deep breath and collected himself. "There are a couple of problems with that."

"Okay. Let's walk through them."

He nodded to himself. "The first problem is that the network went down in the middle of the deployment. This corrupted the software package on the distribution servers. I have to rebuild the package and upload it to the servers all over again."

"How long will this take?" Arthur asked.

"Two hours. Maybe three."

"That's not bad," I said.

Robbie shook his head. "Then there is problem two. We are not, um, technically allowed to push software during the daytime. It's against IT policy, in case it causes a reboot or other disruption to our employees while they are inputting sales."

"We can forget about what we're *technically* allowed to do," Liam said. "If it needs to get done, it needs to get done, and we'll deal with the consequences later."

"That brings us to the final problem," Robbie said. "The network is throttled during the daytime. All downloads are slowed to a crawl, to make sure one person streaming Netflix at work doesn't hog all the network bandwidth."

"So it will download slowly?" Liam asked.

"Too slow," Robbie replied. "It will take hours."

I opened up my laptop and pulled up the project timeline. "How many hours? Can you give me a better estimate?"

Robbie opened the calculator app on his computer. "Sure. The install is five-hundred megabytes. Our throttle speed is fifty kilobits-per-second. That means it will take about an average of..."

He trailed off when he saw the number, then looked up at me in defeat.

"Twenty-three hours."

"Fuck," Liam cursed.

"*Twenty-three?*" Arthur demanded. "This cannot be correct."

A wave of dread rose in my chest as I reviewed the project timeline. We were supposed to be spending all day today doing final checks on the client installs today. Software inventory checks to make sure each computer installed properly. Prep-work on the server to make sure they were syncing. Then Robbie had to configure the cloud backup.

"None of these steps can happen until the software has been deployed," I said.

Robbie nodded.

We're not going to make it, I realized. *We're going to miss our deadline.*

"What time is the presentation tomorrow?" Liam asked me.

"Nine in the morning."

"What about moving it back?" Arthur suggested. "To tomorrow afternoon. Or perhaps Sunday, yes?"

I thought about what the Chief Operating Officer had said about her ski trip. "They're expecting it to be done before lunch," I said weakly. "That's the hard-deadline they've set."

Liam put a hand on my shoulder and squeezed it. "Well, now would be a good time to at least *try* to move it back. Yeah?"

His words weren't forceful, but they were blunt enough to force me into action. "I'll see what I can do," I said with more confidence than I felt.

I rode the elevator up to the fourth floor with two truck loaders carrying kegs of beer. "I don't suppose you could tap that for me now, could you?" I asked.

They both stared at me. "Ma'am, it's eight in the morning."

"It was a joke," I grumbled to myself as we got off the elevator.

The entire fourth floor had been transformed. All the cubicles in the middle of the room had been cleared away, leaving one huge open space with the C-suite offices around the outside of the room. A bar was being set up in one section of the room, and a wooden dance floor was being connected like puzzle pieces next to it. Beth was directing one of the workers who was carrying bundles of electrical cable. She waved at me as I passed on the way to the COO's office.

Katherine Chandrakhan was in a meeting with someone, so her administrative assistant had me wait outside her office. "She is very busy today," she told me with a note of annoyance.

"I won't take long," I replied. "And this is important."

"I'm sure it is," she said doubtfully.

While I waited, I watched the holiday party decorations being brought upstairs and then placed. There were giant Christmas presents wrapped with ribbon surrounding the bar, and candy cane poles being screwed into the ceiling and floor where lights could be strung. A man emerged from the elevator pushing a cart, upon which was a block of ice the size of a refrigerator. *That must be the ice sculpture*, I thought. Last year it was an elaborate ice Christmas tree with LED lights implanted in the ice. I wondered what he would carve this year.

Katherine returned from her meeting half an hour later. "Oh, Ms. Hill," she said when she saw me. Then she turned to her admin and asked, "Did I miss something on my calendar?"

"I didn't schedule anything," I said hastily. "I just need a few minutes of your time."

I could tell she didn't like the sound of that, but she led me into her office and closed the door.

"I'm going to be blunt with you," I said. "We've hit a snag and need more time."

Katherine froze while lowering herself into her seat. "How much time?"

"Half a day. If we could move tomorrow's presentation to the afternoon, everything will be sorted out."

The stern-looking COO pursed her lips like she had bit into a lemon. "That is not possible."

"We ran into a technical issue," I insisted. "It happened last night, some problem with the network. It delayed the client rollout, but only by a day."

"A day? I thought you just said you needed *half* a day."

"Well, yes. Half a day probably, but a full day would be better. We will take whatever you can give us."

Katherine leaned back in her chair and interlaced her long, spider-like fingers. "Ms. Hill. We met just two days ago in that conference room." She pointed. "And you *assured* me that the deadline would be met."

"As I said, this networking problem just happened..." I tried, but she cut me off with a hand gesture.

"I'm afraid we cannot give your team any more time.

Tomorrow's presentation is when the new system must be operational. Work overnight if you must."

She said it so flippantly, as if it was a task that could be completed with a little extra *work*, pissed me off. Hearing Robbie lose his temper downstairs was making my own blood boil. We had worked so hard to get to this point. I couldn't allow it to fail now.

This was my time to throw my managerial weight around.

"With all due respect, the STT project is more important than your ski trip," I said acidly. "You can take a later flight, or dial-in to the meeting from Denver. But the presentation *needs* to be pushed back so we can complete our project tasks. And I'm not leaving your office until I get that extra time."

Katherine's face remained calm throughout my harangue. She was so still that I might have thought that she didn't even hear what I said. Without a word, she began typing on her laptop.

She's having me fired, I realized. *She's contacting Human Resources as we speak.*

"Mrs. Chandrakhan," I began.

She twisted her laptop around. "Do you see these training documents?"

I frowned at the screen. "Yes. I helped Liam write them."

"We—the company, Allegheny Supply—have two dozen technical trainers arriving tomorrow at ten in the morning. We're paying them extra to come in on a weekend to review the documentation. They are spending tomorrow afternoon and evening learning the new InterLync System as it applies to our company, inside and out. Then on Saturday evening these skilled trainers are flying around the country to each of our regional operations centers. This is because on Sunday morning they will be standing alongside Allegheny employees, helping them transition from our old system to the new one. Assisting in entering sales and orders into the new system. Troubleshooting the inevitable learning curve our employees will face.

"But they cannot do this," she said with finality, "unless a fully operational system is ready for them to use tomorrow morning. Delaying that hand-off by even a few hours will hamstring their entire weekend timeline."

"Oh," I said in a small voice. "I didn't know..."

"You are right that this project is far more important than my *ski trip*," Katherine said with fire in her voice. "My family vacation can be delayed by a few hours, or a day, or even a week for all I care. But if your poor management delays the training program that we have spent several million dollars carefully arranging? That means our employees won't be able to seamlessly do their jobs for the final seven business days of the year. Which means our end-of-the-month financial numbers won't meet their targets. Which means *you*, Ms. Hill, will be out of a job. Have I made myself clear?"

"Crystal clear."

I walked back through the party decorations and took the elevator to the third floor. Robbie, Arthur, and Liam were all gathered around Mrs. Caltrop's desk. They whirled excitedly when I entered our office.

"Well?" Arthur asked. "Have you saved us, Leslie?"

"What did they say?" Liam asked.

I relayed them everything that had happened in Katherine's office.

"It would have been nice to know about the training programs," Liam grumbled.

"Would it have changed anything?" Robbie argued. I could tell he was still worked up. "Our deadline was still damn-near impossible. It's not like knowing about the trainers would have made us magically finish faster."

"There has to be a way, Robbie." I smiled weakly at him. "You don't have any tricks up your sleeve to magically make the software download faster, do you?"

He slumped his shoulders. "I talked to the networking team. There's no way to lift the throttling rules outside of the standard maintenance window at eleven o'clock tonight. It's all managed by a third-party company which needs more than twenty-four hours notice to change throttling rules. We're screwed."

I tried not to give in to the crushing feeling that was twisting inside my chest. I glanced at my watch and said, "It's ten-thirty now. Let's keep working and get as far as we can today, regardless."

The four of us got to work as if nothing was wrong. Liam focused on tweaking the documentation so that it was as accurate as possible. I reviewed my overall presentation for the board tomorrow. It was tough to muster the energy knowing what I knew now. The presentation wouldn't matter because we would be late. The trainers would be delayed.

And all the blame would fall on me.

The day passed annoyingly slow, which felt ironic since what we needed was *more* time. Arthur didn't have much work to do since his piece was complete. He helped Liam review the software documentation, and offered to review my board presentation, but aside from that he got up and walked around the building.

Robbie was a mess. I could tell he was working his ass off, but during the momentary breaks when a file was copying he hung his head like a little league pitcher who had given up a walk-off home run.

I called him into my office after lunch. "I'm starting to think about damage control," I said grimly. "How to defend ourselves when the shit hits the fan and blame starts flying."

"Yeah, um, okay," he said.

His eyes were bloodshot. My heart went out to him, because I could tell this was killing him on the inside. *I'll console him later*, I thought. Pretty soon we would have plenty of time for retrospection.

"The IT guy you were yelling at earlier. Victor. You said he took down the network for maintenance without getting approval?"

"They are supposed to mark all major network changes or outages on their team calendar," Robbie explained. "I checked that yesterday afternoon to make sure there wouldn't be any conflicts with our deployment, and the calendar was empty. They didn't warn anyone the work was going to be done."

"How would you feel if I report him to his manager for doing that?" I asked. "The network maintenance was the direct cause of our problems. I might be able to make a convincing argument to the board tomorrow."

Robbie winced. "Um. Here's the thing. I sort of skipped the standard process myself."

"How so?"

"Normally, IT changes are a big deal," Robbie said. "They don't typically allow us to deploy software to everyone all at once. It's risky that way. They make us go slowly and methodically: deploying to a small pilot location, then a larger region, and then finally the entire company. That way if there are any problems with scaling, they can discover them before it goes out to everyone.

"For *our* project, we didn't have the luxury of time to do it in phases like that. We had to do it in one big bang." He sighed. "I didn't think we could win that battle, so I didn't even create a change ticket. I figured it was better to ask forgiveness rather than permission. Leslie, this is all my fault—"

"It's not you," I said harshly. "Don't you dare try to blame yourself. It's the ridiculous timeline that caused this problem, not your work."

He nodded, but I didn't think he believed me.

Late in the afternoon, music began pumping on the floor above us. People in the other departments on our floor began passing by our little team on the way to the elevator. Everyone sounded happy and excited. I dismissed Mrs. Caltrop, but she insisted she wasn't leaving until we were. I knew better than to argue with the stubborn woman, and let her continue doing whatever she was doing.

"There," Robbie said at six-thirty. He slumped back in his chair. "All the files are back on the distribution points and the deployment is configured. Now we just have to wait."

"What's the new ETA?" I asked.

Robbie's fingers flashed on the screen calculator. "Once the throttling comes off, with the size of the package... It should be on ninety percent of computers by five in the morning. Plus or minus an hour. Then I have at least ten hours of configuration..."

He trailed off with a sigh.

I could sense the defeat among our team. We knew we weren't going to meet the deadline. All of our work from the past two months had been for nothing.

"You have all done your jobs wonderfully," I said to everyone. "It's now on my shoulders to try to convince the board tomorrow morning. And if I can't, then I'm going to tell them that it's my fault, and mine alone."

"Leslie..." Liam said.

I met each of their gaze individually, pouring all of my warmth and emotion into their eyes as I could.

"Now," I said with fake happiness. "Let's go enjoy the party."

40

Leslie

"I'm going home to sleep," Robbie said. "I've been running on fumes and coffee all day."

Arthur slapped him on the back. "No no no. You must share at least one drink with your colleagues. I will accept nothing less."

"If I fall asleep standing, carry me somewhere comfortable," he said.

Arthur barked a laugh. "To fall asleep during the holiday party would be an insult to the joy of the season!"

Liam hung back while they walked ahead. "You okay?" he asked.

"Yeah." I took a deep breath and then said, "No, I'm not. But it can't be helped now."

Liam grimaced. "It sucks."

"It sure does."

He put an arm around me as we went upstairs, which was a small gesture but meant more to me than he would ever know.

When the elevator door opened, we were bombarded with loud, thumping music and flashing lights.

"Holy crap," Liam said.

The entire floor had been transformed into a winter wonderland. The outer walls and offices were covered in gift wrapping, giving the illusion that we were surrounded by a wall of Christmas presents tied with bows. Fake snow covered the floor in all directions, and a huge hearth had been erected on one end of the room with an LCD fire roaring inside. At a glance I saw at least three bars serving alcohol, and a long table ran the entire length of the room piled high with food. Dozens of speakers were mounted around the room, and the song currently playing was a techno-remix version of *Santa Claus Is Coming To Town*.

"*C'est magnifique!*" Arthur said with awe.

"This is nuts," Robbie said. "Is that an ice sculpture?!?!"

To our right was a model of the Allegheny Supply headquarters building carved out of clear ice. Details like each individual window and door stood out, shiny as the light reflected off of its surface.

There was a line of people standing in front of the sculpture. An ice tube extending out the front door of the miniature ice building, like a horizontal straw. One man in a suit crouched down and opened his mouth for it. A bartender opened a bottle of vodka and poured a shot into a hole in the roof of the building. We watched as the clear liquid ran through a tunnel carved inside the ice, spinning and swirling, before emerging out the front door and shooting into the crouching man's mouth.

"A vodka slide!" Arthur exclaimed happily. "How exciting!"

"That's dangerous," I said with a laugh. "Maybe after a few drinks."

"Speaking of that," Liam said, "I need one. *Badly.*"

We grabbed drinks from one of the bars—Arthur and I chose wine, while Liam and Robbie ordered beers. Then we got in line for the food buffet, filled our plates, and found a standing table for the four of us to crowd around while we ate. I eyed one corner of the room, where big box items were arranged on tables. From here I could see a

Roomba vacuum cleaner, an Amazon Echo, and a stereo. Probably items for the silent auction.

We ate and drank in silence, then got a second round of drinks. Despite the exciting party raging around us, none of us felt like celebrating. By this time tomorrow, all of us might be looking for new jobs. At the very least, I would be.

"Beth!" I said when I saw our coworker walking by. "This is all amazing! You guys did a great job!"

"Thanks!" the blonde woman said with a giggle. "It really came together, didn't it? Oh, and you're sure you want to volunteer for the big auction later?"

I'd forgotten all about that. "Yeah, of course," I said, not wanting to flake out on yet another aspect of the party. "Count me in."

She grinned at the four of us. "Yay! I'm looking forward to it! Enjoy the party!"

"That woman is a walking exclamation point," Liam said with a chuckle after she left.

"What thing did you volunteer for?" Robbie asked.

I shrugged. "They needed volunteers for something. Probably handing out prizes to the winner of the silent auction."

Arthur left, and returned with an armful of new drinks for all of us.

"Thanks, buddy," Liam said. "I'm going to keep drinking until I stop feeling feelings."

"A noble endeavor, in which I shall join you," Arthur replied, clinking glasses.

I accepted my drink and sighed. "So, the elephant in the room. Our project is doomed. Robbie, walk us through how tomorrow will go with everything."

Robbie removed his glasses and pinched the bridge of his nose.

"The clients will finish downloading the new software at five or six in the morning. As soon as they are complete, I will begin configuring the boundary groups which organize each computer into individual branches, and regions. That will take... oh, I don't know. Ten hours? Maybe longer, since I've never actually done it before. I'm just going off documentation."

"So the new system will officially be complete at, what? Four in the afternoon?"

"Probably more like five o'clock," Robbie said glumly. "And that's the best case scenario. If I run into any problems, it could be late into the night."

"That's what I thought." I tried to keep the resignation out of my voice. "The trainers are arriving at ten in the morning. They're spending all afternoon reviewing the documentation, using the system, and asking questions before flying out Saturday evening."

"Which means by the time we get the system up, they will already be leaving," Liam said.

I nodded.

Liam took a long drink. "Well, shit."

My phone buzzed, and I made the mistake of glancing at it. "Oh, great. I just got an email from Katherine, the Chief Operating Officer. The trainers are coming earlier than we expected tomorrow. So now we have even less time."

I saw the last remaining ounce of hope disappear from my team. They had probably been hoping the trainers might be delayed, or some other miracle that would give us more time. In truth, I had been hoping for exactly that.

"Forget the trainers' arrival," Arthur said. "Is it truly terrible if we are one single day late? The trainers could begin training on the system on Sunday, yes? The only negative would be that the company paid them to do nothing for a day? Such an expense is a drop in the bucket, I assure you."

"That's the thing," I said. "No, it wouldn't be the worst thing in the world. But it would delay the employee transition from Sunday to Monday, which would affect our big rush of sales at the beginning of the week. Which the board is afraid will screw up our end-of-month financial numbers. Our delay will take the blame, whether we deserve it or not."

"*Merde*," Arthur cursed.

I waved my glass of wine. I was starting to feel the alcohol, which was exactly what I needed right then. "But like I said, I'm going to take all of the blame. I'll insist the three of you are not responsible."

"Don't do that, Leslie," Liam said.

"Why not?" I demanded. "I'm screwed either way. I might as well jump on the grenade and shield the three of you."

"You don't know that..." Robbie said.

"I *do* know it," I insisted. "The COO all but said that I'm gone if we cannot meet the deadline. I won't let the three of you lose your jobs too. I may have been an awful manager, but I can try to save you in the end."

Arthur put a hand on my back. "Leslie, do not say this thing. You were not an awful manager!"

"You're the best manager I've ever had," Liam added.

I narrowed my eyes at him. "I'm probably the only manager you've ever slept with."

Liam rocked his head back and forth. "Yeah, true."

"Speaking of that," Robbie said. "We, um, won't be working together much longer. Not if things break bad the way you expect tomorrow. Which means you will, you know, be able to finally date one of us. Without keeping it a secret."

The tightness in my chest related to work disappeared, and was replaced with a new tension. "Yes, um..."

"Surely she would choose the one with the most charming

accent," Arthur said, leaning on his French accent more than usual. "The two of you cannot speak the language of love, no?"

"I speak the language of love, but not with my tongue," Liam replied. "Well, maybe with *some* of my tongue..." He grinned at me.

"I don't want to think about that right now," I said. "When all of this is over we can figure out what to do about *this*." I swung my wine glass in a circle around the group.

Robbie frowned. "Leslie, I don't know if I can go any longer without knowing. I'd rather the band-aid gets ripped off now rather than pulled off slowly."

"Robbie..." I said gently.

"I would also like to know where I stand," Arthur said stiffly.

I glanced at Liam. "And I suppose you demand and answer right now, too?'

He shrugged nonchalantly. "It wouldn't hurt. Although after last night, I think the choice is easy..."

Arthur scoffed. "Last night? You were a mere bystander compared to the affection Leslie and I shared. An *hors-d'oeuvre* compared to the main dish." He gestured down at his suited body.

Robbie's mouth hung open. "You guys were together last night? All *three* of you?"

"It just kind of happened," I admitted. "Robbie, if you're upset..."

He surprised me by laughing. "I'm not upset. I'm jealous that I was stuck in the office instead of joining you."

Liam blinked. "*You* would have been into that?"

"Why are you surprised?" Robbie shot back.

"I don't know. Because you're as meek as a puppy dog."

"Robbie can be quite assertive," I told them. "There's a whole 'nother side to him when he's in his element. You should have seen him before the marathon."

Arthur gazed at Robbie with shock. "Robbie! You are a lover after all!"

Robbie blushed and focused on his beer glass.

The music trailed off and Beth walked out onto the stage by the dance floor. "Hello everyone! How is everyone enjoying the party?"

A cheer went up among the crowd.

"It's time for the surprise auction you've all been waiting for," Beth said into her microphone. "We're calling this the *naughty list*! We have several bachelors and bachelorettes who *you* will be bidding on a chance to dance with! All proceeds go to charity..."

"Wait," I said. "They're actually doing the bachelor auction thing? Seriously?"

"Hmm, I suppose Beth and Charletta decided it was a good idea after all," Robbie said.

"It is less risque than *seven minutes in heaven*, yes?" Arthur grinned.

"Let's get our auction prizes up here on the stage!" Beth announced. "First we have Alex Andropolous, from the Sales Department..."

The crowd cheered as Alex jogged up to the stage.

"You're avoiding the question," Liam told me. His face was deathly serious. "The past two months have been torture for us. I think we all agree we need some sort of answer, Leslie."

Robbie and Arthur nodded. The three of them stared at me, waiting for my choice.

I didn't know what to do. When I looked at Robbie, my heart went out to him and I wanted to choose him. But I had a similar affection when I looked at Arthur. And when I gazed into Liam's understanding eyes, and he gave me his silly half-smile, I wanted to throw my arms around him and hold on tight.

"I..." I said. "I think..."

"And last but not least..." Beth's voice echoed through the speakers.

"Leslie Hill, the manager of the Systems Transition Team!"

41

Leslie

My head whipped around. "What?"

Beth was on the stage, gazing around the crowd. "Where's Leslie? Leslie Hill, I know you're out there!"

Robbie's jaw hit the floor. "You signed up for this?"

"Of course not. I didn't..."

My stomach sank.

Beth had asked for volunteers for one of the events tonight, and I'd agreed without looking at the details. The email was still sitting in my inbox, unread.

"Oh no," I said. "I think I did. Crap, I need to get out of here..."

"There she is!" Beth said, pointing at me. "Come on up here, Leslie! I *know* you're on the *naughty list!*"

People started clapping, including the human auction prizes up on the stage. John Fadringham, my old boss, was suddenly at my side and guiding me forward.

"Come on, don't be shy!" he said happily.

"I forgot I signed up," I whispered to him.

He paused, suddenly as worried as a parent. "Do you want me to cause a distraction? I can spill my drink on you, so you can run to the bathroom and hide."

For a moment, I considered it. I wasn't in the mood to be put on display and bid on. But then I thought, what the hell? It was just a dance. And it was for charity.

And I *had* promised Beth, even though I didn't realize what I was agreeing to.

"I'm good," I told John with a laugh. "Don't let me go without any bids though, alright?"

He grinned. "I'll save you from embarrassment, if it comes to that."

I relented and allowed myself to be guided to the stage. The lights were brighter here than out in the crowd, making me feel like an animal on display. The other people in the auction—most of whom I didn't know—gave me high-fives as I took my place at the end of the line.

"Alright everyone!" Beth announced. "These lovely people on stage are on Santa's *naughty list*, so you're bidding on a chance to *dance* with them. Just one dance, totally innocent. Got it? Now let's get started!"

The crowd cheered again. I squinted through the lights into the dark crowd. Liam had a silly smirk on his face, and Arthur was smiling widely. Only Robbie looked confused or worried, but that was probably just because he was still barely staying awake.

Beth waved the first gentleman over, who was a handsome younger man. "Our first person on the *naughty list* is Christian, from the finance department!"

Somewhere in the back, Arthur shouted, "Christian! You sexy man!" which made the crowd laugh.

"Let's start the bidding at twenty dollars," Beth said.

"Fifty dollars!" Arthur shouted. "I will dance with you even if nobody else will, Christian!"

There was more laughter as Arthur bid on his friend from finance. Fortunately, a woman in the front row quickly bid one hundred dollars, and then another woman bid one-fifty. The first woman raised it to two hundred, which nobody would match.

"Sold, one dance with Christian to Vanessa from accounts payable!"

Everyone hooted and hollered as Vanessa came up on stage, was handed an over-sized length of ribbon, and wrapped it around Christian like they were conjoined twins. They laughed and shuffled off the stage to more applause.

Beth grinned out at the crowd. "Next we have my partner in crime, who helped plan this marvelous night. She's looking stunning in a black cocktail dress and knows how to dance the salsa. I think we can all see why she's on the *naughty list*. Let's give it up for Charletta from the tax department!"

Charletta was indeed stunning in a tight black dress that hugged her curvaceous figure and showed a *lot* of cleavage. She got quite a few bids from the crowd before eventually being won by none other than John Fadringham for five hundred dollars.

"I thought you're my backup!" I said to him as he came up on stage to escort Charletta away.

"Don't sweat it, Leslie. I've got you."

The next guy was someone I didn't know from the legal department. He was cute, and went for two hundred and fifty dollars. The woman after that went for four hundred, then one of the warehouse hunks pulled in a massive nine-hundred dollars from a tattooed woman in the front—who I soon discovered was his wife.

"He's mine, ladies!" she declared while wrapping him in ribbon and grabbing his butt on the way off the stage. The crowd, who was quite inebriated by now, roared at the show.

Two other people came and went, and then it was finally my

turn.

Beth put an arm around me and glared out at the crowd. "Gentlemen. You'd better open your wallets, because this young lady is a rising star here at Allegheny Supply. She's the manager of the Systems Transition Team, which I'm told completed their new system deployment today! Last among the women, but not least, let's give a big round of applause for Leslie Hill!"

The mention of the STT project temporarily dampened my mood, but the huge cheer from the crowd erased that. *Enjoy the moment*, I told myself.

I couldn't curtsy in my pencil skirt, so I gave a formal bow to the crowd.

"Now, we've currently raised a whopping *four thousand, two hundred dollars* for the Children's Hospital of Pittsburgh," Beth said, which drew another cheer from the crowd. "But with Leslie here, I think we can break five thousand for the night. Let's start the bidding at one hundred!"

There was a small pause where Beth's voice echoed from the speakers, and everyone was silent. That voice of self-doubt that all women had in the back of their heads whispered: *what if nobody bids on you?*

But that doubt disappeared as someone yelled, "I'll bid one hundred!"

I grinned down at the man. It was Brian, a guy I used to work with in sales. He was married, and his wife was on his arm, but they were both smiling up at me.

I was feeling the right amount of tipsy, so I pumped my fist and pointed at him, then gave a thumbs-up.

"We've got one hundred. Can someone do one-fifty?"

"One fifty-!" yelled John Fadringham.

Beth lowered the microphone and put her hands on her hips like a stern schoolteacher. "Now, John. You've already won a dance with Charletta."

"I'll dance with them both!" he shouted. The crowd laughed and cheered.

"Two hundred!" came a new voice in the back.

Liam.

I smiled out at him. He smiled back with the same goofy half-smile he'd given me on my first day at the company five years ago, hands in his pockets and shifting from one foot to the other.

"That's two hundred from Liam Harford," Beth said. "Looks like someone wants a bonus from their boss!"

"Three hundred," Arthur shouted.

Liam rounded on him with surprise, but Arthur only had eyes for me. *Mon fleur,* he mouthed to me from across the room, and put his hand over his heart.

Any other time, it would have been an inappropriate display in front of the whole company. But here, it blended in as part of the overall ridiculous act of the entire auction.

"Four hundred," Liam replied, a determined look on his face.

"Uh oh, it looks like we've got ourselves an intra-team bidding war!" Beth said.

"Five!" Arthur retorted stubbornly.

Beth put her arm around my shoulder and lowered her voice in a pretend whisper, even though the microphone caught it all. "Leslie, you didn't force your employees to bid on you, did you?"

When the crowd stopped laughing, I grabbed the mic and said, "Keep bidding or you're both fired!"

That brought the largest roar of laughter and cheering from the crowd all night. It was all in good fun. We were raising money for charity, and it was just a harmless dance they were bidding for.

But soon it began to feel like something deeper was on the line.

"Eight hundred," Liam shouted. There was no humor on his face now.

"*Mille*," Arthur replied. "One thousand!"

Now the crowd began to buzz with excitement. The smile on my face faltered as I realized what was happening.

"Twelve hundred," Liam bid.

"Thirteen."

"Fifteen hundred."

"Two *thousand*," Arthur said triumphantly.

"Oh my *goodness*," Beth said with a nervous laugh. "You guys know you have to actually *pay* this amount, right? Let's not get carried away..."

Liam's face was strained. "Three grand."

"Thirty-five hundred," Arthur replied without hesitation.

Beth glanced at me: *what the hell is going on?*

The buzz in the crowd rose to an excited hum. This went far beyond the bounds of a lighthearted auction for charity. Everyone could tell that something *else* was happening. People were going to talk about this long after tonight.

I could see the conflict on Liam's face. Wondering whether to keep going, if it was worth trying to best Arthur, who had his arms crossed over his three-piece suit and was smiling smugly.

I shook my head at Liam. *Don't do it. This has gone too far.*

I have to, his expression replied. "Four thousand."

"Four *thousand* dollars," Beth said. "We've now surpassed all the other *naughty list* auctions combined!"

"*Cinq mille*," Arthur shouted. "Five thousand!"

The crowd gasped. Liam winced. Arthur grinned at him triumphantly. They shared a few words that I couldn't hear, and Liam shook his head.

"Five thousand dollars!" Beth said excitedly. "Going once... going twice..."

Before she could bang the metaphorical gavel, a new voice cut through the crowd. "TEN THOUSAND!"

"Robbie?" I blurted out.

His voice was clear and confident as he shouted the number. The crowd, who was prepared to accept five thousand as the final bid, lost their *minds*. Everyone was talking now, and several people went up to Robbie to make sure he was okay. That he understood what was going on.

No, Robbie no, I thought. *You don't need to jump into this pissing contest.*

Beth almost fainted. "Ten... oh my. *Ten...*"

I grabbed the microphone from Beth. "He's running on a lack of sleep," I said with a nervous laugh.

Robbie shook his head. "Ten thousand for a dance with Leslie! You heard me!"

Liam and Arthur looked shocked, and remained silent. They weren't prepared to compete with that.

"Ten thousand... I don't think I need to count down to *that*," Beth announced. "Sold! Ten thousand dollars for a dance with Leslie, and the winner is Robbie Godwin, the third member of the STT project!"

The crowd, who was finally at the end of their rope, cheered with excitement and relief. Robbie blushed and looked around awkwardly, then quickly ran to the bar to get another beer.

"That's one heck of a dance!" Beth said. "Leslie, here's the ribbon—I'll let you go down and meet your winner, who appears to need another drink after coughing up five figures! Now, our final male auction is Philip from human resources..."

I took the ribbon from Beth and left the stage in a daze.

42

Leslie

It took me a while to move through the crowd, because everyone kept patting me on the back and making jokes about how *motivated* my team was to work for me. Jokes that were funny in a vacuum, but hit a little too close to home given the reality of the situation.

Ten thousand dollars. I can't believe it.

When I finally reached Robbie, he was talking to Liam and Arthur. Their conversation was calm on the surface, but I could tell there was tension in the air.

"What the hell?" I demanded of him. "Ten *thousand* dollars? For a dance?"

Robbie shrugged in that awkward, but adorable, manner of his. "I wanted to make sure you fetched the biggest amount."

"Oh, we were *well* past the other auction people," I said dryly. "What has gotten into you? *All* of you?"

"It's for charity," Robbie said simply.

"A dance, *and* we are helping children with cancer?" Arthur replied. "This is what you Americans call a *win-win,* yes?"

"Three hundred dollars for Philip, our final auction on the

naughty list!" Beth announced on stage. She did a good job acting enthusiastic about that number, even though it was an order of magnitude lower than the one before it. "Altogether, that brings the total amount raised by the *naughty list* to fourteen thousand, five hundred dollars! Give yourselves a round of applause!"

The crowd cheered loudly, but many people turned and cheered in Robbie's direction. He didn't seem to notice—he was focused on me.

"Are you mad?" he asked nervously.

"Alright, everyone!" Beth announced loudly. "It's time for the auction dances! Let's clear the dance floor for everyone who contributed!"

Robbie's eyes widened. "Oh no. I, uh…"

A laugh escaped my lips. "Don't tell me that after all of that, you can't dance."

His face turned beet red, giving me my answer.

I took his hand. "Come on. We'll make it a slow dance."

Fortunately, the music *was* a slow dance—the song *Lady in Red*, by Chris De Burgh. We entered the dance floor and I put my arms around Robbie innocently, as if this was the school prom and dance monitors were watching us closely for any impropriety.

Everyone was watching us. Not just the dancers in general, but specifically me and Robbie. I could see them whispering to one another, wondering what was *really* going on between us, if anything.

I tried to put them out of my mind as I enjoyed the dance with Robbie.

"Well?" he asked nervously. "Are you mad?"

I smiled. "No, I'm not mad. I mean, I'm a *little* mad. Ten thousand dollars, Robbie? Seriously?"

He grinned bashfully. "Like Arthur said. It's for a good cause."

"It was bad enough that the two of them were measuring their dicks, but you just *had* to jump in and add your dick to the contest."

He frowned. "You seem more than just a little mad."

I sighed. "I guess it doesn't matter. I'm going to lose my job tomorrow, so who cares if people whisper about us. Do you have ten grand to blow on a donation like this?"

He shrugged as we danced. "I don't go out much. I have a lot in savings. I was thinking of buying a motorcycle, but kids with cancer is better."

I burst out laughing. "A motorcycle, seriously?"

"What?"

"You're quiet and shy, but you're absolutely *jacked* with muscle and have tattoos covering your arms," I explained. "You're the weirdest IT nerd I've ever met."

"Should I take that as, um, a compliment?"

"Yes, it's a compliment you big nerd."

He smiled.

"All joking aside," I said more seriously, "if you think I'm going to choose you just because of this..."

"Forget about that," he said. "Honestly."

"I'm serious. One grand gesture isn't going to make my decision any easier..."

I trailed off as he started chuckling.

"What's so funny?"

Robbie shook his head. "I've been thinking a lot in the last day. Sleep deprivation has a way of focusing a person. Leslie, I'm in love with you."

I sighed. It was simultaneously what I wanted to hear, and what I was afraid of him saying. Because deep down, my feelings were the same. It was impossible to ignore that fact.

"I'm falling in love with you too," I whispered.

"I've never felt this way about anyone," he admitted. "Maybe

Sarah Pavlicic in ninth grade. But that was a long time ago, and I was just a teenager. Since we started working together—hell, since that night in the closet at your house, I haven't been able to stop thinking about you. For a while, Leslie, I was able to put aside my feelings and focus on my job. Because being together wasn't allowed thanks to company policy. But then we kissed in the office, and, um..."

"And what happened in the car after our twenty mile run?" I finished for him.

"Yeah. That was amazing. *You're* amazing, Leslie. I think what we have is real. I just wanted to let you know that. Whatever happens, know that I will always care about you."

I felt myself tearing up at his little speech. He seemed more confident and assertive tonight than just about any other time I'd seen him. Like his love for me made him into a different person.

But I was terrified of breaking his heart.

"I have strong feelings for you too," I admitted. It was the truth, more than he would ever know. "But I also feel the same way about Arthur and Liam..."

"Leslie..." he said gently.

"It's stupid, and crazy, and I feel awful about it," I said in a rush as the music played. "But it's the truth. I don't know what I'm going to do Robbie—"

He put a finger over my lips and smiled reassuringly. "Leslie. Don't think about that right now. I paid a lot of money for this dance, so just enjoy the moment with me. Okay?"

I rested my head on his shoulder. "Okay."

People were watching, and whispering, and would continue talking on Monday morning. But right then I didn't give a damn.

The song finally ended, and the music changed. More people joined the dance floor, and Robbie stroked my cheek.

"It's his turn, now," he said.

"What?'

Liam was suddenly at his side, smiling down at me and taking my hand. Robbie handed me off and disappeared back into the crowd away from the dance floor.

"What's this?" I asked.

The next song was faster-paced, but Liam held me close in a rocking slow dance. I didn't stop him. He gave me his signature half-smile and said, "Here's the thing. After Robbie won the auction, he told us that he wanted to share you for the dance. So we're all throwing in three grand or so into the charity."

"Seriously?" I sputtered. "Somehow, that seems crazier than Robbie paying ten grand for one dance."

"Deal with it," Liam said with mock-bluntness. "You're on the *naughty list*, so you don't have a choice."

"I guess I don't," I said.

We danced quietly for a long moment, just enjoying each other's presence.

"Leslie, I love you."

I jerked in his arms. "Liam!"

"I'm serious."

I laughed and looked around. "We've barely been *together* for the last two months," I whispered. "How could you—"

He smiled and shook his head at me, green eyes shining in the dance floor lights. "I've loved you for five years, Leslie. I didn't know it until these past two months, but it's clear to me now. It was fate that brought us together back in October. All of us joining the party planning committee, and then hooking up after our first meeting. Sure, it would have gone easier if Oliver Edwards had been the manager of the STT, but the roughest roads often lead to the most satisfying sights. It should have happened years ago, Leslie. When we were in sales together. But better late than never, right?"

He cradled my cheek in his hand and had tears in his eyes.

"I love you, Leslie Hill. And I wish I had said it long before now."

My throat tightened and made it tough to breathe as I gazed up at Liam Harford. The man who had been my "work husband" when we both started at the company out of college. The person who I had always known was right for me, even if we could never both be single at the same time to make it work.

He means it, I realized. *He loves me.*

And I love him too.

The realization hit me like a thunderclap. My knees buckled.

"Woah there," he said, tightening his grip around my back and supporting my weight. "I didn't mean to make you faint. Do you need to sit down?"

I shook my head. "I'm fine. I think."

"Good," he said with a big smile. "Because the song just ended, and technically Arthur has the next dance. And he would *never* let me hear the end of it if he didn't get his turn." His thumb caressed my cheek. "Think about what I said. I meant every word."

Suddenly Arthur was pulling me from Liam's arms as another new song began. He placed one hand on my lower back and held my other up high like we were dancing a waltz.

"Leslie," he said. My name sounded exotic on his tongue. "I must tell you how much fun I had with you last night. You *and* Liam, to my surprise."

I felt my cheeks redden at the memory of our threesome. "I wondered how you two would feel about it the next day."

He tossed his hair flippantly. "I must admit that I prefer you all to myself. Yet there is something erotic and luxurious about sharing you with another man. When I am quite close with the other man, of course."

"Of course." I smiled. "I really enjoyed it too."

He stared deeply into my eyes and gave me his charming French smile. "I care quite deeply about you, *mon fleur*. I have never been one to settle down, so to speak. I have been called a... a..."

"A flirt?" I tried. "A womanizer?"

"Liam accused me of such things, yes," he replied. "He also warned me not to toy around with you. I have given this much thought. I would very much like to continue seeing you, Leslie. Not only in the short-term, but for a long period of time. I would like for us to *go steady*, as you Americans say."

"I haven't heard anyone use that phrase in a long time," I said with a chuckle. "But I know what you mean. And I agree. It's just that..."

I glanced at Liam and Robbie, who were standing at the edge of the dance floor. Speaking softly to each other about something while watching us dance. What were they up to?

"Forget them," he said. "Think only of me right now, yes?"

"Okay," I said.

I wished I could kiss him as he guided me around the dance floor. I was past the point of caring about my job—if I was going to be fired tomorrow for failing to meet the deadline, then who cared if I kissed one of my employees?

I'll care, I thought. I cared what other people thought of me.

"I told you not to worry about anyone bidding on you!" John Fadringham said as he passed us on the dance floor.

"Thanks for bidding on me anyways," I said with a smile.

He twirled Charletta. "Any time!"

We left the dance floor when the song ended. Liam and Robbie were still watching us, and I was a bundle of confused emotions, so I walked over to the bar to get another wine. When I returned, my three guys were waiting for me.

"We want to talk to you," Liam said. "In private."

"Can it wait?" I asked hopefully.

"No, Leslie," Arthur replied. "It cannot."

We left the party and went into the elevator hallway, but the music was still too loud so we went inside the stairwell instead. There was a weird smell, and the halogen lights were a little too bright after the dimness of the party. The door closed behind us, leaving only the distant sound of bass thumping through the floor.

"Okay," I said. "What's up? Is this about the crazy ten grand bid you guys are splitting? Because I was *definitely* not worth that."

"Oh, you were indeed worth it," Liam said. "But that's not what we want to talk about."

"We do not want you to choose one of us," Arthur said.

"You... You don't?"

Robbie adjusted his glasses and shook his head. "We want you to keep dating, um, all of us. Me, Arthur, and Liam. At the same time."

"We wish to share you," Arthur said.

My jaw dropped.

"You want to *what?*"

43

Leslie

"You want to *what?*" I asked.

"I can tell you're struggling to make a decision," Liam said comfortingly. "Whoever you choose, I'm afraid you will always wonder what could have been with the other two. You will live a life of regret."

"Such a thing will poison a relationship," Arthur said sadly. "This cannot be."

Robbie nodded. "We talked about it. The three of us. And we don't mind sharing you. We all like each other and, um, get along. Working on the STT project proves that."

Liam rubbed my arm. "The project is ending. You won't be our manager soon, either because we're all fired for missing the deadline or because the team is being disbanded since it's no longer needed. You'll be free to date us. *All* of us."

"And if you wish to make a decision in the future?" Arthur added. "You may do so. But only as you wish, with no pressure from us. We promise you this."

"We all care about you, and want you to be happy," Liam said. "So, let's all be happy *together.*"

I stared at them. I felt like they were pulling a prank on me, and would yell, "JUST KIDDING!" at any moment. But they all just gazed back at me serenely. Waiting to see what I would say.

This is crazy. Right?

Suddenly the stairway door opened and two women came walking down the stairs. "Hey, there's the big ticket dancer!" one of them said. "Hope that dance was worth it, boys!"

"Definitely, um, worth it," Robbie said with a smile.

The women pulled out e-cigarettes and started chatting in the stairwell. I jerked my head at my three guys and we walked down a floor and out into the hallway. But we still didn't have privacy—there were more people down here chatting and sharing drinks.

"Let's go into our office," I said, leading the others that way.

Our office space was as silent as a graveyard. It felt like the scene of a battle, one where we had lost. I could still hear people chatting in the hall, so I led my three employees into my office and closed the door.

"You want to *share* me?" I blurted out.

"That's, um, the idea," Robbie said.

Arthur spread his hands. "What is the problem? Is this not every girl's dream? Three strapping men to tend to her every need?"

"I'm just shocked you all agreed to this," I admitted. "Guys are usually territorial…"

"Last night proved something to me," Liam said. "Being with you, and Arthur… I wasn't jealous at all. It was weird at first, and different. But different in a *good* way."

"I want you to be happy," Robbie said. "And you're happiest when you're with all of us. Which makes *me* happy."

I pointed at Arthur and Liam. "They had a chance last night to really test their feelings. You haven't had that chance yet. How do you know you can handle sharing me without getting jealous?"

Robbie licked his lips. "I know of a way we can, uh, test it.

Right now."

"*Ici au bureau?*" Arthur asked him. "Right here in the office?"

An awkward smile spread across Robbie's face. "Why not?"

I still couldn't believe all of this. There was no way they would be fine with me *being* with all three of them. A random threesome with Liam and Arthur was one thing, but to make it a regular thing...

But I tingled with excitement at what he was proposing. Right here, in my office. The three of them.

I'm getting fired tomorrow. What does it matter?

I turned to Liam and kissed him hard, pressing my body against his and grabbing a handful of his ass. With him still in my arms, I turned to face Robbie and asked, "That doesn't make you jealous?"

He shook his head. "No."

I still didn't believe him, so next I pounced on Arthur. The moment I kissed him he jammed his tongue into my mouth, French-kissing me hard in my office until I began to moan.

"Anything?" I asked Robbie.

Robbie smiled nervously. "Not even a little bit. As long as I get a turn, I mean."

I strode toward him slowly, pushing him back until he leaned against my desk. I kissed him deeply, passionately, molding my chest against his and reaching for the front of his dress pants. His cock stood out stiffly against the fabric.

When we were done kissing, we were both gasping for air. "Does that make you two jealous..." I began to ask Arthur and Liam.

But before I could turn around, Arthur was already wrapping me in his arms from behind, and kissing the back of my neck. Liam flipped the switch by the door and the windows fogged in an instant.

Robbie cupped my cheek and pulled my lips back to his, while Arthur nuzzled at my neck and ground against my ass. Wedged between the two of them was like being dunked in a pool of pure ecstasy. Two men who wanted nothing more than to please me, to make me happy.

Liam pulled me from the others and kissed me possessively in a way that took my breath away. He pushed me around the desk and dropped me into my chair, the same chair where he'd fucked my face during office hours a few weeks before. I gazed up at his tall frame, and he smiled down at me with mischief in his eyes.

But it was not my face that he would be pleasuring this time. He dropped to his knees and spread my legs in the chair, then pushed my skirt up to reveal my panties. Liam licked along the inside of my thigh, teasing me with tantalizing kisses, moving closer to my pussy... and then skipping over it to kiss and lick my other thigh. I grabbed a handful of his messy brown hair and tried to pull his face to my pussy, but he resisted.

"You have to wait," he said with a wicked grin.

Before I could respond, Robbie leaned down and kissed me on the lips again. I moaned into his mouth as Liam's tongue licked up my other thigh, along the seam of my panties without going any closer. Then new hands were pulling at the buttons of my blouse, opening it and then removing my bra until my full breasts were exposed to the warm office air. Arthur's mouth closed over my nipple and I hissed with surprise, then sighed with pleasure.

And just as I began savoring that sensation, Liam pulled aside my panties and licked up my pussy from bottom to top.

I moaned with ecstasy as their three tongues worked on me simultaneously. I didn't care that they were my employees, and that we were in my office with the entire company partying one floor above us. None of that mattered.

They were all that mattered.

Liam gave my pussy a final tongue-lashing and then picked me up out of the chair. He swept his hand across my desk, knocking aside a few stacks of paper and my extra computer mouse.

"That was unnecessarily dramatic," I said.

He unbuckled his belt and let his pants drop to the floor. "You liked it."

I grinned up at him. "I did."

I tensed with anticipation as Liam stepped out of his pants and boxers. His cock was stiff and ready. I grabbed Liam's tie and used it like a leash, pulling him between my legs. His cock found my wet entrance and slid inside with ease.

"Oh *fuck...*" I moaned loudly.

Liam held my legs up and began fucking me steadily. "Is now a good time to ask for a letter of recommendation?"

My moans turned into a sputtering laugh. "Keep going and we'll see."

"*Oui, mon fleur*," Arthur said as he appeared at my side. "We shall see indeed."

He resumed kissing and fondling my breasts while Liam fucked me. Solo sex was fantastic... but there was no comparison to a threesome. Being worshiped by two men was twice as hot as just one, and last night's adventure's at Arthur's loft had awoken something inside of me.

This is how a woman is meant to be loved, I thought while watching the handsome men kissing and making love to my body.

But it wasn't a threesome, and there were more than just two men. I rolled my head until I found Robbie to my right, watching the scene with wide, lustful eyes.

"How do you feel?" I asked him. "Do you like this?"

"Oh yes," he answered immediately. "I like this very much."

I squeezed my legs around Liam's waist, pulling him into me and stopping his thrusts. "I want you," I told Robbie. "Take off your pants."

Robbie stood and began undressing. I kissed Liam on the lips and then slid off the desk, then bent over the surface. Liam grabbed my ass with both hands and squeezed my cheeks, fingers digging into my flesh with need.

As soon as Robbie was nude, I grabbed his cock and pulled him toward me. The desk was *almost* too wide... But not quite. While bending over the desk I could barely reach Robbie's dick with my mouth. I wrapped my lips around the tip and gently sucked, gazing up at him through my eyelashes.

A groan escaped his mouth as he looked down at me, eyes wide with lust. "Leslie..."

I kissed his tip and asked, "Does that feel good?"

"So good."

I opened my mouth wider and took more of his cock. His was wider around the middle, but I was still able to fit most of it in my mouth, pushing down until my lips were near his base. I held it there for a moment, then pulled back slowly, ending with a kiss on his head again.

"Does *that* feel good?"

"Are you kidding!" he blurted out. "I'm going to die if you do that again."

Behind me, Arthur had pushed Liam aside and was eating me out from behind. Then he gave my ass a playful slap, and rubbed his cock up and down along my slit, teasing me with his manhood.

"Should I fuck her now?" Arthur asked.

"Hmm, better tease her some more first," Liam said.

"Fuck me," I begged while stroking Robbie with my hand. "Please..."

Arthur grabbed my waist and then completely filled me with one long thrust. The force of it pushed me forward on Robbie's dick, taking half of him in my mouth and pulling a loud groan from his chest.

I rocked back and forth in time with Arthur's pumping cock, giving Robbie a blowjob from those movements alone. Liam grabbed a handful of my hair and pushed my head farther down on Robbie each time. I responded by reaching over and grabbing Liam's cock and stroking it rapidly. Pleasing all three of my men at the same time.

Arthur was speeding up and gripping my waist tighter, a sign that he was close. That was unacceptable to me, so I pushed back on him and then stood up. "I want more of you," I said. "Hold what you've got."

He grinned. "Whatever you desire."

I rounded my desk and pushed Robbie down into one of the guest chairs, then straddled him until I felt his cock tingling against my sex. I guided his cock up into my pussy and drove my hips down until I felt them touch Robbie's thighs, filling my pussy with his wide cock.

He gasped underneath me. "Leslie, oh my God."

I sighed as I rotated my hips around him. "There's that cock I wanted. *Fuck*, you feel good."

He grabbed my ass with both hands and guided me up and down. "I don't think we're doing a good job of sharing."

"I think you're sharing surprisingly well for the first time."

Robbie caressed my face with a tattooed hand. "We can share more, though." He nodded over my shoulder.

Liam stepped up behind me, and Robbie lifted me off of him until his cock slid out. Liam immediately shoved his prick inside my pussy, fucking me from behind.

"Much better," Liam agreed.

"Sharing is caring, they say, yes?" Arthur chimed in on the other side.

Liam fucked me for about ten seconds, then pulled out and let me ride Robbie again. Then it was Arthur's turn to mount me from behind, fucking me hard while I rested on Robbie's body and made out with him.

Back and forth they fucked me, taking turns and switching every ten or fifteen seconds. Being shared by my three lovers heightened everything to a new and exciting level of eroticism. Arthur's dick, then Liam's, then Robbie's inside of me. It was a surprise each time one entered me, and sent pulses of ecstasy surging through my body. And with the way they were taking turns, it allowed them to last for what felt like *hours*.

A never-ending gauntlet of thick, throbbing manhood pounding me in my office.

I was riding Robbie as I began to come. I tightened my inner muscles around him as I cried with pleasure, and then his face twisted with his own ecstasy. I felt his hot juices squirting inside of me, which drove my own orgasm even higher.

The moment Robbie finished coming, Arthur took his place and filled me from behind. "*Oh, mon fleur,*" he roared while gripping my shoulders. "*Je suis au paradis...*"

His orgasm helped sustain mine, and new waves of tingling electricity rocked my body. And before I could come down from those, it was Liam's turn to fill me with his seed, and he bent over my back and kissed my neck while pounding me from behind.

"Leslie," he breathed. "I love you..."

"Yes, yes," I screamed. "Yes, Liam, *yes...*"

We cried with mutual rapture together there in my office, my three lovers and me.

44

Liam

The floor of Leslie's office was not comfortable. It was thin carpet that scratched against my ass, and provided next to no cushioning. It might as well have been hard wood.

But none of us cared, because we were sprawled out together on the floor, too satisfied to move.

"Yep," Robbie mumbled on the other side of Leslie.

"Hmm?" she asked.

"Yep, I don't mind sharing you," Robbie replied. "I, um, enjoyed that very much."

"She is quite the woman, is she not?" Arthur said, his head resting between Leslie's legs.

I leaned over to kiss her neck. "Yes, she is."

I still wasn't sure how we had gotten to this place. Two months ago, I was trying to become Leslie's boyfriend since we were both finally single. Then we weren't allowed to date because she was my boss, and I learned that Robbie and Arthur both had feelings for her too. We had all accepted that, and agreed that we would respect whatever decision Leslie made at the end.

But somewhere along the way, we started feeling like a team. A work team, sure, but more than that. The four of us were a single unit centered around Leslie. We shared one common purpose: to care for Leslie, and to make her first managerial project a success.

And to please her in other, more erotic, ways.

Now? I couldn't imagine Leslie choosing any one of us. We worked better as a group. The four of us had a special kind of chemistry together. It couldn't be explained.

We're going to share her, I thought happily. It felt normal now. It felt *right*.

"Aren't you glad you came to the party after all?" Leslie asked Robbie.

"Very glad," Robbie replied. He was a good-looking guy without his glasses, I had to admit. "I'm not even tired anymore. I think I caught my second wind."

"You'll crash soon," I told him. "I give it about half an hour before you're snoring on the floor. The janitorial crew is going to find you in here, naked, tomorrow morning."

Leslie kissed him, then kissed me. "All the more reason to get up and start moving."

"But I do not want to move," Arthur complained. "I have decided to remain here, on your floor, until the end of time."

Leslie kissed him on the head, then stood. "It's time to get up. Before someone discovers us."

I crawled to my feet and held Leslie's arm. "We're serious, you know. About sharing you."

She blinked those long eyelashes at me. The ones that won me over five years ago. "I know. I'm still wrapping my head around that. But if it involves more gatherings like *this*? Count me in."

We dressed and then opened the door to her office, peeked our heads out, then went into the room and pretended like nothing had happened. Leslie left to go to the bathroom leaving the three of us standing around.

Arthur was grinning at me. "What?" I asked.

"You love her," he said.

"I do," I admitted. "Lately, I've realized that I have loved her for a long time. What about you?"

He shrugged. "I am falling for her swiftly. I think I will get there quite quickly, yes?"

"Robbie's falling in love with her," I said with a smile.

"Why do you say that?"

I patted the IT guy on the arm. "I can tell. The way you look at her... There's no faking that. It's all real."

Robbie blinked as if I had said something profound. He went to his cubicle and logged into his computer, then scrolled through some logs.

"How's it look?" Leslie said as she returned. "Is the software downloading on the clients?"

"It sure is," he said. "You guys go ahead. I'm going to stick around and check some things."

Leslie narrowed her eyes. "You said that last night, and ended up sleeping here."

"I promise I'm just staying a few more minutes. I have to make sure everything goes smoothly tonight, or we're *really* screwed." He smiled weakly.

Leslie looked like she wanted to argue, but then nodded. "Fine. But make sure you go home for at least *some* sleep in a bed, even if it's only a few hours before you have to come back."

Arthur led Leslie out to the elevator. I lingered and watched Robbie.

"Is something up?" I asked quietly.

"No, why?"

"You had a weird look on your face when I mentioned the look in your eye, and how that can't be faked."

He waved a hand. "It's fine. Go home and get some sleep."

I stared at him a moment longer, then followed Leslie and Arthur downstairs.

45

Leslie

The elevator was crammed with people leaving the party, and we barely squeezed inside. Everyone was drunk and laughing and having a good time. After the fun we'd had in my office, it was tough not to smile along with them.

Until I remembered that tomorrow would bring the end of my career.

There was a line of people waiting for Uber rides out front, which the company was providing for free to the employees. We got in line. Most of the downtown Pittsburgh skyscrapers had Christmas lights along their edges, outlining the rectangular buildings against the grey snowy sky. The three of us watched the heavy snow drifting down around us, completing the picturesque winter scene.

"So," Arthur whispered. Fog puffed in front of his mouth as he spoke. "Whose house are we visiting tonight?"

I smiled sadly. "As much as I would love to cuddle, I need some heavy sleep tonight. Tomorrow is going to be a very long day."

"Gonna have to agree with the boss," Liam said. "After staying at your place last night, Arthur, I want my own bed."

Arthur shrugged nonchalantly. "This is fine. I will cuddle with my pillow, yes?"

"Lucky pillow," I said with a wink. The line wasn't moving, so I said, "I think I'm going to walk home."

"It's freezing out!" Liam replied.

"I don't mind the cold," I said. I moved to kiss them goodbye, then remembered I was in line surrounded by my coworkers. "I'll see you guys on Monday."

"We want to be there tomorrow," Liam protested. "To see how they take things, for better or for worse."

"Then take the morning off and come in the afternoon," I said. "You guys deserve at least half a day off."

We said our goodnights, and then I began walking.

The peaceful walk across the bridge to my side of Pittsburgh gave me time to think about everything. Being thrown into the *naughty list* auction abruptly, and then having my three employees bid on me. In front of the rest of the company. *That* was certainly going to feed the rumor mill on Monday morning.

Maybe it was a good thing I was going to get fired tomorrow.

I didn't want to think about my impending Hindenburg-like disaster, so I let my thoughts drift back to what happened *after* the auction. The dances with each of my three men, and what they revealed to me during them. Then their announcement that they intended to share me among the three of them. How could they possibly want to do that? What kind of guy would share a woman with two other men?

It was ridiculous. It was crazy.

Wasn't it?

They had seemed awfully enthusiastic about it in my office. Even Robbie had been surprisingly excited in a way that was more than just going along with it. There was a fire in his eyes while I was riding him on the chair that was more intense than any other time we had been together. More than when we made love in the car after the twenty-mile run, or before the marathon.

If they were serious about being able to share me, with no

major jealousy between them? It would save me from having to choose. Because the blunt reality of my situation was that I *couldn't* choose.

As soon as I got home I changed into pajamas and crawled under my big comforter. I was warm and cozy as the snow fell outside, but I couldn't help but wish my three men were with me. Snuggling with me, sharing our body heat, as we fell asleep and dreamed together.

For the first time since I could remember, I hit snooze on my work alarm the next morning and slept for an extra hour. There was no use going in early since I didn't have anything to do except wait for the Board of Directors presentation to begin. I took my time showering and getting ready around the house, then took an Uber to work since my car was still parked there.

I walked into the office at eight thirty, half an hour before the big presentation. Robbie was the only one there. His sleeves were rolled up, and his tattooed arms were crossed over his chest while he snored in his chair. Poor thing had probably barely gotten any sleep last night before having to turn around and come back into the office early this morning.

Then I realized he was wearing the same clothes he'd had on last night. Which were the same clothes from the night before *that*.

"Robbie!"

He blinked and looked around. "Hey, uh, whaa?" he croaked.

"Did you *stay here*? Again?"

He blinked. "Um. No?" the adorable nerd said unconvincingly.

I rounded the cubicle and put my hands on my hips. "I told you to go home and get some sleep! You promised me you would!"

"I... I don't know. I guess I lied." He let out a huge yawn, then settled back down to sleep.

I let out an exasperated sigh and glanced at his screen. The new InterLync System console was up. It now showed two thousand clients as installed and connected to the server, but their status symbol showed yellow, meaning they had yet to be organized into branches and regions, the work that would take Robbie all day. A progress bar was ticking across the screen indicating he was waiting for one of those jobs to complete.

We were making progress, but we would definitely miss the deadline.

I guess wishing for a miracle was too much.

Arthur appeared in the doorway with a tray of Starbucks coffee. "Oh, Leslie! You are here!"

"I am here," I said slowly. "Why are *you* here? I told you not to come in until the afternoon."

Arthur delivered a coffee to Robbie's desk, then handed me one. "I wanted to be here for my lovely manager. For better or worse, yes? And I wished to help our dear friend Robbie, who was desperately in need of caffeinated assistance."

He kissed me on the cheek. It felt totally natural until I realized he'd done it in the office. Nobody was around... But still.

It won't matter soon enough.

"Do we need to wake him?" I gestured at Robbie.

"No no no," Arthur replied. "He has worked quite hard this morning, and has two hours of down time before the next task. I am monitoring him, do not worry. Focus on your presentation, yes?"

I sipped my coffee and piddled around answering emails for ten minutes, then decided there was no point in delaying things further. I carried my laptop upstairs to the fourth floor. The elevator ride felt like I was being delivered to a firing squad. The doors were going to open, and seven men with rifles were going to put me out of my misery.

If only it were that quick.

The open space on the fourth floor looked like a Christmas-themed bomb had gone off. Confetti covered the floor, along with discarded drink cups and food. The room reeked of beer and wine. A cleanup crew of four were walking around with trash bags, slowly returning the room to normalcy.

I passed the dessert table, then sneaked a cupcake off one of the trays. If I was going to crash and burn in front of the most important people in my company, I was going to do it with a cupcake in my stomach, damnit.

Because like it or not, that was the reality of my situation. We'd missed our deadline. I was going to walk into the meeting and have to deliver bad news. I still didn't know *how* I would do that. Whether to mention it at the beginning, or wait until I'd finished my presentation to tell them. "Oh, by the way—we're still not done. Sorry."

And then I would be fired. Or worse, they might tell me to leave today, and I would have to wait a week or two before I got the official notice. That would be a great way to spend Christmas: waiting for the guillotine to fall.

When I finished my morning-after cupcake, I gathered myself and approached the boardroom. The door was ajar, but another presentation was happening inside. I was still a few minutes early.

I was going to go back for a second cupcake when I recognized the voice inside.

Liam?

I moved closer to the door until I could see him inside. He wore dark dress pants, but instead of a button-down he was wearing a navy polo shirt. Casual for Saturday, I supposed.

"...the batch collection documentation," he was saying. "Our team has detailed that process as thoroughly as we could, so you should have no trouble showing examples when you train the branches tomorrow morning."

What the hell was he doing?

Katherine Chandrakhan saw me peeking in the door. She waved me inside, and I slid through the door and then took the seat next to her.

"What's going on?" I whispered. "Am I late?"

"I saw your sales liaison in the elevator this morning," she explained. "He was kind enough to come up early and help us get a jump start on the documentation review. He's going to work with the head trainers. They have had a *lot* of questions."

She nodded her head toward the other end of the table, where six casually-dressed young people with matching Macbooks were listening intently. Flanking them on either side were the other ten members of the Board of Directors.

Liam noticed me then, and smiled. "Here's Leslie Hill, the project manager for the transition team. She can better answer your questions about the documentation you'll be reviewing today."

I moved to take his place at the front of the room. As he passed me, he leaned close and whispered, "Pretend like nothing's wrong."

"What? Why?"

"Just give your normal presentation. *Trust me.*"

I felt flustered and confused as I connected my laptop to the projector. "Good morning everyone. I'm, uh, glad to see you all flew in safe. As Liam said, I'm Leslie Hill, the project manager for the transition team here at Allegheny Supply..."

I glanced at Liam. He gave me a look: *keep going.*

I trusted Liam completely, so I launched into my presentation as if nothing was wrong. I reviewed every step we had made in the project, and why we had chosen the software we had. I described its benefits and drawbacks, and some of the hiccups along the way. I explained that our deployment timeline was expedited, but otherwise I didn't complain about how little time we had.

It was a short presentation, and took no longer than ten minutes. I reached the final slide and took a deep breath.

"I'm, uh, happy to say that the production environment is completed and ready for our users to begin making sales."

The lie hung in the air like an odor. I waited for someone to call me out on it.

One of the trainers, an attractive woman with short blonde hair, raised her hand. "I have a question about the sales batches on the new system."

"On our old system," I explained, "batches went out at the end of the day, at six o'clock local time. A cascade of batches trickling into the server throughout the evening. The new InterLync system allows us to send batches every hour on the hour. This will allow our operations and credit departments to begin reviewing and approving batches much quicker. Chapter nine of our software documentation outlines this process."

The young woman frowned at her computer screen. "I understand the strategy of it. I'm confused about the actual implementation. Can you show me where those hourly batches are configured in the software?"

I swallowed the lump in my throat and put on a plastic smile. "We, um, can look at the software after the presentation. I'm sure it will take a while to give you access to, um, our system..."

The trainer shook her head. "I'm already in the system and looking at it now." She twisted her laptop so I could see.

I glanced at Liam. "I've already given them access," he explained, punctuated with another look. *Go along with it.*

I crossed the room in a daze. *It's impossible. I was just downstairs. All the clients were yellow.* But sure enough, the trainer was remotely connected to a computer that had the software installed. It was open and running, with a green command prompt showing a list of sales options. Just like one of our employees would see when they used the software.

I moved my finger on her touchpad, clicking through the menu to bring up the software options. It was a computer at our Harrisburg location, and according to this it was fully configured and connected to the server. I stared at the screen as if I was trying to read Greek.

"Well?" she asked. "Can you show me where that setting is

configured?"

"It's right here—batches, then configuration, then options. We have pre-configured it to send them every hour, but that setting can be changed locally if need be."

The trainer nodded. "Very good. I don't expect to want to change those settings, but I wanted to know in case someone asks tomorrow. Thanks!"

"Of course," I said warily. This still felt like a trap. I looked at the other trainers and asked, "You are all connected to your specific regions?"

The man next to her nodded. "I'm remotely connected to the site server in Philly."

"I'm connected to Columbus," said the next person.

"Memphis, here."

"Kansas City."

"San Antonio."

I glanced at Liam. He winked at me.

What the hell happened?

I went back to the front and answered more questions. Katherine had a question about the hand-over documentation for the operations department. The CFO asked me about the licensing plan for the software, and was surprised that we were paying so little for such a huge system upgrade. I told him that was entirely due to Arthur Durand, our finance liaison.

And then the presentation was over, and the board was gathering their things and leaving.

"Excellent job, Ms. Hill," said the COO in a booming, approving voice. "I think I speak for everyone when I say that you've got a bright future at Allegheny."

"Thank you, sir," I said, dumbfounded.

Katherine lingered until the rest of the board had left. "The trainers all have what they need, but will you remain with Mr. Harford in case they have any questions?"

"Right, of course," I said. "Anything they need."

Katherine put her laptop in her bag and then beamed at me. "You're quite amazing for getting this done on time. I know the deadline may have seemed arbitrary and unnecessarily aggressive, but I hope you'll understand why this had to be completed by this morning."

"Right, I do understand."

She disappeared, leaving me alone with the trainers. They were clustering together in the corner of the table, chatting softly and pointing at their screens. Liam was nowhere to be seen.

"I'll be back shortly," I told them.

The elevator ride downstairs felt a lot different than the one going up. I still had a deep sense of foreboding in my stomach, like we had somehow tricked everyone upstairs and they would soon discover that fact.

As soon as I walked into my team's office space, there was a huge pop from a champagne bottle being opened. "*Voila*! Let us celebrate!" Arthur said, hefting a champagne bottle that was overflowing with bubbles.

Robbie was chugging the rest of his coffee. Liam was grinning widely. Like they had just pulled the biggest prank in the world on me, and were waiting to see what my reaction would be.

"Will someone please explain what the *hell is going on*?" I demanded. "How did you get the production environment fully configured overnight?"

Robbie rubbed his palm into his eye and returned his glasses to his nose. "That's the thing: I *didn't*."

"Then what did I just show to the trainers upstairs?"

Robbie grinned. "I had an epiphany last night. When I was talking to Liam and Arthur about... Well, about *you*. We were discussing sharing, and Liam said something about not being able to fake feelings, and a lightbulb went off in my head."

"Fake computers!" Arthur said excitedly while pouring champagne into glasses. "Have you heard of such a thing, Leslie?"

"They're called VMs," Robbie said snobbishly. "Virtual Machines. They emulate a real computer by *sharing* hardware on a server. The same CPU, memory, hard drive, and network adapter. We use VMs all the time in testing, because you can spin one up whenever you want and then disable it when you're done."

"Is that supposed to mean something to me?" I asked. "Because I have no idea what you're talking about."

Robbie waved a hand. "Our bottleneck was the fact that we had to get the full environment up and running for the trainers. They had to have a production computer in each of their respective regions to connect to, and getting the full environment up would take all day. But then I realized: I could *fake* it! I created twenty-four virtual machines here on the primary server, and assigned them IP addresses that correspond to the subnets for each region. Configuring twenty-four is a lot quicker than two thousand. When the trainers remotely connect to them, they'll look just like a device in Harrisburg, Philly, Kansas City, or any other region. They'll never know the difference, and neither would the board."

"That's what I helped them connect to upstairs," Liam explained. "They can mess around all they want today as if it's the real thing. This buys us enough time for Robbie to get the rest of the environment up and running today."

"Then tonight, as the trainers are all flying out to their regions, I'll make the switch," Robbie said proudly. "I'll pull the VMs down, activate all the *actual* computers, and tomorrow morning nobody will know the difference."

Arthur mixed orange juice into the champagne flutes and handed one to me. "*C'est magnifique, no?*"

"You two knew about this?" I asked him and Liam.

"They didn't just know—they helped make it happen." Robbie smiled weakly. "I showed them how to replicate Virtual Machines on the server, and they spent all night helping me build them and put them into production."

It began to sink in. We'd lied to the board and pretended we were finished, when in fact we were still setting up the *real* environment. Like Wile E. Coyote putting up a painting of a tunnel while the real one was still been dug.

But it had worked. Nobody upstairs was the wiser, and the trainers were diligently working at that very moment.

All the stress of the past two months bubbled out of me like carbonation escaping a bottle of soda. I fell apart into a fit of hysterical giggles.

Liam put a comforting hand on my back. "You okay?"

"I'm fantastic," I said. "I've never been better! They bought it. Nobody knows it's fake."

Arthur raised his mimosa. "A toast, then. To Robbie."

Robbie raised his glass. "To all of us. I wouldn't have been able to do it without the two of you."

"And to our fearless leader," Liam said, clinking against my glass.

We celebrated with the drinks as Robbie explained the details of the switch-over that would happen tonight. Then Liam and I went back upstairs to assist the trainers and answer any questions they had. But aside from a few points of confusion, they didn't need us. The documentation Liam had written was verbose and easy to understand.

We did it, I thought with wonder. *I can't believe we actually did it.*

46

Arthur

"I cannot believe we did it," I told Robbie. "It is a miracle, Robbie!"

"Mmm hmm," he replied.

I patted him on the back while he hunched over his keys. "Surely you can show more excitement than this! We have snatched victory from the jaws of defeat, as they say!"

"I still have a lot of work to do today," he said.

I put down my mimosa and spread my arms. "Tell me how I can help. I am your humble servant, yes?"

He glanced up at me. Robbie was a good-looking man, but there were bags under his eyes. Two nights in the office was not good for a man's complexion.

"I could use some more coffee."

"A new pot, coming right up!" I declared.

I spent the day helping Robbie with little tasks. I was not a technical person, but he helped explain how to verify some of the settings on computers all around the country. I had not felt very useful on the project for some time, so assisting him today helped raise my spirits. It made me feel as though I was truly contributing.

I wished to be part of the success rather than a mere bystander.

Leslie and Liam returned downstairs in the late afternoon. "It's done," she said with wonder, like she was still shocked. "The trainers are all caught up, and are leaving to catch their flights to their respective regions."

"Perfect timing, because as soon as this server sync completes the *real* production environment will be ready," Robbie replied. "Then we can pull down the VMs and bring up the real environment."

I slapped him on the back. "Robbie, you are an incredible man! It is no wonder you run marathons—you are unstoppable!"

He smiled sheepishly.

The phone in Leslie's office rang. All of us froze.

This cannot be good.

"Who's calling you on a Saturday?" Liam asked quietly.

Leslie shook her head and walked into her office. We watched through the glass windows as she answered the phone. She nodded, said a few words, and then came back out. Her face was ghastly and pale.

"What is it, *mon fleur?*" I asked. "Did they discover our trickery?"

She took a deep breath. "That was Jen, the project management coordinator. She was passing along the news that the board is thrilled with our results."

I cradled Leslie's head in both of my hands and kissed her forehead. "This is excellent!"

"They're so thrilled that they want to convert our temporary transition team into a full-time management team," she said. "We would be dedicated to the new InterLync system. Management, maintenance, upgrades, training. You name it. The entire team will be extended full-time offers. And I would be able to hire two more bodies."

My immediate reaction was joy. We were being rewarded for our hard work, which was the reason we had all applied for these positions in the first place. But then the obvious problem presented itself.

Leslie would remain our boss. We could not be romantically involved with her without risking everything.

I saw my reaction mirrored on my colleagues' faces. Joy, then grim realization. A somber silence fell over us, ruining the victory we had felt just moments before.

"I need a drink of water," Leslie said. She left our office in a hurry.

The three of us looked at one-another.

"It was one thing to bend the rules on a temporary project team." Liam ran a hand through his messy hair. "But if this becomes a permanent team with permanent jobs..."

"*Fils de pute*," I cursed. "This is not ideal."

Robbie looked crestfallen. "What do we do?"

Liam shook his head softly. "I've waited five long years for a chance to be with Leslie. I'm not going to let a new job ruin that."

"What is it that you propose?" I asked. "Continue breaking the rules until one of us, or *all* of us, is discovered?"

"We can't do that," Liam said. "It was fine for two months during this project, but I can't hide my feelings for Leslie. I can't pretend like we're only colleagues."

"Then what?" Robbie asked.

Liam let out a long, reluctant sigh. "There's only one thing to do. It sucks, but it's the only way. And it's worth it."

We put our heads together and discussed what we would do.

47

Leslie

I went to the water fountain, took a drink of water, and then went into the bathroom to buy myself more time. Everything was happening so fast. This morning, I had walked into work expecting to be humiliated and lose my job.

Now, I was basking in success and being given my own team.

I felt lightheaded. I still wasn't sure if any of this was real.

But now we had a bigger problem.

Our weird shared relationship could begin once the project was dissolved. But if it was converted to a permanent team...

"What am I going to do?" I asked the reflection in the mirror. Continuing my relationships with Liam, Arthur, and Robbie while being their manager was forbidden and exciting, but it was doomed to eventually be discovered. It was only a matter of time.

I returned to my office. My three employees, my three lovers, were all standing around Robbie's desk.

"We have to talk," I said. "If this project team is converted to—"

"We quit."

Liam's words hung in the air, thick with meaning.

"All of us," Arthur added. "We quit the team, yes?"

"What!" I blurted out. "Why would you do that? You all joined the STT project to hopefully move up in the company. Now you have that opportunity!"

Liam smiled sadly at me. His sleeves were rolled up, and he put his hands in his pockets. He was as handsome today as the day we started at the company five long years ago. So much had changed in that time, but some things were still the same.

"We can't keep our relationship a secret," he said. "We'll eventually get caught. And I don't want to keep it a secret anyways. I want to go out in public with you, and kiss you in front of other people. I want..." He paused to clear his throat, and there was a shimmer in his emerald eyes. "I want a *future* with you, Leslie."

I tried to speak, but only a small sound came out. It felt like an elephant was sitting on my chest. "I want the same thing, Liam."

"We all discussed this." Arthur took my hands in his. "We are unanimous in our resolve. Life is more than merely chasing job opportunities, which come and go. The chance to be with one's soulmate? To pursue true love?" He kissed my fingertips. "These are what matter in life, *mon fleur*."

Robbie rose from his chair and wrapped me in a hug. "I'm too tired to think of a romantic speech on the spot. But I don't, um, give a damn about this position. I'll go back to the IT department if I have to."

I looked from one handsome face to the next. This wasn't just a spur-of-the-moment decision, or a grand gesture meant to make me fall in love with them. They were sincere. And serious.

"I..." I said.

There was a knock in the doorway by the hall. All of us whirled to find Katherine Chandrakhan walking into our office space.

"Katherine!" I blurted out. "I thought you were flying out to Denver."

She gazed back evenly. "I wanted to make sure this all got off the ground smoothly. As you said, there are more important things than vacations. I'm flying out in a few hours."

I stepped aside and gestured. "Let me introduce you to the rest of the team. This is Robbie Godwin and Arthur Durand. Meet Katherine Chandrakhan, the Chief Operating Officer."

She shook their hands. Robbie's face turned beet-red. "I, um, apologize for my disheveled appearance. I, uh, worked all night and have not had a chance to go home and change…"

"It's a Saturday, Mr. Godwin. I think we can ignore the dress code, especially in the context of your project's massive success!" Katherine turned to me. "Leslie, I wanted to stop by and tell you in person that you have exceeded the board's expectations in every way. This project could not have gone smoother."

You say that, I thought, but kept a big smile on my face. "Thank you."

Katherine clapped her hands together excitedly. "I think Jen has already spilled the beans, but we intend to convert the STT project into a permanent team. New compensation packages will be sent to each of you, with generous bonus targets. It's nothing less than what you each deserve for the hard work you have shown on this project. Especially you, Leslie. A project lives or dies depending on its manager's competence."

She looked at her watch. "I need to catch a ride to the airport. You should receive those offer letters on Monday morning. Merry Christmas!"

She gave me a final smile, then left our office.

I turned to my three men. "You all just received promotions. For jobs that you intend to quit."

"Looks like it," Liam said. "But it doesn't matter."

"It changes nothing," Arthur agreed.

"You can't be serious!" I exclaimed. "At least wait to see what the offer letter looks like on Monday. You need to know what you're turning down."

Robbie began typing rapidly on his keyboard. "I'm notifying Human Resources of my resignation right now."

"Good idea," Liam said. "I'll do the same."

I started to protest, then realized it was useless. They were determined. They were choosing me over their careers.

It was sweet, and endearing. It made me love them just a little bit more.

Which is why I can't allow this.

I fled from the office and ran to the elevators. Katherine wasn't there, so I took the stairs down to the first floor lobby. Katherine was walking out the front door toward the busy Pittsburgh street, where snow was gently falling from a grey sky.

I burst through the door behind her. "Katherine, wait!"

She whirled, confused. "Leslie?"

There was a stampede of footsteps as Liam, Arthur, and Robbie followed us outside. I felt their presence behind me but ignored them.

"Katherine," I said happily, "I quit."

The COO blinked. "Is this some sort of joke?"

"I'm delighted to have delivered the STT project, but I don't want to take on a full managerial role," I explained. "I'm quitting my position as the manager of the Systems Transition Team, effective immediately."

"Leslie..." Liam whispered behind me.

Katherine's jaw dropped. "When you applied for the STT position, you claimed that your primary motivation was to move into management."

"And over the past two months, I've learned that it's not for me," I replied. "I don't enjoy dealing with budgets, and timelines, and managing people."

She looked at the three men behind me and narrowed her eyes. "Does this have anything to do with the *extraordinary* charity donation last night? Is there something I should know, Leslie?"

I shook my head. "I'd rather move back into an operations role. That's all."

"Leslie, perhaps you should take some time to consider it. We can discuss the promotion when I return from—"

"I've made my decision," I said.

Katherine sighed. "Very well. Send a notification to HR as soon as possible, so that they don't waste time in drafting an offer letter. I'm sorry to hear this, Leslie. We need more women of your caliber in upper management."

"Maybe in the future," I replied.

Katherine shook her head, then walked away.

Liam grabbed my arm and whirled me around. "Leslie! Why did you do that?"

"This is not acceptable," Arthur said. "I cannot allow—"

"It's basic math," I said with a laugh. "You're the finance guy, Arthur. Which number is bigger: three or one?"

Robbie shook his head. "Leslie. Um. You're making a mistake..."

"The only mistake would be to let the three of you turn down amazing job offers," I replied. "It's too late. You all saw me notify Katherine. It's *done*. Now we can be together. There's nothing standing in our way."

Liam held my hand. "You're a stubborn woman, you know that?"

"I'm the boss. What I say goes."

"Technically," Arthur pointed out, "you quit, effective immediately. You are no longer our boss, yes?"

"You're right. Which means I'm free to do this."

I kissed Arthur, then Liam, then Robbie. They wrapped their arms around me in a group hug there on the street outside our Pittsburgh headquarters while the thick snowflakes landed on our shoulders and in our hair.

"It's over," I whispered. "We don't need to hide it anymore."

That felt like the biggest promotion I could have gotten.

Epilogue

Leslie

I stretched out in my bathtub, allowing the almost-too-hot water to seep into my muscles and bones. Snow fell outside the window, and gentle piano music drifted from my phone next to the tub.

"I needed this," I told myself as I sank deeper into the water.

I'd spent the rest of the weekend tying off loose ends and making sure there were no hiccups when Robbie pulled down the VMs and set up the *real* production system. Aside from a few growing pains as Allegheny Supply employees struggled to adapt to the new system, everything went flawlessly on Sunday morning.

And just like that, the STT project was finished.

Since then, I'd done a whole lot of *nothing*. I slept in, made myself breakfast around ten, and then went for a jog. It felt good to go for an easy run for the fun of it, rather than training for a marathon. I could ignore my pace and just soak in the winter feeling while the snow fell around me.

I spent the rest of the time in my pajamas in front of the television, catching up on all the shows I'd missed for the past two months.

And it felt great.

It had only been three days, but I quickly realized how much I *needed* this. Managing the STT project had burned me out. I needed to recharge my batteries.

Fortunately, my three handsome *former* employees helped me recharge at night. Liam on Sunday night, Arthur on Monday, and then Robbie last night. It was the kind of delicious routine a girl could get used to.

The doorbell rang.

I grinned and looked at my phone. *Right on time.*

I climbed out of the tub, dried off, and wrapped the towel around my body. I practically skipped downstairs to open the front door.

Liam, Arthur, and Robbie were standing outside in the snow, with arms full of gift-wrapped presents and grocery bags of food.

"Merry Christmas!" I said happily.

Robbie blinked and adjusted his glasses. "This, um, reminds me of the first time I met you. We were here for the first party planning meeting."

I winked at him. "That was the idea. Except *this time* someone has nailed mistletoe above my door..."

I kissed each of them underneath the mistletoe as they came inside. Robbie kissed me slowly and passionately, while Arthur grabbed a handful of my ass underneath the towel and squeezed so hard I yelped.

When it was Liam's turn, he only gave me a peck on the cheek. "That's all I get?"

He hefted his paper bag. "We've got a full Christmas dinner to cook! I can kiss you more later."

"Food over fondling. I can't argue with that."

Arthur sniffed the air and gasped. "Leslie! What are you cooking!"

"I've got a ham in the oven," I said. "Why?"

Arthur glared at me while unloading groceries. "We told you that *we* would be making *you* Christmas dinner!"

"I wanted to contribute something. After all, you three had to work yesterday and Monday. I'm unemployed."

"I thought you start your new job January second?" Robbie asked.

"It's more like my *old* job. But yeah, I go back next week."

"That's not really unemployment. More like a two-week vacation," Liam pointed out.

"Details, details."

While they started cooking, I went back upstairs and got dressed. When I came back down, the kitchen was full of delicious smells and *Home Alone* was playing on the TV.

"Alright, who can I help?" I asked.

Arthur tossed me a potato peeler. "I require assistance with the mashed potatoes, *mon fleur.*"

"One potato peeler, coming right up!"

Liam was prepping a big turkey, just as he had done on Thanksgiving. He gestured at the TV with a grease-covered hand. "Why didn't Kevin McAllister just call the police? All of this could have been avoided with a single phone call."

"He didn't realize he had been left at home," Robbie replied while making the stuffing. "He made a wish for his parents to disappear, and then he woke up and they were gone. He thought it was legit."

Liam pursed his lips. "Eh, I don't buy it. Even if that's true, he could have called the cops when the burglars were trying to get into his house."

"I have a theory," Arthur said. "Kevin does not call the police because he *desires* to harm these criminals. Perhaps he is a serial killer hunting for his prey, yes? Luring them into his trap so he can sadistically torture them?"

"Damn, I never thought of it that way," I said while tossing a peeled potato into the pot. "Kevin is a psychopath."

"It kind of changes the entire vibe of the film," Liam said. "Not very Christmas-y."

"It's still my favorite Christmas movie," Robbie said. "Can we, uh, watch the sequel next?"

"If you've been a good boy, we'll let you stay up late watching TV," I said with a playful wink.

We worked busily in the kitchen while joking and laughing about the movie. Everyone was just so happy, including me. I couldn't stop smiling. I still couldn't believe how things had turned out.

There was no guarantee that our unusual polygamous relationship would work long-term. But for now, everything was perfect.

"Kevin's mom was a total fox," Liam said.

"Hey! I'm right here!" I protested.

"Don't deny me my childhood crush," he argued, pointing a turkey baster like it was a sword. "Mrs. McAllister is probably the reason I have a thing for redheads."

"Well, in that case I suppose it's okay," I said. "I kind of had a crush on Kevin's dad, too."

"Hey, gross!" Robbie shouted.

"*Him?*" Arthur demanded. "He is an old man!"

"So it's okay for Liam to have a teenage boner for Kevin's mom, but I'm weird for liking Kevin's dad?"

"Exactly!" the three of them yelled at once.

Once all the food was cooking, we gathered on the floor by my Christmas tree and exchanged presents. "My gift first," Arthur said, handing me a bottle-shaped bundle of wrapped paper.

"Gee, I wonder what this could be," I said, holding it up to my ear. "Is it a bicycle?"

"Close..."

I unwrapped the paper and held up the bottle of wine to the light. The label said *Chateau Cambrai*, and the date...

"Nineteen Forty-Six?!?!" I gasped. "This bottle of wine is older than my house!"

"It was the first vintage after the war," Arthur said proudly. "It was not a very good year, I'm afraid, but it has aged marvelously. And it represents new beginnings, which I hope to have with you. Yes?"

I leaned forward and kissed him. "I love it. Should we open it tonight?"

"No no no," he said. "This must be saved for a *very* special occasion. Some other time."

Robbie held his present in both hands and frowned. He looked embarrassed. "My gift isn't as nice as an eighty year old bottle of wine."

"I'm sure I'll love it," I said as I took it from him. It was heavy and shaped like a thick book. I ripped off the wrapping and held it up. It was a shadowbox that held my Allegheny Marathon medal. Behind the medal were two photographs: one of me crossing the finish line, and another of Robbie and me posing after the race with our medals.

"Robbie," I whispered. "This is so sweet!"

"Yeah? It's not too, um, sentimental?"

"It's the perfect amount of sentimental. Thank you."

I leaned across and kissed him. He blushed with pride from ear to ear.

"Last but not least," Liam said, flourishing a small box.

"This is not fair!" Arthur exclaimed when he saw the box. "We agreed no jewelry!"

"It's not jewelry," Liam said.

I took the box and removed the bow. "This looks awfully similar to a jewelry box..."

"Trust me. It's not jewelry."

I opened the lid. It was indeed a jewelry box with a slitted cushion where a ring would fit, but instead there was a small metal ring. I plucked it from the box and held it up.

"What is it?"

"Hey!" Robbie took it from me and squinted at it. "This is a paper roller from a Hewlett Packard multifunction printer. I used to replace these rollers all the time."

I frowned at Liam. "A printer roller?"

"Do you remember when we first reconnected? Two months ago?" Liam asked.

"Yeah. We had lunch together, then met for the party planning committee..."

"Before that." Liam took the roller from Robbie and twisted it in his fingers. "I knew you were single, and needed an excuse to bump into you. So I sneaked into the operations department early in the morning and removed one of the rollers to the paper feed."

My mouth fell open. "You intentionally broke the printer so you could come to my rescue?!?!"

He gave me a lopsided grin and shrugged.

I playfully smacked him on the leg. "You jerk! Do you know how frustrating a broken printer is?"

"I'm sorry! I'm sorry!" He play-fought back against my barrage of smacks. "I needed an excuse to run into you!"

Arthur was laughing uproariously. "This is ingenious, Liam! You are quite sneaky!"

I stopped pummeling him and instead smothered him with kisses. "It's okay," I said between smooches. "It was worth it."

"I thought so too."

"There are easier ways to orchestrate a broken printer," Robbie mused. "I can cause a memory overflow error with just a few keystrokes. Freezes the entire printer for about five minutes before it reboots. I used to do that in college when my professor was printing our exams. While the print job was frozen, I would harvest the data from the memory and get a copy of the exam before everyone else."

"Next time, I'll come to you first," Liam said.

"There had better not be a next time!" I asserted.

Liam shrugged casually. "Just keeping my options open. Beth Carlson is awfully cute, and I never got a chance to do anything with her when we played *seven minutes in heaven...*"

Liam yelped and tried to run away as I pummeled him with pillow-punches again.

Then it was time for the boys to open my gifts. For Robbie, I'd purchased an entry to next year's Pittsburgh Marathon. Arthur received a very expensive wedge of White Stilton Gold cheese, and when he realized what it was he threw his arms around me and tried to make out with me there on the floor.

Liam frowned after opening his gift. "A gift card?"

"A gift card to Lili's Bistro," I said with a grin. "That's where you offered to take me on our first date, which we never got to go on. Now we can. Just the two of us."

Arthur cleared his throat.

"All four of us can go another time," I said. "This is just for Liam and me."

Liam ran a hand through his mop of messy hair. "I love it, Leslie. It's exactly what I wanted for Christmas."

He hugged me tightly, showing me just how much it meant to him.

We all got up and went into the kitchen to finish readying the food. The turkey was golden brown when Liam pulled it out of the oven, and filled the entire house with the smell of delicious spices.

"I got the three of you another Christmas gift," I said while mixing butter into the mashed potatoes.

"Oh?" Robbie asked.

"I have a very special activity planned for after dinner," I replied coyly.

"We aren't, um, going to watch *Home Alone Two?*"

"Trust me, you're going to like this far more than a movie," I said with a wink.

"I have an idea of what it is," Arthur said gleefully. He whispered into Robbie's ear.

Robbie's eyes widened. "Oh. At... the same time?"

"This is the plan, yes?"

"Can..." Robbie glanced at me. "Can Leslie even handle that?"

"Oh yes," I said. "I believe I can."

Robbie's gorgeous face turned red. "The movie can wait. I suppose."

"I don't know," Liam said casually. "I kind of had my heart set on a *Home Alone* marathon..."

I tossed a small sliver of butter at Liam, which bounced off his arm. "Did you just throw *butter* at me?" he said, incredulous.

"What are you going to do about it?" I taunted.

He ripped off the turkey leg and held it like a saber.

He chased me around the kitchen island while Arthur and Robbie laughed and cheered.

Cassie Cole is a Reverse Harem Romance writer living in Norfolk, Virginia. A sappy lover at heart, she thinks romance is best with a kick-butt plot!

Books by Cassie Cole

Broken In

Drilled

Five Alarm Christmas

All In

Triple Team

Shared by her Bodyguards

Saved by the SEALs

Forbidden Crush

Full Contact

Sealed With A Kiss

Smolder

The Naughty List

Made in the USA
Monee, IL
18 December 2019